D0731698

Tragedy in Tahoe

Tragedy in Tahoe

Rylie Sunderland Mysteries Book 1

Rachele Baker

Fleur de Soleil Books

Tragedy in Tahoe

Chapter 1

I t was the start of a whole new chapter in her life. Rylie's five-year-old golden retriever Bella panted excitedly from the back seat. As she drove into the little town of Tahoe City high in the Sierra Nevada mountains, she caught a glimpse of the sparkling blue water of Lake Tahoe between the tall pines. She opened her car window and took a deep breath of the fresh mountain air.

"We're going to have so much fun this summer, Bella!"

Bella wagged her tail and looked at her with a big doggie grin on her face, her tongue lolling out one side of her mouth.

She drove down the west shore of the lake until she saw a small wooden sign announcing the entrance to Whitaker Cottages on the lake side of the road. She turned into the narrow driveway and drove slowly through the tall pines toward the lake. She followed the driveway as it veered to the left in the direction of the cottages and parked in the parking area. As she was letting Bella out of the back seat, a man and woman came out of a nearby building and walked over to her.

"You must be Rylie. I'm Gillian, and this is my husband, Liam." Gillian spoke with a strong Irish accent. Her wide smile lit up her face.

Rylie returned Gillian's smile. "Hi, Gillian. Hi, Liam. Yes, I'm Rylie. And this is Bella. Nice to meet you."

"We really appreciate your coming to help us out this summer, Rylie. We know this is a big change for you. Elizabeth told us that your mother said you've been working as a veterinarian in the same veterinary hospital since you graduated from veterinary medical school. It's such a shame what happened."

"I know," she replied. "It was such a shock when the veterinary hospital where I worked burned to the ground in the Lightning Complex Fire. It put me and a lot of other people out of work. My mother's been worried about me."

"We went to Tahoe a lot when I was growing up. I always loved spending time at the lake. So when Elizabeth Whitaker asked my mother if she knew anyone that could help out as a temporary caretaker at her rental cottages this summer, my mother thought it would be a great opportunity for me. She knows I need some time to figure out what I'm going to do next with my life now that I'm out of a job. I'm happy to help you out. I've never done anything like this before, but I'll do my best to get up to speed as quickly as possible."

"It won't take you long." Liam smiled. "Don't worry. We'll show you the ropes, and we'll be available to answer any questions you might have when you're working."

They showed her to the vacant caretaker's house so she could get settled in and made plans to meet up later that day so Gillian could start training her in her new position.

She went inside with Bella to explore her new home. The gorgeous lake views from the large windows surrounding the open plan living and dining area took her breath away.

"This could work, Bella." She reached down to stroke the soft golden fur on Bella's head. She'd been under so much stress since she'd lost her job. Maybe this was just what she needed. She hoped so.

After she got Bella some water and unpacked everything from her SUV, she drove to the grocery store in Tahoe City to get some food and supplies. When she got back, she found Bella sleeping peacefully on her dog bed.

She put her groceries away, then went over to the building that housed both Liam and Gillian's residence and the reception area. Liam and Gillian had told her that the door to their residence was in back of the reception desk on the far wall. She took in the large stone fireplace, sofa, and upholstered chairs on one side of the room and wood tables and chairs on the other as she walked over to knock on the door to Liam and Gillian's residence.

"Hi, Rylie!" Gillian stepped into the reception area and closed the door behind her. "Did you get all settled in?"

"I still have some things to do, but I did go grocery shopping so I have some food in the house. I can finish getting settled in after you show me what I have to do. I want to be ready to start work on Monday."

"Okay. Let me show you our online reservation system. We currently have five cottages that we rent out to guests, but there are a few more cottages on the property that we might be renovating soon, so there may be more in the future."

Gillian showed her how to book reservations, invoice guests, and accept payments.

"Didn't I see on your website that you have free continental breakfasts in the mornings?" Rylie asked. "How's that handled?"

"One of our local bakeries, the Butter Lane Bakery and Coffee Shop, brings us fresh baked breads and pastries every morning," Gillian replied. "The owner, Colin Matthews, makes the deliveries himself on weekdays. A number of people around here consider Colin to be Tahoe City's most eligible bachelor. He's a handsome devil, I'll give him that."

"I can't wait to meet him." Rylie grinned.

"Would you like a tour of the property?" Gillian asked.

"Definitely," Rylie replied. "It's such a beautiful old Tahoe estate. I know we visited Elizabeth and her family here a couple of times when I was growing up, but that was a long time ago, and I don't remember much."

Gillian took her through the Butterfly Garden, a couple of the rental cottages, and the Card House where she told Rylie that Liam had weekly poker nights with his friends. Then she took Rylie over to the main house.

"Elizabeth keeps the main house for her own use for whenever she and her family come to visit," Gillian said. "But she lets us use it once a month for Locals' Night. That's when we invite all the locals for food and drinks. It's good PR. We get a lot of referrals from people in the community."

The front door of the main house opened into an elegant foyer with honey-colored wood wainscoting accented with dark green linen center panels. She followed Gillian into the spacious living room filled with natural light from the tall windows that showcased gorgeous views of the lake and surrounding forest. Next, they went into the library where the walls on either side were lined with built-in bookshelves filled with books.

"I love this room!" Rylie exclaimed. "I'd love to curl up with a good book in one of those overstuffed chairs in front of the fireplace."

"I'm sure Elizabeth wouldn't mind," Gillian replied. "Why don't you ask her?"

"I will." She tried to read the titles of some of the books as she followed Gillian out of the library. Gillian led the way to the butler's pantry lined with glass-fronted cabinets full of expensive-looking china.

"Now for the pièce de resistance," Gillian said mysteriously. She looked sideways at Rylie. "This house has secrets." She slid her fingers along the side of one of the cabinets. A hidden door swung open. A draft of cold air carrying the odor of damp earth rushed out.

"Oh my goodness! What is this?"

"It's one of the entrances to an underground tunnel," Gillian replied. "The original owner had the tunnel carved out of the granite bedrock under the property in the late 1800's. We think he built it so he could get to the Card House from the main house in the winter. The snow can get pretty deep here in the winter."

She cautiously followed Gillian into the dimly lit, barrel-vaulted granite tunnel. The ground below them sloped downward for a long time before it leveled out.

"How far down are we?" she asked.

"It's about two stories underground," Gillian replied. "There's a large wine cellar down here and some other rooms that I don't really know what they're for. There's also a room called the Absinthe Room that's kind of interesting."

Gillian turned into a small room off the tunnel. "This is it. This is the Absinthe Room."

Rylie stepped into the small granite-walled room. Dark water stains trailed down the granite walls to the fireplace. A faint green glow that seemed to emanate from the back of the fireplace accentuated the black ironwork devils with bared teeth and clawed fingers on the doors of the fireplace screen.

A chill ran up her spine. She tried to shake off the uncomfortable feeling. "This place is a little creepy."

"I know, but I thought you should see it. Let's get out of here."

After a brief tour of the wine cellar, Gillian led the way through the tunnel back to the main house.

Rylie inhaled deeply as they emerged from the tunnel. "Thanks for the tour, Gillian. I'm going to take Bella for a walk down to the lake now and then finish getting settled in."

"Okay. Have fun. See you later."

When she got back to her house, she called her best friend Sophie to tell her about Whitaker Cottages and her new job.

"It sounds cool," Sophie said. "I think this will be a good short-term gig for you. It will give you some time to sort things out so you don't have to rush into another veterinarian position right away."

"That's how I feel, too. And I'm looking forward to having some fun around the lake on my days off."

The next morning, she woke up feeling better than she had in some time. She went into the kitchen to make coffee and get Bella her breakfast. While her coffee was brewing, she showered and got dressed. She quickly drank a cup of coffee and then walked over to Liam and Gillian's house. She wanted to meet the guy touted as Tahoe City's most eligible bachelor when he made his delivery of fresh baked breads and pastries.

As she walked in the door of the reception area, she saw a man chatting with Gillian at the reception desk.

"Rylie! Good morning!" Gillian said. "I want you to meet our local bakery owner, Colin Matthews."

Colin turned around. A few stray curls of his dark brown hair flopped rakishly over his forehead. His brown eyes twinkled as he gave her a warm smile. Gillian was right. He was handsome. Rylie's heart did a little backflip. She felt a flash of annoyance at herself for her schoolgirl type reaction. She tried to compose her features and returned his smile.

"Hi, Rylie. Nice to meet you. I understand you're going to be spending the summer here at the lake."

"Yes. I'm looking forward to it." She felt her cheeks getting warm. She wished she wasn't so bad at hiding her feelings.

"I'd love to chat more ladies, but I've got to get to my next delivery. See you tomorrow!" Colin headed for the door.

"Don't forget Locals' Night tomorrow night!" Gillian called out.

"I wouldn't miss it." Colin shot them a sexy smile as he closed the door on his way out.

Locals' Night was the first thing on Rylie's mind when she woke up the next morning. She was looking forward to seeing Colin Matthews again and meeting some of the locals.

After breakfast, she took Bella for a walk through the Butterfly Garden. A dark-haired guy with a stubble beard that appeared to be in his mid-twenties was raking the dirt path in the garden.

He looked up from his raking as she and Bella approached.

Rylie stopped to greet him. "Hi! I'm Rylie. I'm helping Liam and Gilliam as a temporary caretaker here this summer. And this is Bella."

"I'm Thomas. I heard you were coming. Nice to meet you. I'm the groundskeeper. I grew up in Tahoe City, so I know pretty much everyone around here. If you ever want to know anything about anyone in this town, I'm your man."

"Good to know."

Bella trotted over to Thomas. He smiled and stroked her head and scratched around her ears. Bella wiggled around happily.

"Looks like you have a new friend." Rylie smiled. "Bella's a love sponge. She never gets tired of that."

"She's sweet," Thomas replied.

"It was nice to meet you, Thomas. I'm sure we'll see you around. We've got to get going now. Come on Bella."

"See you later."

She took Bella back to her house and made sure she was comfortable. Then she drove into Tahoe City to spend a few hours wandering around looking at all the shops and restaurants.

When she got back home, she took Bella on a short walk. Then she went inside to get changed for the Locals' Night party. She wasn't sure exactly how to dress for the occasion. She ended up choosing a dark turquoise cotton dress with a slim-fitting top and flared skirt.

She left Bella curled up contentedly in the living room and walked over to the main house to help Liam and Gillian with preparations for the party.

"Rylie! We didn't expect to see you until tonight," Gillian said.

"I thought I'd come over and see if you needed any help getting everything set up."

"Well, that's very nice of you," Gillian replied. "We'd love your help. Have you gotten all settled into your new home?"

"Pretty much. I drove into Tahoe City today and spent some time looking around to see what's changed since the last time I was here. I noticed that the old Tavern Grill went out of business. That's a shame. I used to enjoy going there."

"It's been closed for a while now," Gillian replied. "One of the guys that Liam plays poker with, Patrick O'Farrell, purchased it recently. I'll introduce you to him at the party tonight. Maybe he can tell us more about what he's planning to do with the place."

She helped Liam and Gillian get everything ready for Locals' Night. They filled the buffet table with delicious homemade foods and made sure the bar was well stocked. The living room looked warm and inviting with all of the antique table lamps and wall sconces softly glowing.

Guests started to arrive. Before long, the living room was full of people standing around in small groups chatting with each other. The hum of conversation was punctuated by occasional laughter. The atmosphere was warm and convivial. Gillian walked up to where she was standing and interrupted her reverie.

"How about something to drink?" Gillian asked. "What would you like? Wine? Beer? A cocktail?"

"Some wine would be nice."

"Okay. Let's go get some wine at the bar," Gillian said. "Then I'll take you around and introduce you to a few people."

They chatted over their wine for a few minutes. Then Gillian led Rylie over to a man standing by himself on one side of the room with a beer in his hand.

"Patrick! I'd like you to meet Rylie Sunderland," Gillian said. "Rylie's a veterinarian in the San Francisco East Bay area. She's between jobs right now, so she's agreed to help us out as a part-time caretaker this summer. She and her family are friends of the Whitakers. She walked around Tahoe City today and noticed that the old Tavern Grill went out of business. I told her that maybe you could tell us a little about what you're planning to do with it."

Patrick's face lit up. "I have great plans. I want to completely renovate the existing building and expand it. I plan to serve American favorites like gourmet hamburgers, but I also want to serve some Irish favorites like bangers and mash."

Patrick's face suddenly hardened into a scowl. Rylie followed his gaze across the room to see Colin Matthews holding court with a group of women. Colin caught her gaze. He smiled warmly at her and gave her a wink. She returned Colin's smile and then quickly looked back at Patrick. Patrick had regained his composure, but something had changed in his demeanor.

"Excuse me. I need another beer." Patrick turned and strode quickly away toward the bar.

"That was weird," Rylie said. "Gillian, do you mind if I get something to eat? I didn't have anything for lunch, and I'm starved."

"Not at all," Gillian replied. "I'm hungry, too."

They made their way to the buffet table.

"Hi, Rylie." Colin Matthews startled her by suddenly appearing at her side at the buffet table. "I need to talk to you about something. But not right now. I'll catch up with you later, okay?"

"Okay." She watched as Colin disappeared into the crowd.

A couple of hours later, the crowd started to thin. Rylie helped Gillian clear the dirty dishes from the living room and load them in the dishwasher. Then she went looking for Colin. When she couldn't find him, she went back into the kitchen.

"Have you seen Colin?" she asked Gillian. "He said he needed to talk to me about something."

"No. I haven't seen him in a while. He probably left. I wouldn't worry about it. You'll see him Monday morning when he makes his delivery."

"There's not much more to do here, Rylie. There will probably be a couple people that stay late to chat with Liam, but there's no need for you to stick around if you'd like to call it a night."

"Okay. Thanks, Gillian. This was fun. 'Night."

As she walked slowly back to her house, she wondered why Colin would ask to speak to her and then leave without doing so. It seemed like an odd thing to do.

She was woken up early the next morning by loud knocking on her door. She dragged herself out of bed and headed for the front door with Bella racing in front of her barking ferociously. When she opened the door, she was surprised to see Liam and Gillian standing there. Gillian's eyes were red-rimmed and moist. Liam stood rigidly beside her. A sense of foreboding gripped her.

"What's wrong?" she asked.

"Something's terrible happened!" Gillian exclaimed. A sob escaped her. "Colin Matthews is dead!"

Chapter 2

"What are you talking about?" Rylie replied. "How could that be? I just saw him last night and everything was fine." A wave of nausea passed over her and filled her mouth with the bitter taste of bile.

"I found him late last night in the Absinthe Room," Liam replied. "I wanted to have a beer after everyone left last night, but we were out of my favorite kind. So I went down to the wine cellar to get another six-pack."

"When I walked past the Absinthe Room, I noticed something out of place out of the corner of my eye. I looked over and saw Colin crumpled in a heap at the bottom of the far wall. He looked really pale, and he didn't have a pulse."

"I tried to call 9-1-1, but there wasn't any cell phone reception in the tunnel, so I had to run back to the main house to make the call. The ambulance and sheriff's department got there quickly, but the EMTs weren't able to revive him."

"Do they know what happened? Was it an accident? Did he have a heart attack or something?"

"They don't know at this point," Liam replied. "I'm sure there will be an autopsy. I'm planning to call our friend Brayden Hughes later today. He's the local Medical Examiner. I assume he'll be the one performing the autopsy."

"The detective in charge of the case, Detective Mark Felton, asked us to provide him with a list of all the people who were at Locals' Night last night. Gillian and I are going to work on that today. He'll probably want to talk to you, too, at some point to see if you saw anything that might help in his investigation."

"Wow. Okay." Her shoulders tightened. "Do you think Detective Felton thinks Colin may have been murdered? Do you think we're in danger?"

"I don't know, Rylie," Liam replied grimly. "This has always been a very safe area. We never have murders here. I can't imagine that we'd suddenly have a murderer in our midst. I just don't know."

"We'd better go," he continued. "We've got some guests checking out this morning."

She watched Liam and Gillian walk away with unseeing eyes while her thoughts raced. What if it was murder? Who would want to kill Colin Matthews? He seemed like such a nice guy.

It had to be someone that knew how to get into the secret underground tunnel. She wondered who might know how to get into the tunnel besides Gillian and Liam. Would the people that worked on the property have been shown the hidden entrances to the tunnel? If so, then the groundskeeper, Thomas Scott, or anyone that worked on the property would know how to get into the tunnel.

What about the guys that came to Liam's poker night every week? It seemed likely that Liam had shown them the underground tunnel.

And why did Colin go to the Absinthe Room in the first place? Who'd want to go in that creepy place anyway? Did he go willingly or did someone make him go there?

She wanted answers.

Maybe it would be good to get out of here to get some fresh air and clear my head.

She took Bella down to the private beach and then walked with her along the lakeshore path. Bella had her nose glued to the ground as she happily explored the smells of the forest. The quiet and peacefulness helped to soothe Rylie's troubled mind.

She was still reeling from the loss of her job. She'd moved to Tahoe for the summer to give herself some time to figure out what she was going to do with her life now that she'd lost the only veterinarian position she'd ever had. Then handsome Colin Matthews dies, or was possibly murdered, right on the property where she was staying. Everything suddenly felt out of control.

When she got back to her house, she got Bella her breakfast. She started some coffee brewing, poured herself a glass of orange juice, and made some toast. She sat down at the table to eat her breakfast. Her gaze wandered over the beautiful lake views through the windows as she ate.

What a beautiful setting. It doesn't seem like a setting where someone could possibly have been murdered. I hope they find out what happened soon. Poor Colin. I can't believe this happened.

She finished her breakfast and then puttered around the house looking for things to keep herself busy. A knock at the door startled her out of her thoughts. Bella ran to the door barking loudly.

"Placer County Sheriff's Department," a strong male voice called through the front door. She opened the door to see a handsome man with broad shoulders, curly sandy brown hair, and a stubble beard. He looked like he might be about her age. His kind brown eyes put her immediately at ease.

"I'm Detective Mark Felton. I'm in charge of the investigation into the death of Colin Matthews. Are you Dr. Rylie Sunderland?"

"Yes, I am. Would you like to come in?"

He stepped inside. "I understand that Liam and Gillian came over to let you know that Colin Matthews died in the Absinthe Room last night."

"Yes, they did."

"I'm sorry to have to tell you this, Dr. Sunderland, but we have reason to believe that Colin didn't die of natural causes. We're now considering this a murder investigation."

She felt a little lightheaded.

"Would you like to sit down, Dr. Sunderland?"

"No, no. I'm fine." She threw back her shoulders resolutely and stood a little taller. "And please, call me Rylie."

"Okay, Rylie. Can you please tell me if you saw anything suspicious at the Locals' Night party last night? Or if anyone led you to believe that they might be upset with Colin Matthews for any reason?"

She did a mental run-through of the events that occurred during the party. She didn't remember seeing anything suspicious, but she remembered that Patrick O'Farrell had looked angry when he saw Colin Matthews. She told Detective Felton about her conversation with Patrick O'Farrell.

"What was your relationship with Colin Matthews?"

"I didn't have a relationship with him," she replied. "I just met him Friday morning when he came to make his delivery."

"Gillian told me that Colin told you that he needed to speak to you on Locals' Night."

"Yes, he did," she replied. "But I have no idea what he wanted to talk to me about. Like I said, I just met him on Friday. He said he needed to speak to me and that he would catch up with me later. When I was ready to go, I looked all over for him to find out what he wanted to talk to me about, but I couldn't find him anywhere. Gillian told me not to worry about it because I'd see him on Monday morning when he made his delivery. So I went home."

"Colin had a piece of paper in his pants pocket." Detective Felton held up a clear plastic evidence bag with a piece of paper inside. She read the note quickly, then swallowed hard.

"Is this your name and cell phone number?" he asked.

"Yes, it is."

"Do you have any idea why Colin Matthews would have your name and cell phone number in his pocket?"

"No, I don't. I never gave him my number. I don't have any idea how he could have gotten it."

She looked Detective Felton squarely in the eye and knew he believed her. She had a gut feeling that this was a good man. Someone she could trust.

"Thank you for your time, Rylie. If you think of anything else, or if you become aware of any information that might help in this investigation, please call me right away. Here's my business card with my cell phone number."

After Detective Felton left, she walked over and sat on the edge of the sofa. Bella looked up at her with a compassionate look. She moved to sit on the floor beside Bella and hugged her warm body.

Why in the world did Colin have her name and cell phone number in his pocket? How did he get her phone number in the first place?

And what had he wanted to talk to her about on Locals' Night? It made her crazy to think that she might never know what Colin had wanted to talk to her about.

She wondered if Gillian and Liam knew anything more about Colin's death. Maybe Detective Felton had told them something that he hadn't told her. Or maybe they had found out something from their friend Brayden Hughes, the local Medical Examiner.

She headed over to Gillian and Liam's house with Bella. She spotted the groundskeeper, Thomas, working outside.

"Hi, Thomas!"

Thomas turned around as Rylie and Bella walked up to him.

"I'm sure you heard about what happened to Colin Matthews last night," she said.

Thomas's face was devoid of emotion.

Wow, that's a perfect poker face. I wonder if he ever plays poker with Liam and his friends.

"Yes, I did. A detective from the sheriff's department talked to me this morning."

"I can't believe that a murder happened here," Rylie replied. "It seems so unreal. And scary."

Thomas was quiet for a long moment. "I can't believe it either."

He muttered something under his breath that she couldn't quite make out. She could see that he had no intention of continuing their conversation, so she continued on to Gillian and Liam's house.

That was weird. He seemed like such a nice guy yesterday. Today he seems like a different person. Maybe he and Colin were friends, and he's upset about Colin's death.

She knocked on Gillian and Liam's door. Liam opened the door and greeted her and Bella.

"We're inside having a cup of tea," he said. "Would you like to join us?"

"That sounds great. Thanks, Liam."

She followed Liam into the dining area.

"Hi, Rylie," Gillian said. "Please have a seat. Make yourself comfortable. I'll pour you a cup of tea. Help yourself to some biscuits."

She passed Rylie a plate of English biscuits. Rylie took a sip of the Earl Grey tea that Gillian offered her. She enjoyed the slight citrusy flavor.

"Detective Felton just came to talk to me," she said. "He told me they're considering Colin Matthews' death a murder."

"Yes, he told us that too," Liam replied. "We're pretty shocked."

"He showed me a paper they found in Colin's pocket with my name and cell phone number on it. I have no idea how Colin could have gotten my cell phone number. Did one of you give it to him?"

"No, of course not," Gillian replied. "We would never give out your cell phone number without your permission."

"I didn't think so," Rylie said. "But I had to ask. I'm wondering if Detective Felton considers me a suspect because of this. I certainly hope not. Please don't tell anyone about this. I don't want everyone in town to consider me a suspect in a murder investigation."

"Don't worry," Liam replied. "We won't tell anyone. The less publicity this whole thing gets, the better. And we would never tell anyone anything that could possibly damage your reputation."

"I'll be honest with you," she replied. "I'm feeling a little uncomfortable about being alone in my house out here in the middle of the woods even though I have a dog. Bella has a loud bark, but I don't know how good she'd actually be at protecting me. We don't know who killed Colin. It could have been anyone, even someone who works here."

"I know," Liam replied. "We talked to Elizabeth Whitaker on the phone a little while ago. She's taking this very seriously. She's going to have a company come out to install a security system right away."

"That's a relief. Did Detective Felton happen to tell you why he thinks Colin didn't die from natural causes?"

"All he told us was that there was evidence of a struggle," Liam replied. "He said it will take some time for the autopsy to be completed, but that they had enough information at this point to conclude that his death wasn't an accident."

"I just can't imagine why anyone would want to kill Colin," she replied. "I only just met him, but he seemed like a really nice guy."

"I don't think any of us will ever understand why someone would kill another person," Gillian said. "But someone obviously had a reason that compelled them to go to that extreme."

"I told Detective Felton that Patrick O'Farrell looked really angry when he saw Colin at the Locals' Night party," Rylie said. "I'm sure he'll be paying Patrick a visit. By the way, do you know if Thomas Scott and Colin were friends?"

"I doubt it," Liam replied. "Colin purchased his bakery from Thomas's mother about two years ago for less than what she paid for it. Because of her ill health, she wasn't managing the business well, and it was failing. Colin did her a favor by purchasing the bakery before it went out of business, but

Thomas didn't see it that way. He felt like Colin cheated his mother. He was pretty vocal about it at the time. I don't know if Thomas has been holding a grudge against Colin since then, but it's possible. Thomas's mother still suffers from ill health and ongoing financial problems."

"It seems like Thomas should be considered a suspect then," Rylie said. "Did you talk to Detective Felton about Thomas when he was here this morning?"

"No," Liam said. "I didn't even think about it. I just can't imagine Thomas murdering anyone. He's a good kid and a hard worker. But I guess Detective Felton needs to check every possible lead, so I'll give him a call."

Liam picked up his cell phone from the table and walked into the next room.

She looked at Gillian. "What about the continental breakfasts for the guests? Do you think Colin's bakery will be shut down now?"

"I was worried about that too, so I called the bakery a little while ago," Gillian replied. "Apparently Colin has a sister named Dee who lives in Tahoe Vista. She's stepped up to manage the bakery for the time being. Dee told me that Colin's baker and his other employees will be staying on. She said the weekend delivery guy, Eric Larson, will be doing the deliveries Monday through Friday and that she'll be hiring another delivery person to work on the weekends. She assured me that there won't be any problem having our orders delivered every morning as scheduled."

"That's good. Thanks for the tea and biscuits, Gillian. I need to get out of here. I'm going to head into Tahoe City and wander around for a while. I'll probably eat at one of the restaurants downtown while I'm there."

She took Bella back to their house and went inside. Bella wagged her tail and looked up at her expectantly. She leaned over to press her cheek against Bella's warm muzzle and made kissing noises. Bella wagged her tail happily. Rylie stood up. "I've got to go do some things in Tahoe City, Bella. You're going to stay here and watch the house for me, okay?"

Bella looked a little disappointed, but she seemed to know that she had an important job to do. Rylie felt bad leaving Bella behind, but she didn't know exactly what she was going to be doing in Tahoe City, so she thought it would be best to leave Bella at home. She got in her SUV and drove the short distance to Tahoe City.

Chapter 3

She drove slowly through the cluster of shops and restaurants in Tahoe City. She saw signs for restaurants that she remembered from previous visits such as Rosie's Cafe and Jake's on the Lake. She passed numerous sports shops advertising kayak, bicycle, ski, and snowboard rentals.

She drove to the opposite end of town and parked in the Safeway parking lot. She'd been planning to just wander around town, but she suddenly felt the urge to check out the derelict old Tavern Grill that Patrick O'Farrell now owned.

She tried to look nonchalant as she walked past the Tavern Grill while trying to see as much of it as she could. The parking lot was in bad shape and in dire need of resurfacing. She also thought the parking lot looked pretty small. It didn't look like there would be enough parking if Patrick planned to use part of the parking lot to expand the restaurant.

She noticed an empty lot next to the Tavern Grill parking lot. It was a large lot right on the lake with beautiful views. She knew it must be very valuable land. The lot looked large enough to build a shop or restaurant on and still have plenty of room for parking. She wondered who owned it.

She remembered seeing Colin's bakery, the Butter Lane Bakery and Coffee Shop, on the other side of town. She started walking in that direction.

Maybe Colin's sister Dee will be at the bakery, and I can get a chance to talk to her.

The bakery was set back from the road on the side opposite the lake. Round tables with white umbrellas were scattered around a large deck out front. Brightly colored flowers over-flowed from built-in planters along the sides of the deck.

She stepped inside and breathed deeply of the luscious aromas of baked goods and freshly brewed coffee. Sunlight poured into the room from the large windows. Customers were seated at tables along the right side of the bakery working on their laptops or engrossed in their cell phones. Glass cases displayed fresh baked goods on the left side of the room.

She walked over to peruse the baked goods on display. Everything looked delicious. She discreetly scanned the room to see if she could see anyone that looked like they might be related to Colin.

When she spotted Dee Matthews, there was no mistaking the family resemblance. She watched Dee move around the room. She got the impression that Dee was a take charge kind of person by the way she carried herself and spoke to the customers.

"Can I help you?" Dee asked as she made her way back to the counter after waiting on some customers at one of the tables.

"Everything looks delicious, but I think I'll just have a glass of your freshly squeezed lemonade for now," she replied.

"Sure thing," Dee said. "You'd better snag a table while you can. I'll bring you your lemonade in a minute."

She wanted to sit where she could watch Dee and hopefully get a chance to talk to her, so she selected a table at the back of the bakery. When Dee brought her lemonade, she took the opportunity to introduce herself.

"I'm Rylie Sunderland." She smiled up at Dee. "I'm helping out as a temporary caretaker at Whitaker Cottages this summer. I just moved here a few days ago. Are you Colin's sister Dee, by any chance?"

Dee looked sharply at her. Then her facial features relaxed. "Yes, I'm Dee. How could you tell? Was it the family resemblance?" She smiled sadly.

"I'm afraid so. I only saw Colin a couple times, but you definitely look like him. I'm so sorry for your loss. What a horrible thing to happen."

Dee's face crumpled and tears started to form in her eyes. She straightened her back and composed herself. "That stupid brother of mine. I knew his lack of good judgment would end up costing him someday. I just didn't know he'd pay the ultimate price for his indiscretions."

"I'm not sure what you're talking about, Dee. I know of Colin's reputation for being a bit of a flirt, but there's no real harm in that, is there?"

Dee snorted. "If that's all he did, then you're right, there wouldn't be any harm in it. But he did a lot more than just flirt. I was afraid it would catch up to him someday."

Dee abruptly turned away and strode off to help another customer. Rylie wondered what Colin had done, or who he'd gotten involved with, that made Dee so sure that it would cause him problems. She knew there was a lot more to the story.

She sipped her lemonade as she reflected on what she'd just learned. If Colin had gotten involved with someone that he shouldn't have, surely other people would know about it. This is a small town. And people talk. So it shouldn't be too difficult to find out who Colin was involved with.

She finished her lemonade and went across the street to Commons Beach, She wanted to walk along the lakeside trail to clear her mind and sort through the events of the day. The trail was quiet and peaceful with beautiful views of the lake and surrounding mountains.

As she approached the other side of town where she was parked, she saw Za's Lakefront Restaurant. It was lunchtime, and the restaurant's deck was full of people enjoying drinks and food in the sunshine. Her stomach rumbled. She decided to go in and get something to eat.

She asked to be seated outside on the deck so she could enjoy the fresh air and lake views. The hostess seated her on the deck and then hurried off. She browsed through the menu and saw that they served some of her favorite things including gourmet burgers and artisan pizzas.

When her waiter came to take her order, she ordered a pesto pizza and some sparkling mineral water. Then she settled back to enjoy the view. She scanned the people sitting on the deck to see if there was anyone she recognized. She thought a couple of the people seated on the deck might be people that she'd met at Locals' Night, but she'd met so many people that night that she wasn't really sure.

The waiter brought her mineral water. As she was taking her first sip, she noticed the hostess escorting two men to a table on the other side of the deck. One of them she recognized instantly. Patrick O'Farrell. She'd never seen the other man before. Patrick was seated with his back to her. She had a clear view of the man seated across from him. He was dressed in what looked like a very expensive light grey suit.

No one wears suits in Tahoe. Even the locals dress like they're on vacation.

She imagined that some people might consider Expensive Suit Guy handsome, but there was something about him that was cold and hard. He looked like he was all business.

She struggled not to stare. Patrick was gesturing like he was trying to emphasize a very important point. She wished she could hear what he was saying. She saw a flash of anger pass across Expensive Suit Guy's face. Then Expensive Suit Guy got up from the table and strode angrily out of the restaurant. Patrick threw his napkin on the table and hurried after him.

She quickly pushed her napkin off her lap onto the deck and ducked under the table to retrieve it so Patrick wouldn't see her. She stayed under the table a little longer than it would normally take to retrieve a napkin to give him time to leave. She hoped he'd left by the time she emerged from under the table. When she sat back up, Patrick was nowhere to be seen. She breathed a sigh of relief.

Wow. I wonder what that was all about. Expensive Suit Guy didn't look very happy with Patrick.

She finished her meal and headed home. As soon as she got inside her house, she called her best friend Sophie to fill her in on everything that had happened since the last time they'd talked. Her voice cracked as she told Sophie about Colin Matthews' murder.

"Oh, Rylie!" Sophie exclaimed. "How horrible! Are you sure you want to stay there after a murder just occurred right next to your house?"

"Liam told me that Elizabeth Whitaker is going to have a security system installed throughout the property right away.

And I have Bella. I don't think anyone could break into my house at night without waking her up. And hopefully her barking would scare them off. She sounds pretty ferocious, even if she isn't."

"Still. Be careful, Rylie," Sophie said. "I don't want anything to happen to you."

"I will. Don't worry."

After they said their goodbyes, she let Bella out to go potty and then got ready for bed.

She laid on her back in bed and stared at the ceiling without really seeing it. She tried to go to sleep, but her brain wouldn't turn off. Her thoughts swirled around everything that had happened recently. The loss of her job. Colin Matthews' murder.

She wondered where her clients would take their pets now that they were forced to find a new veterinarian. She'd taken care of many of those pets since they were puppies and kittens. She thought about the great relationships that she'd developed with a number of her clients over the years, not to mention some of the people that she'd worked with. She wondered if she would ever see any of them again.

Her thoughts turned back to Colin Matthews. He'd seemed like such a nice guy. Handsome, warm, friendly. It was so hard to believe that he was dead.

He'd told her that he wanted to talk to her about something and then was killed later that evening. With her cell phone number in his pocket.

She covered her face with her hands. How had everything in her life gotten so out of control? What new challenges would she face tomorrow?

Chapter 4

She woke up the next morning before her cell phone alarm went off. Her whole body tingled with nervous energy. This would be her first day of work at Whitaker Cottages, and she wanted to make sure that everything went right.

She jumped out of bed and headed for the kitchen. She let Bella out to go potty, got some coffee brewing, and put fresh kibble and water in Bella's dog dishes. As soon as she let Bella back in, Bella made a beeline for her dog dishes and quickly consumed every morsel of food. Rylie grabbed a cup of coffee and headed to the bathroom for a shower.

She dressed quickly, then walked over to the reception area with Bella and let herself in. Bella immediately started sniffing her way through everything in the room.

Rylie went behind the reception desk to check the computer to see how many cottages had been occupied the night before. She saw that all five cottages had been occupied, and three of them were scheduled to check out that morning. She hoped she remembered how to check people out on the computer like Gillian had shown her. She did a quick mental rundown of everything Gillian had taught her. It shouldn't be too hard.

While she waited for the baked goods to be delivered for the continental breakfasts, she went into the small kitchen, got some coffee brewing, and got water heating for tea and hot chocolate. When the coffee had finished brewing, she poured it into a thermal carafe and set it next to the carafe of hot water on the long cabinet next to the tables and chairs. She poured milk and orange juice into glass pitchers and set the pitchers next to the carafes of coffee and hot water. She stepped back to inspect her work. Piece of cake so far.

She heard the Butter Lane Bakery delivery van pull up and looked outside. A guy with blonde hair and a blonde stubble beard that looked like he was in his early 20's picked up two trays of breads and pastries and headed for the reception area. He had a distinctive flair in the way he dressed. He wore a sleeveless blue jean jacket over a dark grey sweater with a black fedora perched jauntily on the back of his head. She liked him instantly. She rushed to open the door for him.

The guy smiled as he walked in. "Hi! I'm Eric."

"Hi, Eric. I'm Rylie." She returned his smile. "Nice to meet you. I'll get the serving platters to put the baked goods on so you can have your delivery trays back."

They transferred all the baked goods from Eric's trays to the serving platters. The fresh pastries smelled delicious. Her stomach growled. She felt her cheeks get hot. She hoped Eric hadn't heard her stomach growling. She carefully set the platters of baked goods on the long cabinet next to the coffee.

"I'm going to be helping out as a caretaker here this summer. I'm actually a veterinarian, but the veterinary hospital where I was working burned to the ground, so I needed something to do for a while until I figure out where I'm going to go with my career at this point."

"Oh, wow. Sorry about that. I hope you have some fun at the lake while you're here. I have a golden retriever named Buddy. He usually goes everywhere with me except I'm not allowed to bring him to work."

As if on cue, Bella shoved her muzzle into Eric's hand asking to be petted. Eric looked down at her and then squatted down to her level.

"Oh, you're sweet." He pet the golden fur on Bella's head. "What's her name?"

"Bella. And she's a love sponge. She doesn't ever get tired of being petted like that."

Eric gently scratched around Bella's ears. Bella looked like she was in heaven.

"Maybe I can bring Buddy here one day so he can play with Bella."

"I think Bella might like that," she replied. "It would be good for her. She doesn't get to play with other dogs very often. There's lots of room for them to play around here. Maybe we could take them down to the lake."

"That sound great. I'll think about what day might work for me. What are your days off?"

"I work Monday through Wednesday and have the rest of the week off," she replied. "Let me know what day works for you, and we'll set something up."

"Sounds good. I've got to get going. I've got to get to my next delivery so I don't get behind."

She followed Eric to the door and watched him drive away. What a nice guy.

She turned to look at Bella. "Would you like to have a play date with another golden retriever, Bella?"

Bella looked up at her and slowly wagged her golden-plumed tail. Then she broke out in a big doggie grin and started panting happily. Rylie reaching down and ruffled the soft fur on Bella's head.

She selected a pastry from the platter, got herself a cup of coffee, and settled into a chair in back of the reception desk. Everything seemed to be going well so far. She took a deep breath and slowly let it out. The muscles in her back and shoulders relaxed a little.

A few minutes later, an older gentleman and his wife came in. She smiled and greeted them. They got coffee, juice, and pastries and sat down at one of the round wooden tables.

"We haven't seen you here before," the man said. "We've been coming here for years. I'm Ernie, and this is my wife, Estelle."

"I'm Rylie. Elizabeth Whitaker is a friend of my mother. Elizabeth asked my mother if she knew anyone that could help her out as a temporary caretaker here this summer. Apparently, the other caretaker couple had to move out of state quite suddenly to care for the wife's mother. I'm between jobs right now, so I agreed to help out."

"That's nice of you to help Liam and Gillian," Ernie said. "I'm sure they appreciate it. Say, I noticed a sheriff's department vehicle here yesterday. What was that all about?"

She took a moment to collect her thoughts before replying. She hadn't anticipated dealing with questions about Colin's murder from the guests. She wondered how much she should say. She didn't think letting it be known that a murder had occurred on the property would be very good for business.

"I guess there was an altercation here on Saturday night during the Locals' Night party. I don't know all the details," Rylie replied.

"Hmmph," Ernie snorted. "I'll have to ask Liam or Gillian the next time I see them."

More guests came in to get their breakfasts. She was relieved to be saved from having to answer any more of Ernie's questions. He and his wife left a little while later. Some of the guests loaded up paper plates with baked goods to take back to their cottages, and some of them sat at the tables in the reception area to eat.

After all the guests had gotten their breakfasts and left, she cleaned the tables, washed the dishes, and put everything away. When lunchtime rolled around, she slipped the business cell phone in her pocket so she could go home to eat. She was happy that Liam and Gillian had given her a cell phone that was connected to a wi-fi video doorbell so she didn't have to stay in the reception area all day.

"Let's go get some lunch, Bella!"

Bella eagerly jumped up off the floor where she'd been lying down and raced to the door. She bolted out the door as soon as Rylie opened it.

On the short walk home, Rylie brainstormed ways to learn more about Colin Matthews and see if she could unearth any information that might help Detective Felton in his investigation. She felt very uncomfortable about potentially being on Detective Felton's list of suspects. She wanted to get off that list as soon as possible.

She thought hanging out at Colin's bakery might be a good place to start. She tried to think of a legitimate reason she could give anyone who asked why she was hanging out there. She remembered seeing people sitting at tables in Colin's bakery working on their laptops. That could work. If anyone asked, she could just say she was researching information about how to write a novel because she was interested in writing one. It wouldn't be a lie. It just wouldn't be the whole truth.

When she got home, she rummaged around in her refrigerator for something to eat. She had all the ingredi-
ents to make herself a nice spinach salad with goat cheese,
cherry tomatoes, and cucumbers. As she was making her
salad, she handed Bella a small piece of goat cheese. Bella
swallowed it so quickly that Rylie was sure she couldn't
possibly have even tasted it.

"Bella, silly girl. You're supposed to chew your food before you swallow it so you can taste it. It's better that way."

Bella looked up at her hopefully and swished her tail
back and forth.

After lunch, Rylie put her laptop in her backpack and
went back to the reception area with Bella. The guests
that had reservations to stay in the three vacant cottages
started arriving in the late afternoon. They seemed happy
and excited about all the things they planned to do while
they were on vacation.

Bella assumed the role of official greeter. Every time
someone new came in the door, she walked over to greet
them with her beautiful golden-plumed tail slowly wagging back and forth. The guests ate it up. Bella reveled in
all the attention she got.

By about 7:00 that evening, everyone had finally checked
in and gotten settled in their cottages and the reception
area was quiet. Rylie was startled when the door to Liam
and Gillian's home in back of the reception desk opened
and Gillian walked in.

"Hi, Rylie. How did everything go today? Did you have
any problems?"

"No. Everything went smoothly. Eric from Butter Lane
Bakery delivered the baked goods this morning as scheduled.
And all the guests have been very nice. It took me a little while

to get used to your computer system, but I'm fine with it now."

"Great! I'm glad your first day went so well," Gillian said. "Listen, we wanted to invite you to join us for dinner on Wednesday night. We have Liam's friends over for dinner on Wednesdays before they go over to the Card House with Liam to play poker. This week we decided to invite Aidan and Alain's wives too. Patrick isn't married, and he doesn't have a significant other, so he'll be by himself. We thought it would be nice for you to join us so you can get to know everyone."

"I'd love that! What can I bring?"

"Oh, you don't need to bring anything. We always have more than enough food and drinks to go around. Those men eat like horses." Gillian smiled her broad smile.

"Okay. Let me know if you need any help. I like to cook. I think I'm going to head home now. Everyone's all checked in, and I'll have the business cell phone with me if anyone needs anything."

"Okay. Sounds good. Thanks for all your help today."

"No problem, Gillian. 'Night."

Rylie locked up the reception area and went home. She was tired after a long first day at her new job. She made a light dinner for herself and fed Bella, then gratefully collapsed into bed as soon as her shift was over. She fell asleep fairly quickly but woke up a short time later feeling restless and agitated.

Having someone murdered right next to where you live could do that to you. Who could possibly have wanted Colin Matthews dead? And why?

Chapter 5

S he got up early the next morning, made coffee, and got
  ready for her second day at her new job. Bella seemed to
be enjoying this new routine. She got to spend all day with
Rylie, meet new people, and get lots of attention.

Rylie opened the front door of the reception area just as
the Butter Lane Bakery delivery van pulled up. Eric smiled
at her and said hi as he got out of the van. He brought in
two trays of freshly baked breads and pastries. The aroma was
mouthwatering. She stared at all the delectable goodies.

Eric handed her a buttery croissant. "Here. Try this croissant. I made it myself."

"Yum, this is fantastic," she mumbled as she savored the
flaky croissant. "I thought you just delivered baked goods. I
didn't know you were a baker, too."

"I'm not. But I'm learning how to become one. A little
while after I started working at Butter Lane Bakery, I asked
Colin if it would be okay if I hung out in the kitchen with
Ryan, his baker, so I could learn how to bake. Colin said it
would be okay as long as it didn't interfere with my work as
the weekend delivery guy."

"I told Ryan I wanted to learn how to become a baker. I
offered to help him with anything he needed in the kitchen.

After about a month, Colin offered me a job as an assistant to Ryan. I've had a great time working with Ryan for the past year. He's taught me a lot."

"That's great, Eric!" Rylie said. "What do you have to do to become a professional baker?"

"I want to train where Ryan did." Eric's eyes sparkled with excitement. "I want to attend the Pâtisserie and Boulangerie program at Le Cordon Bleu in Paris. It's a sixteen-month program followed by an internship. It costs 37,300 euros which is about $39,000.00. I've been working hard and saving every cent I can to go toward tuition."

"I'm sure if you keep working hard to achieve your goal, you'll find a way to make it happen. Do you know how to speak French?"

"Not yet. But I'm working on it. Sorry, but I've got to get going now. I've got to get to my next delivery. See you later!"

She finished getting everything set out for the guests' continental breakfast just as the first guest walked in the door. She settled back in her chair behind the reception desk with her croissant and a cup of coffee. She hadn't known that Eric had been working at Butter Lane Bakery in the kitchen or that he'd been with them as long as he had. Interesting.

After all the guests had gotten their breakfasts and left, she put a few pastries on a paper plate and poured some coffee into a disposable cup. She put the business cell phone in her pocket and stepped outside. Bella bounded out the door and headed straight for the Butterfly Garden as if she knew what Rylie planned to do.

It didn't take long to find Thomas. He was in the Butterfly Garden weeding the flowers. He smiled when Bella rushed up and nuzzled him with her soft muzzle. Rylie was relieved to see that Thomas seemed to be in a good mood today.

She smiled as she approached him. "Hi Thomas. I thought you might be hungry, so I brought you some pastries that we had left over from this morning's continental breakfast."

She held out the plate of pastries to him. He stared at it like she was offering him a plate of worms instead of a plate of pastries. Her heart sank.

Finally, his face relaxed. "Those look good. I'm starved."

He accepted the plate from her and took a bite of one of the pastries.

"Mmmm. These are incredible. I guess Colin hired a better baker than my mother did."

She stayed quiet, willing Thomas to keep talking.

"You know that Colin bought the bakery from my mother, right?" Thomas asked.

"I think Liam or Gillian may have mentioned that."

"My mother bought that bakery seven years ago," Thomas continued. "Did you know that it used to be called the Tahoe City Bakery before Colin bought it? My mother has health issues that prevent her from being able to work full time. She bought the bakery so she could support herself without having to work full time. She thought all the day-to-day work at the bakery could be handled by employees and that all she'd have to do is oversee everything."

"Unfortunately, my mother didn't realize how much work was involved in running a business. Or how much help she'd have to hire so she'd only have to work part-time. I don't think she hired a very good baker. Things kept going downhill until one day my mother told me that she might have to close the bakery and file for bankruptcy. I told her she should talk to an attorney first to see what her options were. She decided to sell the bakery after she talked to an attorney. But it wasn't worth much at that point."

"Even so," Thomas continued, "I think Colin took advantage of my mother and the situation she was in. He paid my mother a lot less than she paid when she bought the bakery. My mother ended up in a very bad position financially that she still hasn't been able to recover from."

Her stomach clenched when she saw the intense resentment etched on Thomas's face.

"I'm so sorry, Thomas," Rylie replied. "It sounds like your mother has been through a lot."

Thomas's face softened. He looked at her sadly. She thought she saw a slight glistening of tears in his eyes before he turned his face away from her.

"Yeah," he said. "I try to help my mother as much as I can, but I don't make much as a groundskeeper."

He turned around abruptly and walked away.

She headed back to the reception area with Bella and spent the rest of the morning searching the internet. Around lunchtime, Gillian came into the reception area from the door in back of the reception desk.

"Hi." Gillian smiled warmly at her. "How're things going?"

"Fine. I think I'm getting the hang of this. Bella's having a great time. She's appointed herself the Official Greeter, and she's getting lots of pets and attention from everyone."

Gillian smiled down at Bella. "Bella, are you having a good time?"

Bella rushed over to Gillian wagging her tail so hard from side to side that her whole body was wagging. Gillian laughed, then turned to Rylie.

"Hey, I know you're coming to dinner tomorrow night to meet Liam's poker buddies, but how would you like to also join us for dinner on Thursday night? Our friend, Brayden Hughes, the local Medical Examiner, is coming for dinner that night. We called him to see if he could give us any information about what might have caused Colin's death. He said he didn't want to talk about it on the phone, but that he's planning to be in the area on Thursday and he could talk to us then. So we invited him for dinner. He was happy to come. He's single, and I don't think he cooks much for himself. He's looking forward to having a good home-cooked meal."

"I'd love to join you," Rylie replied. "I can't wait to hear what he's been able to find out about what happened to Colin."

"He told us it can take months for the autopsy report to be completed," Gillian said. "But maybe he can at least shed a little light on what happened."

"I hope so. I'm starving. I'm going to go home and get some lunch. I'll talk to you later."

"Okay. Sounds good. Talk to you later."

After lunch, as she was headed back to the reception area with Bella, she saw a man walking up to the door.

"Hi! I'm Rylie. I'm one of the caretakers here. Can I help you?"

"Are Liam and Gillian here?"

She unlocked the front door and stepped inside with Bella. The man followed them in.

"They're off today," Rylie replied. "Can I help you with something?"

"I'm James Ferguson. I'm a friend of theirs. I need to talk to them. It's important."

"I'm not sure if they're around, but I'll give them a call."

"Okay, thanks."

She called Gillian from the business cell phone and told her James Ferguson was there to talk to her and Liam.

"No problem. Tell James I'll get Liam, and we'll be right out."

The door to Liam and Gillian's house flew open a minute later. Liam quickly crossed the reception area with a broad smile on his face.

"James! Good to see you! How're you doing?"

James smiled as Liam gave him a couple friendly slaps on the back. "Hi, Liam. Gillian. I'm glad you're both here."

James' face turned sober. "I heard about what happened to Colin Matthews. I met his sister Dee for the first time when I went into Butter Lane Bakery this morning. I didn't even know he had a sister."

"We didn't either," Liam replied.

"Dee told me that the sheriff's department is considering Colin's death a murder," James continued. "I'm shocked. Do you know what happened?"

"Not yet," Liam replied. "We're hoping Detective Felton can get to the bottom of it soon. We can't believe that something like this could happen right here where we live. We're concerned for our safety and the safety of everyone that works here."

"I have some information that might prove useful to Detective Felton in his investigation," James said. "I wanted to talk to you about it before I go to the sheriff's department."

"I saw Colin having dinner with Aidan Flynn's wife, Katiana, last week," James continued. "They were in a booth way in the back of the Crystal Bay Steak and Lobster House. I couldn't tell who Colin was with at first. I'd heard rumors that he was having an affair with someone's wife, so I was very curious to see who he was with. I walked through the restaurant as far from their table as possible so Colin wouldn't see me. Then I saw that he was with Katiana Flynn. They were holding hands across the table and having a very intimate conversation. It was obvious it wasn't a casual meeting."

Rylie let out the breath she'd unconsciously been holding. Her mind was spinning. If Aidan Flynn found out that his wife was having an affair with Colin Matthews, what would he do? She'd never met Aidan, but she thought that any man that found out that some guy was having an affair with his wife would be furious.

Could Aidan have gotten angry enough to commit murder?

Liam and Gillian shared a look and then turned their attention back to James.

Liam spoke first. "Thanks for letting us know, James. Let me give you Detective Felton's cell phone number in case he's not at the sheriff's department when you go over there."

"Thanks." James shook his head sadly. "This whole thing is so crazy. Stuff like this doesn't happen around here."

"I know," Liam agreed. He handed James a piece of paper with Detective Felton's number on it. Then he reached for Gillian's hand and held it in his own.

Rylie looked at Liam and Gillian and felt her heart squeeze. She'd like to have a relationship like that someday.

"I'd better get going," James said. "I'm going to head over to the sheriff's department right now. It was nice meeting you, Rylie."

"Nice meeting you, too."

Quiet filled the room after James left. No one spoke for a long moment.

Gillian looked at Rylie. "You haven't met Aidan or Katiana yet. Katiana is one of the most beautiful women I've ever seen. I'm not surprised that Colin would be attracted to her. We heard rumors that Colin was having an affair with Katiana.

But Colin and Aidan were friends. They'd both been coming to Liam's weekly poker nights for a long time. We couldn't believe that Colin would do something like that to Aidan."

"Even if Colin was having an affair with Katiana," Liam growled, "I don't think Aidan would kill Colin if he found out about it. I'm sure he'd be angry. But I really don't think he'd go to that extreme. Aidan may not come across as the friendliest guy in the world, but he's a good man."

A woman that was staying in one of the guest cottages came in the front door of the reception area. Rylie walked quickly over to the woman to see what she needed. Liam and Gillian quietly slipped back into their home behind the reception desk while she answered the woman's questions about what boat cruises were available nearby. She was finding it hard to concentrate on giving out tourist information.

After the woman left, she sat down in the chair behind the reception desk to mull over what she'd just learned about Colin and his suspected affair with Aidan Flynn's wife, Katiana.

Bella put her head on Rylie's lap and looked up at her with dark brown eyes full of concern. She stroked Bella's head, then leaned over, wrapped her arms around her, and leaned into her soft golden fur. She breathed in deeply and then slowly let it out.

"What are we going to do now, Bella?"

Chapter 6

S he woke up while it was still dark the next morning. She looked over at Bella sleeping peacefully on the floor by the side of her bed. She was glad she had Bella for many reasons, but right now she was glad she had Bella for protection. Bella was a sweet golden retriever and she loved people, but she had a deep, powerful bark that would scare anyone that might be thinking about breaking into her home.

She lay in bed listening to the noises of the forest and lake. She heard some ducks quacking intermittently in the distance. She envisioned squirrels and other small forest creatures scurrying through the woods looking for food.

She got out of bed and started some coffee brewing. She let Bella outside to do her business, filled her dog dish with fresh kibble mixed with some canned food, and got her some fresh water. She let Bella back inside before she went to shower and get dressed. Bella made a beeline for her dog dish and polished off her breakfast in a matter of minutes.

It occurred to Rylie that the sunrise over the lake must be beautiful. She checked her cell phone. It was 5:30 in the morning and a cool 36 degrees.

"Bella, let's go watch the sunrise before we go to work today!"

Bella wagged her tail enthusiastically. Rylie put on a warm jacket and went outside. Bella bolted out the door and headed for the path that went down to the lake. It always amazed Rylie how Bella seemed to instinctively know where they were going and led the way.

The sky was just starting to lighten as the sun crept towards the horizon. She shoved her hands in her jacket pockets to keep them warm and walked toward the lake with Bella happily trotting in front of her.

The mountains surrounding the vast expanse of the lake were darkly silhouetted against the warm yellow glow of the rising sun. The sky above the yellow glow was deep purple, and the lake shone a luminescent lavender. It was absolutely beautiful. She sat down on one of the beach chairs to take in the show put on by Mother Nature. She felt a sense of reverence and peace that only being alone in nature could provide.

After a little while, she checked her cell phone. "Come on, Bella. We've got to go to work."

She headed to the reception area to get everything set up for the guests' continental breakfast. There was a small stack of Sierra Sun newspapers on the ground outside the door. She wondered why they hadn't been there on Monday or Tuesday, but then she remembered that the Sierra Sun was only published on Wednesdays and Fridays. She brought the stack of newspapers inside and set them on the coffee table in the seating area in front of the fireplace.

Then she noticed the headline on the front page.

Butter Lane Bakery Owner Colin Matthews Found Dead at Whitaker Cottages

Her jaw dropped. She quickly grabbed the stack of newspapers and shoved them behind the reception desk where they wouldn't be seen. She desperately wanted to read the article, but it would have to wait until she got everything set up for the guests' continental breakfast.

She got some coffee brewing and poured milk and juice into pitchers. Eric came in with two trays of freshly baked breads and pastries from Butter Lane Bakery. He helped her transfer the baked goods onto serving platters.

"Say, would tomorrow afternoon be a good time for me to bring Buddy over to play with Bella?"

"That would be great, Eric. I hope Buddy and Bella get along. Bella hasn't spent very much time with other dogs, I'm afraid. I think she identifies with people more than dogs."

Eric smiled. "Buddy loves other dogs. He's very friendly. I'm sure he and Bella will have fun together. Would 3:00 be okay?"

"Sure."

Guests started coming in to get their continental breakfasts. Rylie concentrated on smiling and trying to act normal even though her insides were churning while she waited to see what was in the Sierra Sun article. As soon as she was alone in the reception area, she picked up a copy of the paper.

Butter Lane Bakery Owner Colin Matthews Found Dead at Whitaker Cottages

Butter Lane Bakery owner, Colin Matthews, was found dead late Saturday night at Whitaker Cottages in Tahoe Pines. He was discovered unresponsive by one of the property caretakers in a room called the Absinthe Room located in a granite tunnel that runs below the property. Local emergency personnel arrived at the scene promptly but were unable to revive him. The Placer County Sheriff's Department has confirmed that Colin Matthews' death is being considered a homicide.

Colin Matthews purchased the struggling Tahoe City Bakery two years ago from Camilla Scott and turned it around to become one of the most popular local hangouts in Tahoe City. A review of the Placer County Environmental Health Department records shows that, in the week before his death, Colin applied for a permit to build a 100-seat restaurant on the vacant lot that he owned next to the old Tavern Grill.

She gasped. She knocked on the door to Liam and Gillian's house in back of the reception desk. Gillian answered the door a moment later.

"What's wrong, Rylie? You look like you've just seen a ghost!"

Rylie held up the Sierra Sun newspaper with the glaring headline "Butter Lane Bakery Owner Colin Matthews Found Dead at Whitaker Cottages." "This! There was a stack of these on the ground outside the front door when I got to work this morning. I hid them in back of the reception desk so none of the guests would see them until I got a chance to read the article and show it to you guys."

Gillian's face drained of color. "Liam! Come here! You need to see this!"

Liam appeared quickly and read the headline. "Oh no." He took the newspaper from Rylie's hand and started reading.

"Let's go sit at the kitchen table," Gillian said. "We'll turn on the doorbell so we'll know if anyone comes into the reception area. Would you like some coffee or tea, Rylie?"

"Yes, please. I'd love a cup of your Earl Grey tea."

Gillian filled a tea kettle with water, put it on the stove to boil, and put some Earl Grey tea bags in a china teapot. Then she joined Rylie and Liam at the kitchen table. Liam handed her the newspaper as she sat down.

They waited quietly as Gillian read the article. When she'd finished reading, Gillian looked up at them sadly. "This is a small community. The news that Colin was murdered was going to come out eventually. But I thought the sheriff's department would want to keep it quiet until they had more information."

"What I don't want is for this to become a media circus with reporters swarming all over the place," Liam said gruffly. "Or for our guests to be afraid to keep their reservations."

They looked at each other solemnly. The shrill whistle of the tea kettle pierced the air. Gillian jumped out of her chair and went over to the stove to pour the boiling water into the teapot.

The business cell phone rang. Rylie stepped away from the table to answer it.

"I understand," Rylie said. "Can you please hold a moment?"

She looked gravely at Liam and Gillian. "This guy has a reservation for next week. He said he just found out that there's been a murder on the property, and he wants to cancel his reservation. He says he can't afford to jeopardize his family's safety. What do you want me to do? Are we going to waive our normal cancellation policies because of Colin's murder and allow guests to cancel their reservations without any cancellation fees?"

Liam and Gillian exchanged a glance. "I guess we'll have to." Liam sighed. "I'll call Elizabeth and let her know what's going on." He pulled out his cell phone and went into the other room.

Rylie finished talking to the guy on the phone and came back to sit at the kitchen table with Gillian. Gillian set a steaming cup of Earl Grey tea in front of her. Rylie added sugar and milk to her tea and stirred it slowly, absorbed in her thoughts.

She looked up at Gillian. "Did you see the part where it said that in the week before his death, that Colin applied for a permit to build a new restaurant on the vacant land that's adjacent to the old Tavern Grill?"

"Yes. I wonder if that has something to do with why Patrick looked so angry when he saw Colin at Locals' Night?" Gillian twisted the wedding ring on her finger.

"I wonder if Detective Felton has read this article and whether he knew about Colin's application for a permit to build a new restaurant?" Rylie said. "I think we should call him."

"I do, too," Gillian said. "I'll have Liam call him when he gets back from talking to Elizabeth."

The doorbell rang and Rylie went to see who was in the reception area. There was a man from the security system company waiting at the reception desk. He told her that Liam was supposed to take him around the property so he could see where security cameras and monitors needed to be installed.

"I'll let Liam know you're here," Rylie said. She texted Gillian.

A little while later, Liam came into the reception area, greeted the man, and took him outside to show him around the property.

Rylie locked the front door and took Bella back to their house for lunch. She made herself a tuna salad sandwich. She bent down to give Bella a small piece of tuna. Bella wolfed it down quickly and looked hopefully up at Rylie for more.

"Sorry, Bella. You only get one piece. The rest is for me."

Bella wagged her tail slowly back and forth and laid down by the dining table in case Rylie happened to drop anything while she ate. Rylie's thoughts turned to the dinner at Gillian and Liam's house she'd be going to later with Gillian, Liam, and Liam's poker buddies. She was looking forward to meeting Aidan and Katiana Flynn. She wanted to see if they seemed close or like their marriage was in trouble. If Katiana was having an affair, surely she'd be less than affectionate with her husband.

That afternoon, a number of people called to cancel their upcoming reservations after hearing the news of Colin's murder. Rylie looked through the reservations on the computer for the rest of June, July, and August. They'd been almost completely booked for the whole summer just a couple of days ago. Now there were lots of empty spaces on the calendar. She felt bad for Elizabeth Whitaker. Her business was going to take a big hit through no fault of her own.

At 6:00, Rylie went home with Bella so she could change into something nice for dinner at Gillian and Liam's house. She chose a royal blue and black knit dress. After she slipped it on, she turned from side to side in front of the full-length mirror in her bedroom to see how she looked. The royal blue brought out the blue of her eyes and looked good with her blond hair. Satisfied with her appearance, she headed for Gillian and Liam's house with Bella trotting in front leading the way. This was going to be an interesting night.

Chapter 7

Rylie helped Gillian set the table while Liam put out a bottle of Irish whiskey, opened a bottle of cabernet sauvignon, and put a couple bottles of chardonnay on ice. Liam and Gillian's home felt warm and welcoming. She watched them working together to get things ready for dinner. Their closeness was evident. She felt very fortunate to have met them and for the friendships they were developing.

If only this dinner wasn't marred by the fact that one of Liam's friends might be a murderer.

Liam went to answer the door. He came back a few minutes later with Aidan and Katiana Flynn in tow.

"Did you meet Aidan and Katiana at Locals' Night, Rylie?" Liam asked.

"No, I didn't." She smiled at the couple.

Katiana gave Rylie a small hug. "Hi, Rylie. Nice to meet you."

"Nice to meet you too, Katiana, Aidan."

She tried to place Katiana's accent and decided it sounded Russian. Gillian had been right about Katiana's beauty. Katiana's long, dark brown hair hung in soft waves nearly down to her waist and perfectly framed her heart-shaped face and full red lips. A vintage platinum, ruby, and diamond necklace hung from her elegant neck. But what struck Rylie most about Katiana was the deep sadness that radiated from the depths of her dark brown eyes.

Katiana's husband, Aidan, was a little scary. His eyes were devoid of expression. A five o'clock shadow accentuated the hard line of his mouth. And the rigid way that he carried himself gave her the impression that he was ready to punch someone.

Alain and Margaux Dubois arrived shortly thereafter. She remembered meeting them briefly on Locals' Night and having been struck by the contrast between them. Whereas Margaux was thin with aristocratic facial features and an air of quiet dignity, Alain was muscular and bald with a dark stubble beard. They just didn't seem to fit, but she felt like it was due to more than just the difference in their outward appearances.

Once Patrick O'Farrell arrived, Liam escorted his friends into the living room for drinks. She stayed in the kitchen with Gillian to finish getting everything set up for dinner. Gillian had made a traditional Irish stew with big chunks of tender lamb, potatoes, and carrots suspended in a thick, flavorful gravy. It smelled amazing. She couldn't wait to try it.

"Ok, everyone! Come and help yourselves!" Gillian called out.

Everyone filled their blue stoneware bowls with the fragrant stew and took a place at the long wooden table in the dining area. Baskets lined with blue and white checked tea towels filled with freshly sliced baguettes and blue stoneware butter crocks were scattered along the length of the table.

She took her first bite of tender lamb floating in rich gravy. "Gillian, this is delicious!"

"Thanks, Rylie." Gillian smiled.

Everyone complimented Gillian on the wonderful meal. Rylie took a sip of her wine and looked around the table. Everyone seemed to be enjoying themselves. She ate quietly and listened to the conversations around her. No one said anything about Colin's death. It was like there was an unspoken agreement among the people at the table to fully appreciate the meal without any drama. She was grateful for that. This was a meal that deserved to be savored.

When everyone was done eating, the men got ready to go to the Card House for their weekly poker game. Liam asked Gillian if she would like help cleaning up the kitchen before he left.

"Oh, no, honey," Gillian replied. "I've got plenty of help. You go to the Card House and play poker. And try not to come home broke this time." She smiled at her husband as if they shared a private joke.

Liam gave her a wicked grin and kissed her lightly on the cheek before following his friends out the door.

Rylie helped Gillian with the dishes while Katiana and Margaux cleared the table and put the leftovers away. The cleanup didn't take long with all of them working together.

"Would you ladies like more wine, some Bailey's Irish Cream, tea?" Gillian asked. "I'll be happy to get you whatever you'd like."

"Bailey's Irish Cream sounds good," Rylie replied.

The other women thought Bailey's sounded good, too. They got their drinks and moved into the living room.

Katiana sat up straight and looked around the room. She was clutching her drink tightly. "I know everyone's been avoiding talking about Colin tonight. But it's all I can think about. I was horrified when I heard about his death. Then to find out that he was murdered! How could something like that happen?"

Rylie saw Katiana's grief. It was easy to believe that this woman could have been in love with Colin. "Were you and Colin close?" she ventured.

Katiana looked at her as if seeing her for the first time. She could see Katiana weighing her words carefully before replying.

"Aidan and I have known Colin for a long time. We considered him a good friend."

Rylie and Gillian exchanged a brief glance.

Margaux studied Katiana. "There have been rumors that you and Colin were having an affair."

Rylie's jaw nearly dropped to the ground at Margaux's brazen comment, but she managed to quickly recover her composure. She looked at Gillian and saw the shock registered on her face.

Katiana pulled herself up in her chair and faced Margaux squarely. Rylie was surprised to see Katiana's transformation into a strong, fiery woman with a fierce temper.

Maybe she is a match for her scary husband.

"I'm a married woman. I take my marriage very seriously," Katiana said. "Aidan would kill me if he ever thought I betrayed him. Not to mention that he would probably kill any man who dared to touch me."

Rylie watched as Katiana realized what she had just said. All the color drained from Katiana's face. No one in the room said a word.

"Do you think Aidan would kill Colin if he found out that you were having an affair with him?" Margaux asked. Rylie nearly choked.

Katiana couldn't hold it together anymore. Tears started to stream down her face. She jumped up out of her chair and grabbed her coat. "I have to go!" She ran out of the room. They heard the front door slam behind her.

Gillian, Rylie, and Margaux sat in stunned silence for a long minute.

"Wow. I didn't expect that," Rylie said. "Didn't Katiana and Aidan come in the same car? How will Aidan get home? And what are we going to tell him about why his wife ran off?"

Margaux got up from her chair. "I have to go now, too. It's been a long day and I'm tired."

"I understand. Let me walk you out," Gillian said.

"Now what?" Rylie asked Gillian when she returned. "Two of the men are stranded here without the cars they came in."

"I don't think we need to worry about it," Gillian replied. "I'm sure Liam will be happy to take Aidan and Alain home. They both live nearby. We should go let Liam know what's going on. Bella can come with us to keep us safe."

They walked to the Card House engrossed in their own thoughts with Bella leading the way. Gillian knocked loudly on the door. "Liam, it's me and Rylie!"

"Come in!" Liam shouted through the closed door.

The men were all seated at the poker table with their cards in front of them. They looked impatiently at the women.

Gillian looked at Aidan. "I wanted to let you know that Katiana decided to go home early. I'm sure Liam will be happy to give you a ride home when you're finished playing poker."

"What the hell happened?" Aidan demanded.

"We were talking about Colin's death," Gillian replied. "And Katiana got upset."

Rylie was impressed with Gillian's strength under Aidan's angry gaze and inwardly applauded her.

Aidan's glare deepened. Gillian continued, "Katiana said that you and she considered Colin a good friend. She couldn't believe that something like this could have happened."

Aidan looked slightly placated but was obviously still fuming.

Gillian turned to Alain. "Margaux left early, too. She said she'd had a long day and she was tired."

Alain looked a little surprised but didn't say anything.

"Women!" Patrick said. "That's why I'm not in a relationship. Women just complicate your life."

"You're not in a relationship Patrick," Liam said, "because no woman could put up with you for very long."

"Hmmph," Patrick replied.

"Thanks for letting us know, Gillian," Liam said. "I'll make sure Aidan and Alain get home safely after we're done playing poker."

Rylie and Gillian headed back to Gillian's house. Bella stayed close. They went inside and got comfortable around the table in Gillian's warm kitchen.

"What do you think of Katiana's outburst?" Rylie asked. "I thought Katiana looked very sad when I met her. And that Aidan looked very angry. Do you think Aidan may have found out about her affair with Colin? Do you think Aidan's capable of murder?"

Gillian gave her a strained look. "I don't know, Rylie. It's horrible to think that someone you consider a friend could be capable of such a thing. But I just don't know."

"Love and jealousy are powerful emotions," Rylie said. "I think it's possible that those emotions could be powerful enough to incite someone to act in ways that they normally wouldn't."

"I know Aidan has a temper. But I just can't believe that he'd kill someone," Gillian replied.

"I'm not saying that Aidan killed Colin. But I think we've got to consider all the possibilities until we know for sure who did."

"I know. You're right," Gillian said. "I just hope this whole ordeal is over soon."

She noticed that Gillian's Irish brogue became more pronounced when she got tired.

"I'm so sorry, Gillian. I know this must be really hard on both you and Liam."

"You've been thrown into the middle of it too."

"We'll get through this. We have to. And the sooner we can find out who killed Colin, the better it will be for everyone. I'm going to call it a night. You should get some rest too. You look exhausted."

She headed home with Bella. "I'm glad I have you Bella."

She reached down to stroke Bella's head as they walked side by side. Bella looked up at her and slowly wagged her beautiful golden tail. Rylie felt her heart warm with love for Bella.

Her thoughts went back to Colin Matthews' murder. Maybe she could find out something when she hung out at Butter Lane Bakery tomorrow.

Chapter 8

After three consecutive fifteen-hour shifts, she was more than ready to get away from Whitaker Cottages on her day off the next day. She got breakfast for Bella, then showered quickly and got dressed.

Bella wagged her tail and looking at her hopefully as she got dressed.

"I'm sorry, Bella. I've got to go to Tahoe City today and do some things. You're going to stay here and watch the house for me, okay?"

She leaned over and pressed the side of her cheek against Bella's muzzle and made kissing noises. Bella wagged her tail a little faster.

She put her laptop in her backpack and headed for Butter Lane Bakery. The flowers on the bakery's patio were blooming in a brilliant profusion of colors. She went inside and stopped to inhale deeply of the delicious aromas of baked goods and freshly brewed coffee. Sunshine poured through the windows and gave the bakery a welcoming atmosphere. A lot of the tables were already occupied by customers with their laptops and coffee.

She stepped up to the counter to peruse the selection of pastries and baked goods. She decided she had to have one of the dark chocolate croissants on display. Dee Matthews smiled at her. "Do you know what you want, Rylie?"

"Everything looks so delicious, Dee. But I've decided that I have to have one of your chocolate croissants. And I'd like a caffè latte too, please."

"Coming right up. You'd better go find yourself a seat before there aren't any left."

She looked around the coffee shop. She wanted a table with a good view of the other tables and the checkout counter. Fortunately, there was still a table available on the back wall that would give her a little bit of privacy and allow her to discreetly watch everyone. She set up her laptop on the table and laid her cell phone next to it. Dee arrived a few minutes later to deliver her chocolate croissant and caffè latte, then hurried off to help the next customer.

Rylie sat quietly for a few minutes. She took a sip of her caffè latte and an appreciative bite of her chocolate croissant. She decided that she should at least make a show of searching the internet for information on how to write a novel.

When she looked up from her laptop a few minutes later, she saw Alain Dubois with an attractive, well-toned man walk into the bakery. She tried to discreetly watch the two men without appearing to be staring.

Then Alain spotted her. He smiled and waved. "Hi, Rylie!"

Alain and the man purchased a bag of baked goods and a couple of coffees to go. Then Alain walked over to her table with the other man close behind.

"Rylie, this is Graham Sinclair," Alain said. "He's the project manager for several houses that I own around the lake. One of my businesses is to buy houses that are in poor condition, renovate them, and then sell them for a profit."

"That is as long as I do my job and make sure the renovation budgets are kept in check," Graham said. He exuded a warm and friendly personality. She liked him instantly.

Alain put his arm around Graham in a friendly gesture. "Yes, as long as you do your job." He smiled at Graham.

She watched their facial expressions and body language. Graham had a look of adoration on his face as he gazed into Alain's eyes. She recognized that look. These men were more than just friends. These men were in love with each other.

She remembered thinking that there was something not quite right about the relationship between Alain and his wife Margaux. Now it all made perfect sense. She wondered if Margaux knew her husband was in love with someone else.

Is Margaux the type of woman to get jealous? Or is she the type of woman that would look the other way? She thought Margaux might be the type of woman that would look the other way, but she really didn't know her well enough to be sure.

She snapped out of her thoughts and turned her attention back to Alain and Graham. They were both looking at her. Alain no longer had his arm around Graham.

"We've got to get going. We have to get to our first job site," Alain said. "If we don't monitor the construction crew closely, things start to go wrong."

"I understand. It was nice meeting you, Graham." Rylie smiled. "I'm sure I'll see you around."

She resumed her internet search on her laptop. The next time she looked up, she saw Katiana Flynn walk into the bakery. Katiana met her gaze briefly, then turned her attention to the baked goods on display without acknowledging her. She continued to discreetly watch as Katiana selected a pastry and ordered some coffee.

After ordering, Katiana looked around for someplace to sit. Rylie waved. "Katiana! You can sit at my table. I have room." Katiana looked less than enthusiastic about her offer but made her way over to Rylie's table. "Hi, Rylie. How are you?"

"I'm fine. How are you? Have a seat. I'm really sorry if we upset you last night when we were talking about Colin Matthews."

Katiana studied her for a minute before replying. She sat down on the chair opposite Rylie. "Colin was a good man. He didn't deserve to die."

"Of course he didn't. I only got the chance to talk to him briefly, but he seemed like a really nice guy," she replied. "I wish I'd gotten the chance to get to know him better. I can't imagine why anyone would want to hurt him, much less kill him."

Tears threatened to overflow from Katiana's eyes.

"How about we talk about something else? Something more positive," Rylie suggested.

"Ok. What do you want to talk about?"

Dee quickly dropped off Katiana's pastry and coffee. Rylie smiled at Dee and then looked back at Katiana. She tried to think of a way to steer the conversation into something less volatile.

"I've been trying to place your accent. Where are you from?" she asked.

"I'm from Russia. I moved here when I was 23 years old after I got my degree in English Language and Literature. I couldn't find a job in my country. I thought there might be more opportunities for me in the United States. So I started applying for jobs in the U.S."

She wondered what life had been like for Katiana in Russia.

She seems so sad. Is her sadness only because of Colin's murder? Or is there more?

She didn't want to pry, so she was careful with her questions.

"So I assume you found a job here?"

"Yes. I was hired as a personal assistant to a Russian woman who'd married a very wealthy American businessman."

"Interesting."

"I left that job when I married Aidan."

Katiana stopped to sip her coffee and take a bite of her pastry. "So, what's it like being a veterinarian? I had a cat when I was growing up. My mother left me alone a lot. She had to work. My father committed suicide when I was two years old. So it was just me and my mother. And my cat."

"I'm sorry about your father."

"It was a long time ago. It's hard to miss someone that you don't even remember."

"I understand. In answer to your question, working as a veterinarian can be challenging, but it can be rewarding too." Rylie smiled. "My favorite part is when clients bring in cute puppies for their puppy shots. Cute puppies always make my day."

Katiana smiled a soft smile that didn't quite reach her eyes. A movement on the other side of the bakery caught Rylie's eye. She looked up to see Aidan Flynn standing in the open doorway. He spotted his wife at her table and strode angrily toward her. He grabbed Katiana's arm and lifted her roughly from her chair.

"What are you doing here? I told you not to come here," he growled.

"I'm having coffee with a friend." Katiana met her husband's stony gaze without flinching. "Let go of me!"

She pushed her husband's chest as hard as she could with her free hand. Aidan didn't let go of Katiana's arm. They glared at each other.

A giant of a man suddenly towered over the couple. "I think the lady wants you to let go of her arm, buddy," he said.

Aidan looked up at the man scornfully for a long minute. Rylie held her breath. Then Aidan dropped Katiana's arm and stalked out of the bakery.

She let out her breath slowly. Everyone in the bakery was staring at them. The whole bakery was quiet. Then the buzz of conversations resumed. The giant man walked away and sat back down at his table.

"I have to go," Katiana said. She gathered up her purse and headed for the door.

I would love to know the rest of that story, she thought as she watched Katiana leave.

A little after one o'clock, Rylie packed up her laptop and left to get some lunch. She drove down the west shore of the lake to Sunnyside Restaurant. She wanted to sit out on their lakeside deck while she ate.

Sunnyside was packed as usual, but they managed to seat her quickly at a table out on the deck with a wonderful lake view. She was excited when she saw crab cakes on the menu. The waiter showed up soon after she was seated. She placed her order and then sat looking out over the lake and thinking about everything that had occurred since she'd arrived at Whitaker Cottages.

I've only been here a week, but it seems like I've been here a lot longer. So much has happened since I got here.

The waiter brought her lunch, and she ate while watching everything that was happening on the lake in front of her. It was a beautiful sunny day. The lake stretched out in a sparkling pale blue expanse to the mountains cradling its border on the opposite shore. She watched a couple people go by on stand-up paddleboards. A few boats went by at slow speeds while the people on board waved at the people on Sunnyside's deck.

She felt herself slowly starting to relax. She hadn't realized how tense her shoulders and back muscles were until her muscles started to unwind. She started to think about the fun things that she wanted to do at the lake before the summer was over.

A well-dressed man that looked vaguely familiar appeared at her table.

"Hi, Rylie." He smiled at her. "I'm Blake Cunningham. We met on Saturday night at Locals' Night."

She thought back to the Locals' Night party. It seemed so long ago. She vaguely remembered meeting Blake. What she remembered most was that there was something about him that put her off and made her feel uncomfortable.

"Oh, yes." She tried to summon up a smile that would appear genuine. "I remember you told me that you've got a really sweet German shepherd."

Blake beamed at her recollection. She cringed inside. She hoped her feelings didn't show. She wondered how she was going to get this guy to go away and leave her to enjoy her lunch.

"I'm on my way back to my office," Blake said. "But I'd love to take you to lunch sometime. What do you say?"

"I'm not really looking to date anyone right now," she replied. "But thank you for the offer."

"Oh, it wouldn't be a date. Just a casual lunch. I'm sure you don't want to spend your entire summer all by yourself out there in the woods at Whitaker Cottages. There are so many great restaurants around here. Have you been to the Bridgetender Restaurant by Fanny Bridge? They claim to have the best burgers and Bloody Marys in Lake Tahoe."

Rylie grinned in spite of herself. "You had me at burgers and Bloody Marys. I love a really good burger. I consider myself a burger connoisseur. And I love Bloody Marys as long as they're made from scratch and not from Bloody Mary mix."

Blake smiled triumphantly. "I can tell you from personal experience that the burgers and Bloody Marys at Bridgetender's are some of the best I've ever had. How about tomorrow? Would you like to meet at Bridgetender's tomorrow - say around 12:30?"

She considered Blake's offer for a moment before replying. She had absolutely no romantic interest in Blake, but since he was a local, he might be able to provide her with information that could prove useful to Detective Felton in his murder investigation.

"Okay," she replied. "See you then."

"Great! See you tomorrow!"

She watched him make his way through the crowd on the deck. She wondered if she'd done the right thing by agreeing to meet him for lunch. He gave her the creeps. She wasn't sure why.

She finished her lunch and then checked her cell phone to see what time it was. It was almost time to meet Eric for the play date they had set up for Bella and Buddy.

Chapter 9

S he got back to her house a little before 3:00. "Bella! Eric and Buddy are coming over so you can meet Buddy and get a chance to play with him! Does that sound like fun?"

Bella bounced up and down and wagged her tail. She was game for whatever Rylie was suggesting. Rylie gave her a quick brushing so she'd look pretty when Eric and Buddy arrived.

Right around 3:00, there was a knock at the door. Bella rushed to the door barking and wagging her tail. When Rylie opened the door, she was greeted by Eric and a large strawberry blonde golden retriever. Buddy wagged his tail and gave Bella with a big golden retriever grin. It was obvious that Buddy loved everybody and had a great disposition. Buddy stretched his neck out to sniff Bella from where he stood. Bella looked cautiously interested.

"Hi, Rylie!" Eric said. "This is Buddy. He's very excited about getting a chance to play with Bella."

"Hi, Buddy! I'm going to bring Bella's frisbee with us. Bella loves playing frisbee. Does Buddy like to play frisbee?"

"Oh, yes. He loves it!"

"I got Bella a soft rubber frisbee so it doesn't hurt her mouth when she catches it."

"That's a great idea."

She showed Bella her frisbee. Bella bounced around excitedly. "Let's go outside and play, Bella!"

She stepped outside and Bella bounded happily after her. Buddy moved close to Bella, pushing his muzzle into her neck to encourage her to play with him.

"Let's go down to the lake," Rylie suggested. "The hard-packed part of the beach will be a great place to throw the frisbee for them."

"Sure. I brought a tennis ball we can throw for them too."

They headed for the lake with Buddy and Bella romping around in front of them.

"I hung out at Butter Lane Bakery for a while this morning," she said. "I'm researching information about how to write a novel. I have no idea if I can write a book, but I'd like to try."

"That's interesting. Do you like to write?"

"I do. It seems to come naturally to me. I think it might be really fun to write a novel. I should have some time this summer to at least pursue the idea and see where it goes."

"That's great, Rylie. I think it's important to pursue things that we're passionate about. So many people just live their lives taking care of their day-to-day responsibilities without taking time out for themselves to do the things they really enjoy doing. I don't ever want to become that kind of person."

She looked over at Eric. He seemed to be very insightful for someone so young. She was thirty-two years old, and she'd just started to realize the truth of what Eric was saying. She was impressed with his maturity. She could see that she and Eric could become very good friends.

When they got to the beach, Bella and Buddy ran around sniffing everything in sight. A small bird landed on the beach and attracted both dogs' attention. Bella and Buddy took off at a sprint toward the little bird, but it flew away long before they reached it. All in good fun.

"Bella!" Rylie called out. "Want to play frisbee?"

Bella and Buddy ran over with big grins on their faces and their tongues lolling out the sides of their mouths. She threw the frisbee in a straight line just above the dogs' heads. Bella and Buddy charged after it. Bella neatly plucked the frisbee out of the air at a dead run. Then she turned and pranced back toward Rylie and Eric, celebrating her catch. Buddy hopped around joyfully next to Bella, obviously eager to have a turn with the frisbee that Bella held proudly in her mouth.

"Good job, Bella!" Rylie exclaimed. Bella wagged her tail and took a few appreciative chomps on the frisbee. Then she dropped the frisbee on the ground about ten feet away from where Rylie and Eric stood.

"I've never been able to get Bella to bring her frisbee, or her tennis ball, all the way back to me," she said. "I'm not sure why she drops it so far away."

Buddy took advantage of the opportunity to grab the frisbee and make off with it. He enjoyed a few good chews on the soft rubber.

"Hey, Buddy!" Eric called. "Bring the frisbee!"

Buddy came running back to Eric with the frisbee in his mouth and dropped it neatly at Eric's feet.

"Good boy, Buddy!" Eric said. "Okay, you guys. Are you ready to catch the frisbee again?"

Bella and Buddy stood poised for flight waiting for Eric to throw the frisbee. Eric threw the frisbee the way Rylie had with the frisbee sailing just above the dogs' heads. Both dogs bolted after it.

Buddy got to the frisbee first this time. He snatched the frisbee out of the air and chomped down on it with glee. Bella bounced up and down next to Buddy and touched the frisbee with her nose a couple times. Buddy dropped the frisbee right in front of Bella so she could have it. Bella scooped up the frisbee instantly and triumphantly ran off with it in her mouth.

Rylie laughed. "What a gentleman! Buddy sure knows how to charm a girl!"

Eric grinned. "It looks like Bella is having a great time with Buddy. I told you Buddy gets along great with everyone. He's just a happy, easygoing kind of guy."

"Golden retrievers are the best dogs," she replied. "They're so happy and loving. I love Bella with all my heart."

"I feel the same way about Buddy."

They took turns throwing the frisbee for the dogs a few more times.

"I think they're getting a little tired," she said. "Why don't we relax on some beach chairs for a while and let Bella and Buddy run around on their own?"

"Sounds good."

They walked over to where the beach chairs were lined up facing the lake. Eric sat back on a lounge chair and stretched out his legs. "I don't get to sit and enjoy looking at the lake very often. It's so beautiful and peaceful here."

"Yes, it is. Something about looking out over a large body of water like Lake Tahoe or the ocean has always had a very calming effect on me."

She got comfortable on a lounge chair next to Eric and gazed at the lake. "This is definitely one of the most beautiful places on earth."

The lake shimmered with varying shades of blue as it stretched toward the mountains on the far shore.

"It's hard to believe that something so horrible as a murder could happen in such a beautiful and tranquil place," Eric said. "I still can't believe Colin's gone. He was a good friend as well as my boss. He was the one that helped me get started on a career as a baker. I wouldn't be where I am today if it weren't for Colin."

She could feel Eric's pain and sadness. She felt so sorry for both Eric and Colin.

"We've got to find out what happened that night and who killed Colin," she said. "Did Colin have any enemies that you know of? Did you ever hear him arguing with anyone?"

Eric thought for a while before answering. "I heard that Thomas Scott, the son of the previous owner, felt like Colin cheated his mother when he bought the bakery from her. But I never saw Thomas in the bakery when I was working there. I don't know him very well. I just know what people in town were saying."

"Colin was such a nice guy," he continued. "He had the kind of personality that drew people to him. Especially women, I guess. There always seemed to be a bunch of attractive women hanging out at the bakery on the days Colin worked."

"Do you know if Colin had a girlfriend?"

"As far as I know, I don't think he ever really settled down into a relationship with just one woman," Eric replied. "Although I'm sure there were a lot of women that would have liked to have been in a relationship with him. I think he was considered one of Tahoe City's most eligible bachelors."

"I heard the rumors, like everyone else, that Colin was having an affair with Aidan Flynn's wife," Eric continued. "I did see her in the bakery from time to time, but I never saw Colin alone with her. I've also heard that Aidan Flynn has a reputation for having a very bad temper, so I think Colin would've been taking a huge risk to get involved with his wife."

"You know what? I do remember Colin having an argument with someone! It wasn't at the bakery though. Colin took me over to see his land on the other side of town where he planned to build a new restaurant. His land is right next to the old Tavern Grill that Patrick O'Farrell bought. When we were walking around Colin's lot, we saw Patrick and another guy walking around the Tavern Grill."

"Patrick came over to talk to us. I guess he wanted to buy Colin's land. Colin told me that Patrick needed more land for additional parking to get the permits he needed to expand the Tavern Grill. When Patrick first came over to us, he seemed friendly enough. He asked Colin if he was sure he didn't want to sell his land to him. He said he would make it worth Colin's while. Colin made it clear that he wasn't the slightest bit interested in selling."

"Then Patrick got mad and started yelling at Colin. I don't remember everything he said, but he was really angry. Colin said we had to go, and we left before things got out of hand. I just remembered that," Eric said. "Do you think I should tell Detective Felton about it?"

"Definitely. We need to give Detective Felton any information we have that might help him in his investigation. I have his cell phone number. I'll give it to you so you can call him."

"Thanks. I'll put it in my contacts right now and call him when I get home."

"Okay."

She told Eric about the piece of paper in Colin's pocket with her name and cell phone number on it. "I'm worried that Detective Felton considers me a suspect. I have no idea how Colin could have gotten my cell phone number. Do you know anything about it?"

"No. I'm just as baffled as you are."

"This is personal information. Please don't tell anyone. The last thing I need is for everyone in town to consider me a suspect in Colin's murder."

"Don't worry. I won't tell anyone."

"Since Colin was so friendly and outgoing, I'm sure he made friends on his bakery delivery route. I was thinking it might be interesting to talk to some of the people on his route to see if I could learn anything that might be helpful to Detective Felton's investigation. Would you mind if I joined you on your delivery route tomorrow morning? I promise I'll be very discreet and not cause any problems. We could just say I had a day off and wanted to meet some of my neighbors."

"I don't see any problem with it, but I'll have to run it by Dee. I'll call her when I get home and let you know. Are you going to Colin's memorial service at Granlibakken on Saturday?"

"I hadn't heard anything about it. Maybe it's only for family and close friends."

"No, I think it's for anyone that wants to attend," Eric said. "I'm sure no one would be upset if you came."

"I'll talk to Gillian and Liam and see what they think about it. I only met Colin a couple times, but I still feel horrible about his death. I'd like to go to his memorial service."

Eric got out the tennis ball that he brought with him and threw it for Bella and Buddy a few times. Both dogs had a great time running after the ball. It made her happy to see Bella having such a good time and making friends with another golden retriever.

"This was so much fun, Eric," she said. "We'll have to do it again sometime. I think both Bella and Buddy had a great time."

"Definitely." Eric smiled. "I'll check to see if there's a time Buddy and I can come over next week and let you know. I'll call you later tonight after I talk to Dee."

"Sounds good."

Eric and Buddy headed to their car. She walked with Bella back to their house. She wanted to shower and change before going to dinner at Gillian and Liam's house later that night. She was anxious to talk to Brayden Hughes. She wanted to know how Colin had died, but she was a little apprehensive about learning the details.

Chapter 10

As soon as Bella got inside, she went over to her water bowl and took a long drink. Then she laid down in the middle of the living room and panted happily. Rylie could tell that Bella was a little tired from all the activities that afternoon.

She took a shower and then looked through her closet to decide what to wear to dinner at Gillian and Liam's house that evening. She chose a form-fitting forest green dress made of lace over a fabric lining. After she fed Bella her dinner, she got a mineral water out of the refrigerator and got comfortable on the sofa in the living room so she could relax a little before she had to leave.

She decided to call Sophie to update her on all that had happened.

"Hi, Sophie."

"Rylie! How are you?"

"I'm okay," she replied. "I still feel uncomfortable here because of what happened, especially when I'm alone in my house at night, but Detective Felton told me the sheriff's department is having patrol cars drive by and keep an eye on the property. So that's good. And Elizabeth Whitaker had a security system installed throughout the entire property including in my house."

"That's a relief," Sophie said. "And I'm glad the sheriff's department is patrolling the area."

She told Sophie about everything she'd discovered about Colin Matthews since the last time they'd talked.

"Sounds like you're becoming a bit of an amateur sleuth. I hope you're being careful."

"I am. But I have to do whatever I can to help Detective Felton and his team find out who killed Colin. I need to get my name off the list of possible suspects. I just wish I knew how Colin got my cell phone number."

She felt some of the tension drain from her shoulders as she talked to Sophie. She was glad she had Sophie in her life.

After she hung up with Sophie, Bella came over and stood in front of her, wagging her tail and looking at her expectantly.

"You can come. Gillian and Liam love you, and they're happy to have you come with me when I visit. Tonight we're going to meet someone new. His name is Brayden Hughes. He's the local Medical Examiner. Do you want to go to Gillian and Liam's house with me?"

Bella eagerly wagged her tail and broke out in a doggie grin.

"Okay, Bella. Let's go to Gillian and Liam's house!"

Bella bounced around excitedly and sprinted out the front door as soon as she opened it. She followed as Bella led the way to Gillian and Liam's house. Liam opened the door and welcomed them.

Gillian turned around from where she was working in the kitchen and smiled.

"It smells amazing in here, Gillian! What are you making?"

"I'm making pot roast with carrots, onions, and potatoes."

"Yum! Can't wait!"

They heard a knock on the door. Liam went to answer it. A very tall, good-looking man stood in the doorway.

"Brayden!" Liam exclaimed. "Good to see you, man! It's been too long!"

He introduced Brayden to Rylie and Bella.

"Hi, Rylie," Brayden said. "Nice to meet you."

Brayden's hazel green eyes were kindly and intelligent. He carried himself with an air of self-confidence tempered by humility.

"Nice to meet you too, Brayden."

Brayden squatted down to Bella's level and Bella rushed over to greet him. She wagged her tail, delighted by the attention Brayden gave her. Rylie smiled as she watched Bella's antics.

"Would either of you like something to drink?" Gillian asked. "Wine, beer, mineral water?"

"I'll have a glass of wine," Rylie said.

"I'll have a beer," Brayden replied.

"Let me help you, Gillian." She went into the kitchen. "I can get the drinks. Where are the wine and beer?"

"There's zinfandel on the counter over there. If you'd rather have sauvignon blanc, it's in the refrigerator. There's Guinness and hefeweizen beer in there too."

"Brayden, would you rather have Guinness or hefeweizen beer?" Rylie asked.

"I'll have a hefeweizen. Thanks," Brayden replied.

She brought Brayden his beer and then went back into the kitchen to help Gillian get everything ready for dinner. She set the table with Gillian's beautiful midnight blue stoneware and sliced a couple fresh baguettes.

Gillian put the pot roast on a large stoneware platter and arranged the steaming potatoes, carrots, and pearl onions around it.

"That looks delicious, Gillian," she said.

"Okay guys, come and get it," Gillian said.

Brayden and Liam joined Rylie and Gillian in the dining area, and everyone took a seat at the long wooden table.

Brayden eagerly eyed the pot roast in the center of the table. "Gillian, this looks and smells incredible!"

"Thanks, Brayden. I hope you like it," Gillian replied.

Everyone served themselves and started in on the delicious meal.

"How did you and Gillian meet Brayden?" Rylie asked Liam.

"Brayden stays in one of the cottages from time to time when he comes up here on vacation," Liam replied. "It's only about two and a half hours from where he lives in Folsom, so he manages to get up here a few times a year."

"I love it here," Brayden said. "I especially like it in the summer, but I come here to ski in the winter sometimes too."

"I grew up in northern California, so I've been coming to the lake pretty much all my life," Rylie said. "But I hadn't been here in years until I came to help Gillian and Liam this summer. It's so beautiful here and there's so much to do. I'm looking forward to getting out and exploring the area on my days off."

"Where are you staying tonight, Brayden?" Liam asked. "I hope you aren't planning to drive back to Folsom after dinner tonight."

"I'm staying at a friend's house in Tahoe City. I have a meeting at the sheriff's department early tomorrow morning."

Everyone enjoyed the delicious dinner. Then Brayden got up and started clearing the table. Rylie got up and joined him.

"Oh, you don't have to do that, Brayden," Gillian said. "Rylie and I can clean up while you and Liam go and chat in the living room."

"Don't be silly, Gillian," Brayden said. "You worked hard to make this incredible meal. You go sit in the living room and relax with your husband. Rylie and I will clean everything up."

"Yes, you go sit down and relax, Gillian," Rylie agreed. "We'll have everything cleaned up in no time."

Gillian looked helplessly from Rylie to Brayden. "Okay. I guess I can sit down and relax a little."

Rylie worked with Brayden to get the leftovers put away and the dirty dishes loaded into the dishwasher. Then they joined Gillian and Liam in the living room.

"I guess we need to address the elephant in the room," Liam said. "We're hoping you can help us make some sense out of everything's that's happened here recently, Brayden. Colin's murder has left us all in shock. What can you tell us about his death? I know it's an active murder investigation and you probably can't tell us everything. But Colin was our friend. The fact that he was murdered right here where we live really upsets us. And we're concerned about our safety and the safety of the people that work here."

Brayden straightened in his chair. A muscle flexed in his jaw. "It may take months to get all the test results back from the autopsy. But I can tell you that Colin Matthews died from injuries sustained when his head struck the granite wall in the Absinthe Room. His head hit the wall pretty hard."

Rylie looked over at Liam and Gillian. Gillian looked a little green.

"Are you okay, Gillian?" she asked.

"Yes, I'm fine. But I might like a cup of tea. Would anyone else like some tea?"

She went with Gillian to the kitchen to make some tea and then rejoined the men in the living room.

"I'm sorry, Gillian," Brayden said. "I know this must be hard for you. It's horrible that this happened at all, not to mention that it occurred right where you live. The sooner the person who did this is put behind bars, the better it will be for everyone."

She watched Liam quietly take Gillian's hand. It was clear they had the kind of deep love that she'd like to have someday. A pang of loneliness washed over her. She forced her thoughts back to the present.

"Here's what we know at this point. There were at least two other people in the Absinthe Room with Colin Matthews on the night he was killed."

She looked at Gillian and Liam and saw the look of shock on their faces.

"What are you saying, Brayden?" Liam asked. "That Colin was attacked by two people at once? How can that be?"

"At this point, we have no idea if both people were in the room at the same time or if they were in the room at different times. My gut tells me that the two people were in the room at different times, but I have no way to prove that."

"The bruising on Colin's face indicates that he was punched in the face two times," Brayden continued. "Once on the left side and once on the right. A right-handed person would tend to punch someone on the left side of their face whereas a left-handed person would tend to punch someone on the right side. That's why I believe there were at least two other people in the Absinthe Room on the night that

Colin was murdered. One was left-handed and the other was right-handed."

"I can't imagine how three people could go into the tunnel on Locals' Night without us noticing," Liam said.

"We were busy taking care of our guests," Gillian said. "In all the times that we've hosted Locals' Night, it's never occurred to me to worry that one of our guests might go into the tunnel. Only a few people even know how to get into the tunnel other than you and I. I know you showed your poker buddies the tunnel, so Colin would know how to get into it. Oh, and I think you showed Thomas the tunnel one time."

"Maybe Colin brought one or both of the other people into the tunnel with him for some reason," Rylie said.

"There's more," Brayden said. "The bruising on the right side of Colin's face was worse and noticeably larger in size than the bruising on the left side. Based on that, I think that the left-handed person that punched Colin had larger hands and was stronger than the right-handed person."

"I think it may have been the left-handed punch that threw him back into the wall with such force that it ended up killing him. I was able to find a small amount of skin under two of Colin's fingernails. I submitted the sample to the lab so they can extract DNA and see if the DNA matches anyone in the database."

They sat quietly absorbing all that Brayden had told them.

"Well, thank you for letting us know what you know so far, Brayden," Liam said. "I have to say that it's a bit disconcerting to know that at least two other people were in the Absinthe Room with Colin that night. I'm not really sure what to make of it. Do you know if Detective Felton has any suspects?"

"No, I don't," Brayden replied.

Gillian got up from the sofa. "This is a lot to process. We really appreciate your taking the time to come here and let us know what you've found out so far, Brayden. Would anyone like something else to drink?"

"No thanks, Gillian," Brayden said. "I've got to get going. I have to get up early tomorrow. Thank you for a wonderful dinner. It was delicious."

Brayden got up, said his goodbyes, and left. She looked at Liam and Gillian. They both looked tired and stressed.

"Bella and I are going to call it a night, too. Thanks for a wonderful dinner, Gillian."

"You're welcome, Rylie. I'll walk you out," Gillian said.

She walked back to her house deep in thought about all she'd just learned. She was looking forward to meeting the people on the Butter Lane Bakery delivery route with Eric the next day. Maybe she'd get lucky and learn something that could help Detective Felton find Colin Matthews' murderer, whoever that was.

Chapter 11

She got up early the next morning so she could meet Eric at the Butter Lane Bakery to go with him on his bakery delivery route. While Bella was outside doing her business, she put some fresh kibble in Bella's dish and got her some fresh water. Bella ran to her dish as soon as Rylie let her in. Bella happily munched on her breakfast while Rylie made herself some freshly brewed coffee and an English muffin.

After breakfast, she showered and got dressed. Bella was laying on the floor watching her as she prepared to leave.

"I'm going to go with Eric, Buddy's daddy, on his delivery route this morning, Bella. You remember Eric and Buddy, right? You be a good girl for me while I'm gone, okay?"

Bella thumped her tail up and down on the floor a few times.

The first blush of sunrise was just beginning to lighten the sky as she parked in the Butter Lane Bakery's parking lot. She spotted Eric carrying a couple of large trays of baked goods to his delivery van.

"Morning!" she called out.

"Morning! Do you want to step inside where it's warm while I finish loading the van?

"Okay."

A short while later, they set off down the west shore of the lake so Eric could deliver his baked goods to motels, bed and breakfast inns, and restaurants along the way. When he stopped at Sunnyside Restaurant and Lodge, she purchased some coffees to go. She handed one to Eric as she got back in the van.

"Thanks," Eric said. He sipped his coffee appreciatively.

They chatted briefly with the people that greeted them as Eric made each delivery, but they didn't stay long enough to have in-depth conversations with anyone. She was hesitant to bring up the subject of Colin Matthews' murder with the people they met on Eric's route. It didn't seem appropriate under the circumstances.

Maybe I should have thought this through a little better before I asked Eric if I could join him. I can't just walk up to perfect strangers and ask them if they know anything that could help Detective Felton in his murder investigation. Or if they know anything that could help me clear my name.

They stopped to deliver baked goods at Sierra Vista Cottages in Homewood.

"Wow! This place is gorgeous!" she said. "I don't think I've ever seen this place before."

"There have been rental cottages here for a long time, but they probably didn't look like this the last time you saw them," Eric replied. "It was sold to new owners about five years ago. They tore down all the old run-down cottages and built new ones. They built the nicest Tahoe rental cottages I've ever seen. You should see the interiors. They decorated them with contemporary furnishings, but they still have that old Tahoe charm that everyone loves."

She walked with Eric into the reception area. An attractive young woman with long blonde hair and a contagious smile greeted them from behind the reception desk.

"Olivia! This is Rylie Sunderland," Eric said. "She's a veterinarian from the East Bay. She's between jobs right now, so she's helping out as a temporary caretaker at Whitaker Cottages this summer. She wanted to get out and meet some of the neighbors, so I told her she could ride along with me today."

She liked Olivia instantly. "Your place is really nice. I've never seen it before. I haven't been up here in a while."

"Thanks," Olivia replied. "It was a lot of work, but we're so happy with the way it turned out. I'd be happy to show you around when you have time."

A dark-haired man with a stubble beard came into the reception area. He looked at Rylie and their eyes met. She nearly choked.

"Laurent?"

"Rylie! So good to see you!" Laurent exclaimed.

"I see you've met my husband?" Olivia said.

"Rylie's a good friend of mine from college," Laurent said. "We lost touch with each other after we graduated and she went to vet school. How are you, Rylie?"

He closed the distance between them and gave her a big hug. It felt warm and comfortable. She opened her eyes to glance at Laurent's wife. Olivia was watching them with amused interest. She relaxed a little when she saw that Olivia didn't seem to be the jealous type.

"Laurent! What are you doing here? I can't believe you bought a property in Lake Tahoe!" she said. "You've done an amazing job with this place. I'm really impressed. I can't wait to get a tour."

"Rylie, I'm sorry, but I've got to get to my next delivery," Eric said. "Do you still want to come with me? Or do you want to stay here and visit with your friends for a while?"

"I don't want to impose. I can call you later to set up a time to visit and chat with both of you," she said to Laurent.

"We have time now, if you want," Laurent replied. "I'll be happy to give you a ride home later."

"Great! Thanks for letting me tag along with you today, Eric. Talk to you later."

"Have fun then," Eric said. He waved goodbye and walked out to his delivery van.

Laurent put his arm around her shoulders and gave her a squeeze. "Come on in our house, Rylie. We live right in back of the reception area."

"Can I get you something to drink?" Olivia asked.

"No thanks. I'm fine for now," she replied. "I want to hear about everything you've been doing since college, Laurent. And I want to know how you two met and all that."

She got comfortable on the sofa while Laurent filled her in on the years since they were in college together.

Her mind wandered occasionally to memories of times she'd spent with Laurent all those years ago. He was so handsome. He'd always had a bunch of girls vying for his attention when they were in college. For some reason, their relationship had never been romantic, but they'd been very close. In the years since college, she'd thought of him from time to time and wondered why their relationship never progressed into something more. Laurent was always her "what if."

Their talk eventually turned to more recent events. She was surprised to discover that Laurent had been good friends with Colin Matthews. He was obviously grieving Colin's death.

"Colin took too many chances. He thought he was invincible," Laurent said.

"What do you mean?" she asked.

"He had his hands in a lot of things, including some things that he shouldn't have gotten involved in," Laurent replied. "Let's talk about something more cheerful, shall we? How about I give you a tour of some of our cottages? We have one, two, three, and four-bedroom cottages."

She was disappointed not to learn more about Colin Matthews, but she didn't think she should press the issue with Laurent right now. Better to ease into the subject without putting him on guard. After her tour of the property, Laurent drove her back home and dropped her off with the promise that they would get together again soon.

She went in her house to get Bella. "Come on, Bella!"

Bella bounded out the front door and headed for Gillian and Liam's house. She followed close behind.

Gillian opened the door looking much more refreshed than she had the night before.

"Hi, Rylie," Gillian said. "Come on in! Would you like a cup of coffee or tea?"

"I'll have a cup of coffee. Thanks."

Liam called out a greeting from the kitchen.

"Have you been busy with guests this morning?" she asked.

"Not really," Liam replied. "It's been pretty slow since the story about Colin's murder was broadcast all over the news."

"I'm so sorry, Liam," she said. "Is Elizabeth upset by the loss of business?"

"I think she understands that it's not our fault," Liam replied. "But I'm sure she isn't happy about it. She had asked me a while back to hire a contractor to get two more of the cottages renovated so they can be used as additional rental units. She told me the other day that she still wants to go through with it. Alain Dubois is coming over this morning so I can show him what needs to be done and get his recommendations on the best contractors for the job. He has a lot of experience with local contractors. I trust that whomever he recommends will do a good job for us."

"I'd like to see the cottages that need renovations too," she said. "Would you mind if I tag along with you and Alain when you go through the cottages?"

"Not at all."

"Eric Larson told me there's a memorial service for Colin tomorrow," she said. "He asked me if I was planning to attend. I told him I would check with you to see what you think about me attending. I don't want to intrude if it's only meant for family and friends. Are you both planning to go? Do you think it would be appropriate for me to attend? I'd like to go even though I didn't know Colin very well. I feel really bad about his being killed."

"I think it would be lovely if you attended Colin's memorial service," Gillian said. "It's for anyone that wants to attend. Why don't you plan on going to the service with us?"

"Thanks, Gillian. That would be great."

Liam jumped out of his chair when they heard someone knocking on the door.

"Alain!" Liam said. "Come on in for a minute. You remember Rylie, don't you? She'd like to see the cottages that need renovations so I invited her to come along with us. I think Bella wants to come too."

Alain smiled at Bella wagging her tail happily and looking at him expectantly. He bent down and stroked her golden head. "Aren't you a pretty girl?" Bella wagged her tail a little faster.

"She loves people," Rylie said. "And she never gets tired of getting petted."

Liam led the way to the two old cottages that needed renovations.

"I don't think these cottages have been renovated since they were built in the late 1800s," Liam said. "They're in pretty bad shape. Elizabeth would like us to get them fixed up so we can use them as additional rental units. We want to hire a contractor that will do a good job but not overcharge us. Who would you recommend?"

Alain thought for a moment. "I think either Bob Sanchez or Tony Bartoletti would do a good job for you. Both of them do good work and are reasonably priced. I think Tony tends to be a little busier than Bob. It might be harder to get him than Bob. But either of them would be a good choice."

"What about Steve Randall?" Liam asked. "I've heard he does good work."

"He does do good work," Alain replied. "There's no question about it. I've used Steve for a couple of my renovation projects. But I stopped using him some time ago because he bids below everyone else and promises a completion date sooner than everyone else, but then his jobs end up costing more than his original bid and taking longer to complete than he promised."

"I was talking to Colin the week before he was killed," Alain continued. "He told me Steve had submitted a bid to build the restaurant he planned to put on his vacant lot by the old Tavern Grill. He rejected Steve's bid because he knew about Steve's reputation to overpromise and underdeliver. He planned to go with one of the other bids he received."

She looked at Liam. She could tell he was thinking the same thing she was.

"Did you tell Detective Felton about this?" she asked. "I don't know how much of a temper Steve Randall has, but if he was angry with Colin because Colin rejected his bid, then I think he might need to go on the list of possible suspects."

"I know Steve has a temper," Alain replied. "But I certainly don't think he's a murderer."

"I don't think Rylie's accusing Steve of being a murderer, Alain," Liam said. "Detective Felton has asked us to let him know if we discover any information that could help him with his investigation into Colin's death. I agree with Rylie. I think it's important that you call Detective Felton and tell him what you just told us. Then he can talk with Steve Randall and get more information from him. I have Detective Felton's cell phone number. I'll give it to you when we're done here. I'd really appreciate it if you'd give him a call."

"Okay, Liam," Alain replied. "We've been friends a long time. I trust your judgment on this."

Alain turned to Rylie. "I know you're just trying to help, Rylie. I'm sorry if I overreacted when you suggested I should call Detective Felton."

"Don't worry about it," she replied. "This whole thing has been hard on all of us. Liam, Gillian, and I have been thrown into the middle of Colin's murder investigation because it occurred right here on the property. We want to do whatever we can to help Detective Felton find the murderer as soon as possible."

"I understand," Alain said. "I'll call Detective Felton when we're done here."

She pulled her cell phone out of her pocket to check the time.

"I'm sorry gentlemen, but I've got to go," she said. "I'm meeting someone for lunch. I've got to go get changed."

"Oh?" Liam teased. "Would this be anyone we know?"

"Yes." She felt the color rise in her cheeks. "Blake Cunningham. Gillian introduced me to him at the Locals' Night party."

Liam raised an eyebrow. She laughed. "Don't get any ideas, Liam! I'm not at all interested in Blake. He convinced me to meet him at Bridgetender's for lunch today because they claim to have the best burgers and Bloody Marys in Lake Tahoe. I love a good burger."

Liam and Alain exchanged a look.

"Come on, you two!" She smiled. "Seriously. I'm not the slightest bit interested in Blake. I agreed to have lunch with him because he's a local and he might know something that could help Detective Felton with his murder investigation. I've got to go. See you later. Come on, Bella!"

She headed back to her house with Bella trotting in front of her. She decided to stay in the jeans she was wearing but change her top to something a little dressier. She put on a deep green chiffon blouse.

"Okay, Bella. I'm going to go out to lunch with Blake Cunningham. You haven't met him. Anyway, I won't be gone long. When I come home, we'll go for a nice walk."

Bella wagged her tail hopefully.

"You watch the house for me while I'm gone, okay?" She headed for the door.

Chapter 12

She drove into Tahoe City and pulled into the Bridgetender Tavern parking lot. As she walked toward the restaurant, she saw Blake standing out in front. He caught her eye and smiled as he walked over to her.

"Hi, Rylie. Nice to see you. You look very pretty today. Are you ready for some burgers and Bloody Marys?"

She returned his smile. "Sure. I love a good burger."

"Would you like to sit outside or inside?"

"It's such a beautiful day. Let's sit outside."

They followed the hostess down a cobblestone walkway. She stopped at a rustic wooden table with bench seats and a sand-colored umbrella. After they sat down, she handed them some menus and asked what they'd like to drink.

"I'll have an iced tea with lemon," she said.

"What? No Bloody Mary?" Blake said.

"Not today."

"I'll have an iced tea with lemon then, too," Blake said.

She browsed through the burger selection on the menu. "I'm going to have the blue cheese and bacon burger."

"I think I'm going to have the burger with Monterey jack cheese and sautéed mushrooms," Blake said.

A waitress appeared at their table with their drinks and took their orders.

"You know, in all the years I've been coming to the lake, I've never been to this restaurant before. I'm not sure why," she said.

"I come here for lunch from time to time. It's convenient for me because it's close to my office."

"I remember you told me on Locals' Night that you're a real estate attorney. What kind of real estate do you specialize in? Commercial or residential?"

"Mostly commercial," Blake replied. "But I do residential deals from time to time, especially for clients that I've worked with on commercial deals."

"Did you work on any real estate deals with Colin Matthews?" she blurted out. She instantly regretted not having been more discreet.

Blake looked at her for an excruciatingly long moment before responding. "No, I never worked with Colin Matthews on anything. I knew him, of course. This is a very small town. I feel really bad about his death. That type of thing doesn't happen around here."

She studied Blake's facial expression. His face was grave and slightly wary.

"Let's talk about something more cheerful," Blake said. "Tell me about yourself."

She sensed that Blake knew a lot more about Colin Matthews than he was letting on. But she knew she'd have to be much more discreet if she hoped to learn anything from him that might prove useful to Detective Felton in his investigation.

She told Blake about growing up in the San Francisco East Bay area and about her work as a veterinarian. The delight she experienced when she got to snuggle a warm puppy brought in for their puppy shots. The heart-wrenching task of having to put a pet to sleep. The satisfaction she got from helping sick or injured pets recover and feel good again. The long hours.

The waitress delivered their burgers. The delicious aromas coming from her burger made her mouth water. She took a bite. It tasted as good as it smelled.

"I know all about working long hours," Blake said. "My family was very poor when I was growing up. We lived in a bad neighborhood in the Bronx in New York City. I learned to fight in the streets when I was just a kid. It was either that or get the crap kicked out of me every day when I went to school. I clawed my way out of that life by working hard in school. I managed to get a scholarship to go to college. I've had to fight for everything I have in life, so I never take anything I have for granted."

She looked at Blake with newfound respect. He was dressed in nice clothes and wore an expensive-looking watch. She was surprised to learn that he was from a poor family and grew up in a bad neighborhood. She knew he must have worked very hard to get where he was today.

But at what cost? Did he have to step on people on the way up?

"That's an incredible story, Blake," she said. "Now you're a successful attorney living in one of the most beautiful places on earth."

"Yes," Blake replied. "I'm very grateful for that."

She saw an older gentleman with a pronounced limp hobbling quickly over to their table. He pointed a finger at Blake. "You son of a.... No one gets away with what you did to my daughter! I'll make sure you pay for what you did!"

Blake looked blankly at the man. It was obvious he had no idea who the man was.

A well-dressed woman rushed over to their table. She wobbled a little on the cobblestone path as she tried to navigate it in high heels. She came up next to the older gentleman and put her arm around him.

"Pop! Please don't!" she cried.

"Karalyn!" Blake exclaimed. "What the?"

"Sorry for the intrusion, Blake," Karalyn said curtly. "Come on, Pop." She succeeded in turning her father around and escorting him back toward the parking lot.

Rylie suddenly realized she was sitting with her mouth wide open. She quickly closed her mouth and looked over at Blake. Blake stared after the woman and her father.

"What was that all about?" she asked.

Blake looked at her with a perfect poker face. There was no expression in his eyes or facial features. It was as if the light inside him had gone out, and she was looking at a shell of the man she'd just been having lunch with.

"That was about a commercial real estate deal gone bad," he said. "And that was Karalyn Ashford, a very wealthy client of mine. Or should I say, a very wealthy former client of mine. And the older gentleman, apparently, is her father."

She sensed an undercurrent of tension, and possibly fear, in Blake in spite of his expressionless face.

He looked at his watch. "I'm sorry, Rylie, but I've got to get back to the office. I hope you had a good time before Karalyn and her father showed up. Please enjoy the rest of your lunch."

He left his burger barely touched on his plate and put some twenty-dollar bills on the table as he stood to leave. He walked briskly down the cobblestone path to the parking lot.

She finished her meal in silence, then walked out toward the parking lot. Just past the parking lot, she saw Fanny Bridge with its perpetual row of fannies facing the highway as people peered over the edge of the bridge into the Truckee River below.

She noticed the bike path that ran along the Truckee River and decided to go home and get Bella so she could take her for a walk along the river. Bella would love it and it would give her some time to sort through all the thoughts that were racing through her mind.

Chapter 13

As she walked in the front door of the house, Bella rushed up to greet her with a happy doggie smile on her face.

"Hi, Bella! Want to go for a walk?"

Bella wagged her tail enthusiastically.

She changed into a short-sleeved t-shirt and sneakers while Bella ran back and forth excitedly from the bedroom to the front door of the house.

"Where's your leash, Bella?"

Bella ran into the bathroom where she knew her leash was stored in a drawer. She stood in front of the drawer impatiently while Rylie got out her leash and some poop bags.

"Let's go, Bella!"

She buckled Bella into her seat belt in the back seat, drove to Tahoe City, and found a parking place. She let Bella out of the SUV and they set off down the paved bike path that ran along the Truckee River. Bella strained on her leash while eagerly sniffing everything within reach.

They walked past serene stretches of the river interspersed with short sections of lively rapids. Bella got excited when she saw brightly colored inflatable rafts filled with people in the middle of the river. She bounced up and down, wagging her tail and barking. The people on the rafts laughed at her antics.

Rylie kept up an invigorating pace. It felt good to stretch her legs and exert herself. After a while, she stopped to rest a moment.

"What a beautiful spot, Bella."

Bella stood close to her. She bent over and stroked Bella's soft fur.

"You're such a good girl, Bella."

Bella slowly wagged her tail and panted happily. She loved going on walks and this was an especially nice walk with lots of things to see and smell.

Rylie resumed walking toward River Ranch Restaurant. She walked a little slower now, taking the time to look around. Bella spotted a squirrel and started bouncing up and down excitedly. Rylie looked to see that there were no bicyclists nearby, then let out Bella's retractable leash so she could chase the squirrel. She knew Bella didn't expect to actually catch it. She just enjoyed the chase. The squirrel was safely up a tree long before Bella got to where it had been standing.

They made it to River Ranch Restaurant in a little over an hour. She was thirsty, and she knew Bella was too. She walked up to the hostess on the outdoor deck and asked to be seated outside.

"Would it be possible to get a bowl of water for my dog?" she asked.

The hostess smiled. "Of course! No problem. Seat yourself wherever you'd like on the deck. I'll find you when I have some water for your dog. She's so pretty!"

"Thank you." Rylie smiled.

She turned to scan the deck for an open table. She was surprised to see Thomas Scott seated by himself. She made her way through the tables with Bella by her side.

"Hi Thomas! I'm surprised to see you here. I thought you'd be working today."

"Oh hi Rylie! Hi Bella!" Thomas smiled. "I only work a half day on Fridays. I usually leave on Friday afternoons to drive to Berkeley to spend the weekend with my girlfriend. She goes to school at UC Berkeley. But she's on the east coast right now visiting her father, so I'm by myself this weekend."

"Oh. Wouldn't your girlfriend enjoy coming up to the lake sometimes?"

"She does come up for the weekend sometimes when she can get away. But I go down to Berkeley most weekends."

"Do you mind if Bella and I join you?"

"Sure, have a seat," Thomas said. "Did you walk here on the bike path or did you drive here?"

"We walked here from Tahoe City. I needed to get out and get some fresh air and exercise. And Bella's always happy to go for a walk. Now we're both thirsty, so I thought we'd stop here to rest and get something to drink. I hope they have lemonade. I've been thinking about a tall, icy glass of lemonade for the last mile."

"I don't know if they've got lemonade. But they should have something to quench your thirst."

The hostess appeared with a big bowl of water for Bella. Bella looked at the bowl of water hopefully. The hostess set the bowl down on the deck. Bella gratefully took a long drink.

"Thank you so much!" Rylie said. "I should have brought some water bottles with me for our walk, but I didn't think about it. Bella gets really thirsty when we go on walks."

She ordered some lemonade. After the hostess left, she looked over at Thomas. He seemed more relaxed than he'd been when she'd seen him at work. And something seemed different about him.

"It's nice to have some time off work to relax, isn't it?" she said.

"Definitely," Thomas replied.

A waitress dropped off Rylie's lemonade as she hurried on her way to another customer. Rylie took a long drink.

"Ahhh. That tastes good," she said.

"Look, Rylie. I'm sorry if I've been less than friendly lately. My mother hasn't been doing well. And all the stress of Colin's murder investigation has been taking a toll on me. Detective Felton brought me in for questioning. I told him I was in Berkeley with my girlfriend all last weekend. Plenty of people saw me and were happy to vouch for me. When he found out I had a solid alibi, he let me go."

"Thanks for letting me know, Thomas," she said. "I'm sorry you had to go through all that."

"I need to get out of Tahoe," Thomas said. "I've been here all my life. It's time. I got a job in Berkeley near my girlfriend's apartment. I gave Liam and Gillian my two-week notice when I picked up my check after work today. I'll be making four times more money at my new job than I'm making here."

"That's great, Thomas! What are you going to be doing?"

"I got a job working for a solar energy company," Thomas replied. "It's something I'm really interested in."

"It sounds like this will be a good move for you, Thomas. I'm happy for you."

Thomas looked at her and smiled. His face, free from the stress and worries that he'd been dealing with, looked vibrant and youthful. She was amazed by the transformation. She was also greatly relieved to find out that there was no way he could have killed Colin Matthews.

She finished her lemonade and looked down to see what Bella was doing. Bella was relaxing on the deck near her feet.

"I think we're going to head back now," she said. "Thanks for letting us sit with you, Thomas. Good luck with your new job."

"Thanks, Rylie. See you later."

She headed back toward Tahoe City on the bike path with Bella leading the way. She walked at a slower pace on the way back, enjoying the scent of pine trees and fresh river water in the air. She decided she'd like to rent one of the colorful inflatable rafts they watched float down the river as they walked.

When they got back home, she went over to Gillian and Liam's house with Bella.

She knocked. Gillian opened the door. "Hi Rylie. Hi Bella. Come on in!"

She stepped inside. Bella stopped to greet Gillian. She wagged her tail when Gillian pet her head. Then she ambled inside.

"I just saw Thomas Scott at River Ranch Restaurant. He said Detective Felton took him in for questioning. He told Detective Felton that he was in Berkeley with his girlfriend all last weekend. Plenty of people saw him."

"We just found that out too," Gillian replied.

"I'm glad Thomas has been cleared of suspicion," Liam said. "There was no way I could see that kid doing something so horrible."

"Can I get you something to drink?" Gillian asked.

"Sure. Anything cold and wet will do. Can I have a bowl of water for Bella, too? We just got back from a long walk on the bike path by the Truckee River, and I know she's thirsty."

"Sure. No problem."

She told Gillian and Liam about her lunch with Blake Cunningham and about Karalyn Ashford's father storming up to their table and yelling at Blake. She told them Blake said it was because of a commercial real estate deal gone bad.

"Do you know anything about a commercial real estate deal that Blake Cunningham may have handled for Karalyn Ashford?" she asked.

"No," Gillian replied. "This is the first we've heard about it."

"I got the impression that there was a lot more to the story than what Blake let on," she said. "Blake put on a poker face after Karalyn left, but I sensed that he was really upset. I also got the weird feeling that Blake was scared about something. He doesn't strike me as the kind of guy that scares easily. He left in a big hurry right after Karalyn and her father left."

"We don't know Karalyn Ashford all that well," Liam said. "We just know that she's wealthy and she lives in Incline Village."

"It may not be anything that we need to concern ourselves with," she said. "But I thought I'd let you know about it in case there was any chance that it might have something to do with Colin's murder."

"I think it's wise to stay on the lookout for anything that might possibly help Detective Felton with his investigation no matter how unrelated it may seem," Gillian said.

"Me, too," she replied. "What time are you planning to go to Granlibakken for Colin's memorial service tomorrow morning so I can make sure to be here on time?"

"The service starts at 11:00," Liam said. "I'm not sure how bad parking will be, so let's plan to leave here at 10:30."

"Okay," she replied. "Hey, it just occurred to me! Who's going to answer the phone and take care of the guests tomorrow if all three of us are at Colin's memorial service?"

"Elizabeth and her family will be arriving here early tomorrow morning to spend a few days," Liam replied. "They'll be staying in the main house. Elizabeth is very concerned about Colin being murdered here. She wants us to fill her in on everything that happened on the night that Colin was killed and since then. She also wants to see the security system I had installed."

"I told Elizabeth about Colin's memorial service tomorrow, and she said she'd be happy to take care of the guests so we can attend," he continued. "There's going to be a reception with food and drinks after the service, so we'll probably be gone for at least a couple hours."

"I wonder if Elizabeth might have information that could help Detective Felton in his investigation?" she said. "Even though she wasn't here that night, she might know something that could prove useful."

"That's an interesting thought," Gillian said. "We'll make it a point to take Elizabeth through the tunnel and into the Absinthe Room while she's here. We'll show her where the murder took place and get her thoughts."

"Can I come with you when you do that?" she asked. "I'd love to hear what Elizabeth has to say."

"Sure," Gillian replied. "I think you should be involved. We all have a huge stake in finding out who killed Colin."

"Thanks, Gillian. I'm beat. I'm going to call it a day. I'll see you tomorrow."

She headed back to her house with Bella. Bella immediately went to check her food and water dishes. She sniffed the inside of her empty food dish and then looked up at Rylie.

"Okay, Bella. I can take a hint."

She got Bella some kibble and fresh water and then curled up on the sofa with the television remote. She wanted to relax and watch something mindless on TV for a while.

Life had certainly not been restful since she came to Lake Tahoe just over a week ago. Colin's murder and the subsequent investigation had taken precedence over everything else and kept her mind off losing her job. But she knew that at some point she would have to examine her feelings about the loss of her job and about losing control of her life as she knew it. She was going to have to figure out what she was going to do with her career and her life going forward.

Chapter 14

S he was deep in thought as she made coffee and got Bella
her breakfast the next morning. She showered and got
dressed in some jeans and a t-shirt. She toasted a sesame seed
bagel and poured herself a large glass of orange juice.

After she finished her breakfast, she looked over at Bella
laying on the living room floor.

"Want to go down to the lake, Bella?"

Bella looked very happy at the prospect. She bounded out
the door as soon as Rylie opened it. She trotted back and forth
across the path to the lake with her nose to the ground sniffing
everything in sight.

When they got to the lake, Rylie stopped to enjoy looking
out over the water in its shimmering shades of blue. The
tranquility of the lake had a calming effect on her.

Bella trotted off down the lakeside path. A group of Mallard ducks swimming on the lake came into view. Bella
bounced up and down on her front legs and barked excitedly.
The ducks veered a little further from shore but didn't seem
overly concerned. They kept up their soft quacking to each
other and kept paddling.

Rylie set off on a brisk pace down the path with Bella
leading the way. They walked for about half an hour before

Rylie slowed down and started to look around and enjoy the scenery.

She thought about the loss of her job that she'd had since she graduated from veterinary medical school and about the friends she'd made at work that she'd probably never see again. Her life had been completely upended when the veterinary hospital burned to the ground, but she'd landed on her feet. She'd moved to a new area, taken a temporary job doing work she'd never done before, and was making new friends. She was finding the strength to put the pieces of her life back together and make a new life for herself.

Eventually she turned around and headed back toward the private beach. She walked slower on the way back. A Steller's Jay spotted Bella and landed on a branch above their heads to squawk his reproach at Bella's invasion of his domain. Rylie looked up at the jay. He had a crest of feathers that stood straight up on the top of his head that gave him an impish look. Bella ignored the jay and kept walking down the forest path. The jay hopped along the branch squawking repeatedly until he was satisfied that he had chased Bella out of his domain. She smiled at the jay's antics.

When they got back to the house, she took a quick shower before she got changed into the midnight blue dress she had chosen for Colin's memorial service.

"I'm going to go to a memorial service for Colin Matthews this morning, Bella. You're going to stay here and watch the house for me, okay?" Bella looked at her with an understanding look and slowly wagged her tail.

She walked over to Gillian and Liam's house. Gillian answered the door looking stunning in an emerald green dress that accentuated her hair's natural red highlights.

"You look fantastic, Gillian!" she said. "That dress really goes well with the color of your hair."

"Thanks, Rylie!" Gillian blushed a little. "Ready to go?"

It was a short drive to the Granlibakken Resort set in a forested valley a mile from Tahoe City. The memorial service was being held on the sprawling Big Pine Lawn. The lawn was surrounded by massive Ponderosa and Jeffery pines. Rows of white chairs had been set up on the lawn facing a terraced hillside. The top terrace created a natural stage for the service. White orchids in deep purple ceramic pots had been placed along the tops of each terrace behind the large boulders that formed the terrace walls. Soft music playing in the background blended with the hum of people talking to each other in small groups around the lawn. The sun beamed down from a brilliant blue sky and bathed the lawn in a warm glow.

The beauty of the site seemed almost spiritual. She looked at Liam and Gillian and could see they were moved too.

Dee Matthews walked up to the microphone on the top terrace. "The service will begin shortly. We'd like to ask everyone to find a seat."

They found some seats roughly in the middle of the rows of chairs. She looked across the aisle and saw Aidan and Katiana. Patrick O'Farrell was seated a couple rows in front of Aidan and Katiana. Alain and Margaux were seated a few rows in front of where she, Gillian, and Liam were seated.

She saw Eric Larson getting ready to sit in one of the seats near the front and caught his eye. She gave him a small, sympathetic smile. Eric looked at her sadly and took his seat. She felt really bad for him. She knew he thought the world of Colin.

It's such a tragedy that someone so well loved by so many people had his life cut short like that. Her heart ached for Colin's friends and family.

Dee spoke into the microphone again. "For those of you who may not know me, I'm Dee Matthews, Colin's big sister. I've met a lot of you this past week at the bakery. Thank you so much for coming out to remember my brother. I know it would mean the world to him."

"My brother was the kind of guy that people were naturally drawn to. He was kind and warm and funny," Dee continued. "He had so many hopes and dreams. He was always a dreamer, ever since he was little. But he didn't just dream. He worked hard to make his dreams become reality. I had a great deal of respect for my brother. I miss him terribly." Dee's voice choked on her last sentence. She stopped for a long moment to compose herself before continuing.

"I want to give everyone here the chance to remember Colin and share their special memories of him. First, we'll hear from Eric Larson, who's been working with Colin at the bakery for over a year."

Eric walked up to the stage and faced the crowd. He tried to put on a brave face, but it was obvious he was grieving.

"I started out as just a delivery guy," Eric began. "But when I told Colin that I wanted to become a baker someday, he gave me the opportunity to work with his baker, Ryan. I'll always be grateful to Colin for that. I've learned so much in the time that I've worked there. Colin was a very good friend to me. I'll always remember him."

Eric walked off the stage. She felt a lump in her throat and the sting of tears in her eyes.

A small gasp escaped her when she saw Karalyn Ashford walk onto the stage. A man carrying a guitar case followed her and stood off to the side.

"Colin was a very good friend of mine," Karalyn said. "And the best way I could think of to honor him today was to sing the song that has been playing over and over in my head since his death: Fire and Rain by James Taylor. James Taylor wrote Fire and Rain to express his feelings of grief and loss when he found out that one of his close friends had taken her own life. And no one can emulate the way that James Taylor fingerpicks this song on the acoustic guitar like my friend, Spencer Morgan, who will accompany me."

Karalyn began to sing in a beautiful clear voice filled with emotion. Every time she sang the last line of the chorus, she could tell that Karalyn's heart was bleeding.

It looks like Katiana Flynn wasn't the only woman in love with Colin.

She tried to look discreetly at Aidan and Katiana across the aisle. Aidan looked tense and angry. Katiana had tears streaming down her face as she listened to Karalyn Ashford's beautiful voice sing the melancholy song. Karalyn's voice resonated with pain and grief. Rylie felt some tears escape her eyes and make their way down her cheeks. She looked over at Gillian and saw that Gillian's face was also streaked with tears.

Colin's baker, Ryan, got on the stage after Karalyn had finished her song. He spoke about his friendship with Colin and his respect for Colin both as a businessman and as a person. Alain Dubois got on the stage next. He told an amusing anecdote about something that happened one night when he was playing poker with Colin and the other guys at Liam

Gallagher's place. She was relieved that Alain had lightened the mood a little with his story.

Liam walked onto the stage as Alain finished. "Colin was a good man. But he was a terrible poker player. He never did manage to master a good poker face." Several people in the crowd chuckled.

A few more of Colin's friends got up on the stage to share stories and memories of him including her friend Laurent. When everyone had finished sharing their memories, Dee stepped up to the microphone and invited everyone to enjoy a delicious buffet of appetizers prepared by Granlibakken's amazing chef.

Rylie stood up, grateful for the opportunity to stretch her legs. Liam put his arm around Gillian when she joined him in the aisle between all the chairs.

"Come on, Rylie," he said. "Let's get something to eat. I'm starved." They started making their way over to the buffet table.

She came face to face with Katiana as she stepped into the aisle. Katiana looked gaunt and pale.

"Hi, Katiana. How are you?"

"Colin's death has been hard on all of us," Katiana replied in a small voice. Aidan stepped up next to his wife and put his arm around her shoulders possessively.

"Hi, Rylie," Aidan said in a hard voice that sent a chill up her spine.

"Hi, Aidan." She tried to force a smile. "It was a lovely service, wasn't it?"

"It was," he replied. "Come on, Katiana. Let's go get something to eat."

He steered Katiana toward the buffet table. Rylie let out the breath she'd unconsciously been holding. There was something about Aidan that made her very uncomfortable. She walked quickly in the direction of the buffet to catch up with Gillian and Liam.

The buffet table was overflowing with a lavish assortment of appetizers including miniature quiches, bruschetta, olive tapenade crostini's, mushroom puffs, and prosciutto-wrapped melon pieces. There were also large platters of assorted cheeses and fruits and decorative displays of shrimp arranged on beautiful cut crystal bowls filled with cocktail sauce.

Liam ordered their drinks from the bar. They filled their plates with appetizers from the buffet and sat down at one of the round white wooden tables scattered around the lawn.

She sampled the delicious food and sipped her white wine spritzer. She watched as other people got their food and chatted with each other. There were a lot of people that she didn't know whom she assumed were either Colin's friends or family members. When she spotted Laurent at the bar, she excused herself and went over to talk to him.

"Hi, Laurent. How are you? Where's Olivia today?"

"Hi, Rylie. Unfortunately, Olivia had to stay behind to watch the cottages. We weren't able to find anyone to take over for us today."

"Can we find a table somewhere relatively private so we can talk?"

"Sure."

They threaded their way through the tables filled with people until they found a table away from everyone else on the edge of the lawn near the pine trees.

"I'm so sorry about Colin, Laurent. It's obvious that you were very close."

"Colin was a good man," Laurent replied. "I'm sorry you didn't get the chance to know him."

"How did you guys meet?"

"I met him after he bought the old Tahoe City Bakery. He renamed it the Butter Lane Bakery and turned it into a thriving business. After I tasted some of his delicious pastries, I arranged with him to deliver fresh baked goods for our guests every morning. He was always so friendly when he came to make his deliveries. We just hit it off. After a while, he invited me to go out on his boat with him. We took his boat all over the lake and explored places I'd never been before. It was great fun. It became a fairly regular thing. We usually went out on his boat about once a week. I really enjoyed those times with Colin."

He stopped talking while he tried to compose himself. She put her hand over Laurent's where it rested on the table and waited quietly for him to pull himself together.

"Can you think of anyone that would want to hurt Colin?" she asked.

"No, I can't. I've been racking my brain trying to figure out who'd want to hurt him," Laurent replied. He looked around to make sure they were far enough away from the other tables that they wouldn't be overheard.

"The only person I can possibly think of is Aidan Flynn. Colin was having an affair with his wife, and they weren't as discreet as they should have been. They were spotted having romantic dinners from time to time. They always went to a restaurant far away from Tahoe City, but they stayed around the lake, so it was inevitable that someone would see them. Colin knew how I felt about their relationship. I don't know Aidan Flynn very well, but I know he has a reputation for having a very bad temper. Maybe he confronted Colin and things got out of hand. I just don't know."

"Detective Felton showed me a paper they found in Colin's pants pocket with my name and cell phone number on it," she said. "I'm afraid they consider me a suspect because of it. Do you have any idea how Colin could have gotten my name and cell phone number?"

Laurent's jaw dropped open. "Oh no! Rylie! I'm so sorry! That was me! Last Friday when Colin came to deliver our baked goods, he told me he'd just met a cute blonde veterinarian named Rylie who was helping out at the Whitaker Cottages for the summer. I thought it had to be you, but I wasn't sure. I couldn't imagine how you could have gotten a whole summer off. I gave Colin your name and number. I asked him to find out for sure if it was you and if it was, then I wanted him to try to arrange a meeting so I could surprise you. I'll go to the sheriff's department as soon as I leave here and give them a statement so you're cleared of any suspicion."

She breathed a deep sigh of relief. "That must be what Colin wanted to talk to me about on Locals' Night! He said he needed to talk to me about something and that he'd catch up with me later. Then he disappeared, and I couldn't find him anywhere. I feel so much better now that I know what he wanted to talk to me about. And I'm very relieved that I won't be on the list of possible suspects once you give your statement to the sheriff's department."

Laurent left a little while later, and she went back to join Liam and Gillian at their table. Karalyn Ashford walked past and set her plate on the empty table adjacent to theirs.

"You're welcome to join us at our table," Gillian said.

Karalyn looked at Gillian blankly, then managed a small smile. "Thank you, that's very kind of you." She moved to join them at their table. "I don't believe we've met."

"I'm Gillian Gallagher. And this is my husband, Liam. We're the primary caretakers at Whitaker Cottages."

Karalyn froze for a minute before she recovered her composure. "Nice to meet you."

"And this is Rylie Sunderland," Gillian continued. "Rylie's helping us out as a temporary part-time caretaker this summer. She's actually a veterinarian from the East Bay, but she's between jobs right now."

"Hello, Rylie," Karalyn said. "Wait, I remember you. I saw you having lunch with Blake Cunningham at Bridgetender's yesterday."

"Yes," she replied. "I met Blake at the Locals' Night party last Saturday. He convinced me to join him for lunch at Bridgetender's when he told me that Bridgetender's was famous for their burgers. I love a good burger. But, just to set the record straight, I do not have any romantic interest in him whatsoever. He's not my type at all."

Karalyn smiled a genuine smile that lit up her face and made her look years younger.

"You did a wonderful job singing that James Taylor song," Rylie said. "You've got an amazing voice."

"Why thank you, Rylie." Karalyn smiled sadly. "I hope Colin was looking down from heaven and enjoying it too."

"How did you meet Colin?" she asked.

"We met quite a few years ago at the Shakespeare Festival at Sand Harbor," Karalyn replied. "We were both there with some of our friends. We were sitting at tables right next to each other, and we happened to strike up a conversation. When I went to use the ladies' room with one of my friends, she told me Colin had a reputation of being a ladies' man. She warned me to be careful and not to take his flirting too seriously."

"He invited me to go to lunch with him the next day. It turned out to be a very long lunch. We talked for hours. But I couldn't get my friend's voice out of my head telling me to be careful. So I gave him the friend vibe and didn't flirt with him. I don't know if that was the right thing to do or not. We ended up becoming very good friends, but our relationship never progressed past the friend stage. I think I might have liked to explore something more, but the timing never seemed right."

"I'm so sorry, Karalyn," she said. "I only met Colin a couple times, but it was easy to see how warm and charismatic he was. I'm sorry I didn't get the chance to get to know him better."

"Liam and I knew Colin for years. He was a good man," Gillian said.

Karalyn stood up abruptly, her eyes glistening with tears. "I'm sorry, but I've got to go. I made plans to meet someone in Incline Village this afternoon. It was very nice meeting all of you." She quickly walked away.

Dee Matthews walked by their table.

"Hi, Dee!" Rylie called out.

Dee looked over. "Oh, hi Rylie!"

"Dee, this is Gillian Gallagher and her husband Liam. They're the primary caretakers at Whitaker Cottages. I think you spoke to Gillian on the phone earlier this week."

Dee turned her gaze to Gillian and Liam and smiled. "Nice to meet you in person, Gillian. Nice to meet you too, Liam."

"Why don't you sit down for a few minutes with us, Dee?" Rylie asked. "You look exhausted."

Dee hesitated for a moment. "Sure. Why not? Thank you."

She took a seat at the table.

"Have you had anything to eat yet?" she asked.

"No, not yet. I've been busy trying to make sure that everything goes smoothly with the memorial service and reception."

"I'll go fill up a plate with appetizers for you," Liam said. "What would you like to drink?"

"Thank you, Liam. That's very nice of you. I'll have a mineral water."

"It was a lovely service, Dee," Gillian said.

"And you had it in such a beautiful and special place," Rylie added. "This was an absolutely perfect spot to have it."

Dee smiled a tired smile. "Thank you. I'm glad it's over and that everything went smoothly. Now I've got to get all of Colin's business affairs in order. He left everything to me in his will. So now I've got my hands full learning how to run a bakery. And I might end up having to take responsibility for his latest business venture. I'm not sure I'm up to it."

They waited quietly for Dee to continue.

"I found out a few days ago that Colin took on a business partner to work with him on the restaurant that he planned to build on his vacant lot on the other side of Tahoe City," Dee said.

"Oh wow," Rylie said. "How did you find out?"

"A man I didn't know came into the bakery on Tuesday and introduced himself. He said he was Colin's business partner in the restaurant deal. His name is Garrison Taylor. I was pretty suspicious about the whole thing, so I asked him to provide me with legal documents proving that he was Colin's partner."

"That was definitely a good idea," she said. "Was he able to produce those documents?"

"Yes, he was," Dee replied. "He brought in the partnership agreement that he and Colin had signed as well as documents proving that he had purchased a one-half interest in Colin's land. He had receipts showing that he paid for one-half of the expenses incurred so far including getting the plans drawn up and applying for permits. I had my attorney look through everything. He assured me that all the documents had been professionally prepared and that everything is in order."

"So are you going to work with Garrison Taylor on Colin's restaurant project?" she asked.

"That's the thing," Dee replied. "I don't know. I called Garrison after my attorney assured me that everything was legal and asked him what he wanted to do going forward. He offered to buy out my interest in the project. Apparently, he owns two other restaurants around the lake. So he definitely knows what he's doing."

Rylie instantly saw a red flag go up. She shared a look with Gillian and knew Gillian was thinking the same thing.

"Dee," she said, "I understand that Colin's partnership with Garrison Taylor is legal, but doesn't it make you a little suspicious that Garrison Taylor showed up out of nowhere and offered to buy out your half of Colin's interest in the restaurant project? I've never met Garrison Taylor, and I don't know anything about him, but I think that anyone who had reason to benefit from Colin's death needs to go on the list of possible suspects."

"I'm right there with you," Dee replied. "I saw a red flag go up as soon as the words came out of Garrison's mouth. After I hung up with Garrison, I called Detective Felton right away. Detective Felton questioned him. Garrison told Detective Felton that he was in Incline Village all day and night on the night that Colin was killed. Detective Felton called me back the next day and said that Garrison's alibi checked out. He's not considered a suspect in Colin's murder investigation."

Liam came back to the table with a plate piled high with appetizers and a tall glass of sparkling mineral water with a slice of lime. He set down the plate and glass in front of Dee.

"Thank you so much," Dee said. She eyed the plate hungrily. "I didn't even know I was hungry until just now. Those appetizers look delicious."

Dee bit into one of the appetizers and smiled. "These are wonderful. The chef here at Granlibakken is fabulous."

Rylie and Gillian waited patiently for Dee to eat some of her food. They filled Liam in while Dee ate.

"To make matters more complicated, Patrick O'Farrell came into the bakery yesterday and offered to buy Colin's vacant lot from me," Dee said.

"I know Colin had no interest in selling his lot to Patrick, so I'm pretty sure I'm not going to sell to him. But I set up a time to meet Patrick for lunch on Monday at noon at The Grille at the Chateau restaurant in Incline Village. I'm planning to meet Garrison at the restaurant at 11:00 so I'll have time to talk with him before Patrick shows up. I need to figure out what I want to do before I talk to Garrison on Monday morning. It's a really big decision."

They sat quietly absorbing all that they'd just learned from Dee. Then Rylie spoke up.

"Dee, I know you don't know me very well, but you might feel more comfortable meeting with Garrison and Patrick if you had someone with you for moral support. I'd be happy to go with you when you meet with them on Monday."

Dee stared at her for a long moment.

"Rylie has a good head on her shoulders," Liam said. "She's smart and observant. It wouldn't be a bad idea to have someone on your side when you meet with those guys."

"I might just take you up on your offer, Rylie," Dee said finally.

"Oh, I just remembered! I have to work on Monday." Rylie looked despondently at Liam and Gillian.

"We'll be happy to take care of the guests on Monday so you can go to lunch with Dee," Gillian said. "It's absolutely no problem."

"Thanks, Gillian! I'll work until mid-afternoon on Thursday to make up for taking time off on Monday. Will that work?"

"That's fine, Rylie," Gillian replied.

"It's settled then," Dee said. "I'll pick you up at 10:00 on Monday. That will give us plenty of time to get to Incline Village in time for my 11:00 meeting with Garrison. I've got to go mingle now. See you Monday, Rylie."

"See you then."

"We really should be getting back," Liam said. "We told Elizabeth we'd fill her in on all the events surrounding Colin's death this afternoon."

"I'm ready. Let's go."

Chapter 15

L iam turned off into the long driveway that led to Whitaker Cottages. "Rylie, would you like to join us when we talk to Elizabeth and fill her in on everything we know so far about what happened the night Colin was killed? Or do you just want us to call you when we're ready go to the Absinthe Room with her?"

"I'd like to be in on the whole conversation with her."

"Of course," Liam replied. "You're as much a part of this as we are. We're going to go change out of our good clothes before we go see Elizabeth. Why don't you meet us at our house in about fifteen minutes?"

"Okay. Do you think Elizabeth would mind if I brought Bella?"

"I'm sure it would be fine," Liam replied.

"Great! See you in a few minutes."

Bella bounced around excitedly when she opened the door to her house.

"Hi Bella! Were you a good girl while I was gone?"

Bella wagged her tail so hard that her entire butt swayed back and forth. Rylie smiled.

"Do you want to go see Gillian and Liam? We're going to go to their house in just a few minutes."

Bella raced to the front door and stood poised to launch out the door as soon as Rylie opened it. When Rylie headed to the bedroom, Bella followed close behind.

She changed into some jeans and a t-shirt and then walked over to Gillian and Liam's house with Bella trotting ahead of her. Liam and Gillian came outside when she knocked on their door, and they walked over to the main house together. Elizabeth opened the door with a smile.

"Rylie, so nice to see you again! Hi, Liam. Hi, Gillian. Please, come in!"

"Hi, Elizabeth. Nice to see you again, too."

Bella looked up at Elizabeth wagging her tail.

"Is this your golden retriever?" Elizabeth asked Rylie.

"Yes, this is Bella." Rylie smiled.

"She's beautiful."

"Thanks for watching the place so we could all go to Colin's memorial service," Liam said. "Did you have any problems while we were gone?"

"No, not at all," Elizabeth replied. "Actually, no one called or came to the reception area while you were gone. So it was pretty easy."

"That's good, I guess. But it's not good that it was so slow on a Saturday in the middle of June," Liam said.

"Having a murder take place on your property isn't exactly good for business," Elizabeth said grimly. "I'm glad you got the security system installed and that there haven't been any more problems since then. But I want to make sure that everyone that works here is safe and that nothing like that ever happens here again."

"We appreciate that, Elizabeth," Liam said.

Elizabeth led the way to the kitchen and invited them to sit at the large wooden dining table. She got drinks for everyone and then joined them at the table.

"Liam, I appreciate your calling me and trying to keep me informed about everything that's happened here recently," Elizabeth said. "But I wanted to sit down with you and Gillian to get the whole story from beginning to end. I'm glad Rylie's here too. I want to know all the details."

Liam recounted the events that occurred on Locals' Night. He told Elizabeth that the groundskeeper, Thomas Scott, had been cleared of suspicion.

"Detective Felton hasn't told us who he considers suspects. But the people that we think might be suspects at this point are, unfortunately, two of my friends," Liam said. "They both come here to play poker with me in the Card House once a week. Patrick O'Farrell and Aidan Flynn."

Liam explained how it seemed likely that Colin Matthews had been having an affair with Aidan Flynn's wife Katiana.

"I guess it's possible that a jealous man with a hot temper might kill someone that he found out was having an affair with his wife," Elizabeth said. "Or maybe they got into a heated argument and it just got out of hand."

Liam told Elizabeth about Patrick O'Farrell wanting to purchase the vacant lot that Colin owned so he could get the permits he needed to renovate and expand the old Tavern Grill and about how Colin refused to sell to him.

"I don't remember if I told you this," Rylie said. "But I saw Patrick meeting with some guy in an expensive suit when I was having dinner at Za's Lakefront Restaurant last Sunday. Patrick was gesturing like he was trying to emphasize an important point. Expensive Suit Guy got mad and walked out of the restaurant. Then Patrick walked out too. I shoved my napkin off my lap onto the deck and ducked under the table to retrieve it when Patrick walked by so he wouldn't see me."

"Who do you suppose the guy in the expensive suit was?" Gillian asked.

"I have no idea. But I was thinking he might be an investor in Patrick's restaurant project."

"There's another person I think we should add to our list of suspects," Liam said. "Steve Randall."

Liam told Elizabeth about what Alain Dubois had told him about Colin rejecting Steve Randall's bid on his restaurant project.

"So you think that if Steve was angry with Colin for rejecting his bid that he might have killed him over it?" Elizabeth asked. "That seems a little extreme."

"I know. It does," Liam said. "But until we know for sure who killed Colin, we have to consider every possibility no matter how far-fetched it might seem. I asked Alain to call Detective Felton and tell him exactly what he told me."

"I think there's someone else that needs to go on our list of suspects," Rylie said. Everyone looked at her expectantly. "Blake Cunningham."

Liam raised an eyebrow. He exchanged a glance with Gillian.

"Karalyn Ashford told us at the service today that she was very close with Colin," she said. "I think she may have been in love with him based on the things she said and the way she sang that James Taylor song."

"I know. I was thinking the same thing," Gillian said.

"I already told Gillian and Liam about this Elizabeth, but I think you should know about it too," she said. "Blake Cunningham invited me to have lunch with him at Bridgetender's yesterday. I agreed to it because I thought that since he's a local that he might know something that could help Detective Felton with his investigation. And just for the record, I have absolutely no romantic interest in him. When we were having lunch, Karalyn's father came storming up to our table and said no one gets away with what Blake did to his daughter. Blake told me it had to do with a commercial real estate deal gone bad that he had handled for Karalyn. If Karalyn was as close with Colin as she said, wouldn't she have told him about it? What if Colin confronted Blake about it, and it escalated into a fight?"

"I know Karalyn," Elizabeth said. "We work together on the annual fashion show fundraiser for the League to Save Lake Tahoe that's held in Incline Village every summer. Did you ask Karalyn if she spoke to Colin about the real estate deal?"

"No, I didn't."

"Then I'll call her and ask her," Elizabeth said. "We've been friends for a long time. She won't have any problem talking to me about it."

"There's something else you need to know Elizabeth," Liam said. He told Elizabeth about what Brayden Hughes had told them about Colin having been punched in the face by two different people on the night of his death.

Elizabeth made a small gasping noise. She suddenly looked very pale.

"Let me get you a cup of tea Elizabeth," Gillian said.

Gillian poured water into a teacup and put the teacup in the microwave while she went looking for tea.

"The tea's in the cabinet to the right of the refrigerator Gillian," Elizabeth said.

"I found it."

Rylie looked at Elizabeth. Elizabeth looked like she might pass out. She moved over onto the chair next to Elizabeth and put her arm around her.

"Do you want to go lie down on the sofa for a few minutes?"

"No, no. I'm fine. This is all just a little much to take in. I didn't know how bad it was until now. Poor Colin. I can't believe something like this could have happened here."

Gillian returned with a cup of tea for Elizabeth.

"Have a sip of tea Elizabeth. It'll help you feel better."

"I'm going to call Karalyn and find out if she spoke to Colin about the real estate deal that Blake Cunningham handled for her," Elizabeth said. "If she tells me she did, I'll ask her to call Detective Felton and tell him about it right away."

Elizabeth got her cell phone and called Karalyn. Her eyes widened as she listened. She asked Karalyn to call Detective Felton as soon as possible.

"I think you may be onto something Rylie," Elizabeth said. "Karalyn told me she'll call Detective Felton right away. I know she wants Colin's murderer to be found as soon as possible, just like the rest of us."

"Why don't I walk you around the property and show you the security system I had installed Elizabeth?" Liam asked. "It'll be good for you to get out and get some fresh air. Then we'll come back and get Gillian and Rylie and go to the Absinthe Room."

Liam and Elizabeth left. Rylie and Gillian sat quietly for a few minutes.

"Didn't you say Elizabeth was bringing her family with her this weekend?" Rylie asked.

"I guess she decided to come by herself. I think she considers this a business trip strictly for the purpose of finding out the details concerning Colin's murder. I'm glad she wants to be involved and that she's concerned for our safety."

Bella walked over to Rylie and put her head on her lap. She stroked Bella's golden fur absentmindedly while her thoughts raced.

"Bella can tell you're upset," Gillian said.

"Yes, she's my best buddy. I can always count on her to be there for me."

When Liam and Elizabeth came back from walking the property, they stopped in the kitchen to get Rylie and Gillian.

"Are you ladies ready to go to the Absinthe Room?" Liam asked.

"Yes," Rylie said. "Bella can go with us and keep us safe. Come on, Bella!"

Liam led the way to the butler's pantry. He slid his fingers along the side of one of the maple wood cabinets. The secret entrance to the underground tunnel swung open and a gust of cold, damp, earthy air rushed out. He made his way down the tunnel with Rylie, Gillian, and Elizabeth close behind. Bella stayed by Rylie's side as they walked.

When they got to the Absinthe Room, Liam stopped to remove the yellow sheriff's department tape from across the entrance.

"Is it okay to remove that now?" Gillian asked.

"Yes. I spoke to Detective Felton yesterday. He said it would be okay. They've already taken photos and collected all their samples," Liam replied.

He stepped into the Absinthe Room. Rylie, Gillian, and Elizabeth followed. Bella walked into the room with her nose to the ground sniffing everything in sight. Rylie's eyes immediately went to the bloodstains on the far wall. There was a bloodstain near the bottom of the granite wall and another further up the wall. She reasoned that the bloodstain further up on the wall was from when Colin fell backward into the wall and hit his head on the hard granite and that the bloodstain further down the wall was from after he had crumpled to the floor. She felt a chill go up her spine.

"Elizabeth," she said. "Do you know why there's a slight green glow that emanates from the back of the fireplace in this room?"

"No I don't, dear. I've never really paid much attention to it."

"I've been wondering about it," Rylie continued. "Maybe it's from some bioluminescent bacteria or something. Do you know why they call this the Absinthe Room?"

"I would assume that the gentleman who built this place in the late 1800s invited his guests into this room to drink absinthe. Absinthe wasn't banned until 1912. When I purchased the property, I found all the accoutrements for serving absinthe in the butler's pantry including a set of absinthe spoons, absinthe glasses, and an absinthe water fountain."

"I'd love to see the absinthe accoutrements some time," Rylie said.

"Please feel free," Elizabeth replied. "I think there may even be some old bottles of absinthe in the butler's pantry that were left by the original owner. They're bottled in dark, light-resistant bottles to prevent the absinthe from oxidizing over time."

Rylie looked over at Bella. Bella seemed extremely interested in something on the ground in the corner of the room. She walked over to see what Bella was so interested in. She bent over to examine the floor where Bella was sniffing and saw a slight flash of something metal partially buried in some disintegrated grout between the large flat stones covering the floor. She squatted down to get a better look and saw it was a Zippo lighter.

"Hey, look what Bella found! A Zippo lighter! I don't want to touch it in case it might be evidence in Colin's murder investigation."

Liam, Gillian, and Elizabeth all walked over and peered at the lighter.

"I'll call Detective Felton," Liam said. "I don't think any of us should touch it. You're right, Rylie. It might be evidence. I want to have Detective Felton come here to remove it properly without destroying any fingerprints that might be on it."

"Good girl, Bella!" Rylie said. "You did a good job!"

Bella looked lovingly up at her and wagged her tail happily.

"Let's get out of here," Liam said. "I want to get Detective Felton out here as soon as possible."

After they all filed out of the room, Liam attempted to re-hang the sheriff's department tape across the door as best he could before they went back to the main house.

When they got back to the kitchen, Liam said, "It's been a long day for all of us, Elizabeth. I think Gillian and I are going to head home. We'll take over watching the cottages the rest of the weekend. If you need anything, please don't hesitate to call us."

"I'm going to head home now too, Elizabeth," Rylie said.

She and Bella walked with Liam and Gillian as far as their house and then continued on to their house. When they were comfortably settled in the living room, she put her arms around Bella's neck and hugged her. Bella's warmth was comforting. Bella slowly wagged her tail. Rylie felt some of the tension drain from her body.

"I love you, Bella. You're such a good girl."

She didn't feel very hungry, but she was sure Bella would be. She got Bella her dinner and then got some brie and crackers for herself. She poured herself a glass of cabernet sauvignon and curled up on the sofa with her snack.

Her cell phone rang. She looked to see who it was before answering. She picked up her phone.

"Hi, Gillian."

"Hi, Rylie. I wanted to let you know that Detective Felton will be coming tomorrow morning at about 9:00 to get the lighter. He said he can't enter it as evidence in Colin's case since there's no proof it was there on the night of the murder. It could've been dropped there at any point since then. But he still wants to collect it. I thought you might like to join us when we go to the Absinthe Room with him."

"Definitely. I'll see you a little before 9:00 tomorrow then."

"See you then."

Chapter 16

Rylie rolled out of bed as soon as the light hit her eyes the next morning. She was eager for Detective Felton to get the Zippo lighter from the Absinthe Room. She hoped he would submit it for fingerprinting and DNA testing even though there was no proof that it was there on the night of Colin's murder. Maybe this was the break they needed to finally find out who killed Colin Matthews.

She headed for the kitchen to get some coffee brewing. She let Bella outside to do her business. She liked to make special breakfasts for herself on Sunday mornings. This morning she decided to make a frittata with goat cheese, freshly grated Parmesan cheese, sautéed onions, asparagus, and crimini mushrooms.

Bella sniffed the air with interest went Rylie let her back inside.

"Smells good, huh Bella? Your breakfast is over there in your dish. I put a little bit of goat cheese on top for a special treat."

Bella rushed over to her dish and made quick work of her breakfast.

Rylie ate her breakfast a little faster than she normally would on a Sunday morning. Bella sensed her mood and lay on the kitchen floor watching her while she ate. They headed over to Gillian and Liam's house a little before 9:00.

Gillian opened the door with a smile. Bella wagged her tail and poked her muzzle into Gillian's hand.

"There's no mistaking what this girl wants!" Gillian giggled as she pet Bella.

An SUV pulled into the parking lot outside the reception area. Detective Felton got out and walked over to them.

"Thanks for coming Detective," Liam said. "Please come in. Would you like a cup of coffee or tea?"

"Oh, no thanks. I've had a lot of coffee already this morning. But I will step inside for a minute."

Liam ushered Detective Felton inside and they all sat down around the dining table.

"Laurent Theroux came to talk to me yesterday afternoon," Detective Felton said. "He told me that he was the one that gave Colin Rylie's name and cell phone number. I want you to know, Rylie, that you're no longer considered a possible suspect in this investigation. Personally, I never really thought of you as a suspect anyway." He smiled at her.

"That's wonderful news Detective," Gillian said.

"Are you ready to go collect the Zippo lighter, Detective?" Liam asked.

"Absolutely. Let's go."

Elizabeth Whitaker opened the front door before they'd even gotten up the front steps of her house. She looked anxious and strained. She reached down to give Bella a couple gentle scratches around her ears.

"Please come in. I'll take you to the butler's pantry, but I'm not going to accompany you into the tunnel today. I'm about to have a cup of tea in the library. Gillian, would you like to join me while Rylie and the men go to the Absinthe Room?"

Gillian smiled. "Sure, Elizabeth. That sounds nice."

Rylie, Bella, Liam, and Detective Felton headed down the granite tunnel. Detective Felton removed the sheriff's department tape from the door to the Absinthe Room. Rylie showed him where the lighter lay partially buried in some disintegrated grout in the corner of the room between the large flat stones covering the floor.

Detective Felton looked at the small piece of exposed metal.

"It's to the left of the door, so it may have belonged to the left-handed person that punched Colin on the night he was killed," he said. "Maybe it fell out of his, or her, pocket."

He bent over to get a better look and took some photos before he touched it. Then he put on some nitrile exam gloves and picked up the lighter to examine it more closely.

The lighter had an antique silver finish with an engraved image of the Tree of Life on the front and the Flower of Life on the back. The bottom of the lighter was stamped with the Zippo logo.

"I've seen one of these special edition Zippo lighters before," he said. "These are expensive. I think they cost about a hundred dollars. I'll send this to the lab first thing tomorrow morning."

He slipped the lighter into a clear plastic evidence bag and sealed it. He looked over at Bella sitting quietly next to Rylie.

"Did Bella sniff everything in this room when she was here with you yesterday?"

"Yes. She always sniffs everything whenever we go anywhere."

"Okay. But just to be safe, I'm going to search this room one more time to make sure there's nothing else we missed. Could you all please step out of the room?"

"No problem," Liam said.

When Detective Felton had finished searching the room, they went to join Elizabeth and Gillian in the library. He showed Elizabeth and Gillian the Zippo lighter in the clear plastic evidence bag.

"That's a very unique lighter," Gillian said. "I think it may have had some kind of special significance to whoever owned it. The Tree of Life and Flower of Life are symbols used in cultures all over the world, and they have specific meanings in each culture."

"I hope the lab can get some good fingerprints or DNA from it," Elizabeth said. "Maybe we can finally find out who killed poor Colin and put this whole matter to rest."

"I'll be sending the lighter to the lab tomorrow Mrs. Whitaker," Detective Felton said. "But I want to make it very clear that no matter what they find, I can't enter it as evidence in Colin's case because it wasn't found by my team during the initial crime scene investigation."

"I understand, Detective," Elizabeth said.

"Now that I've collected the lighter, I'm planning to spend the rest of the day at Vikingsholm," he continued. "I spoke with Dee Matthews a few days ago and asked her if Colin had any places that he liked to go on his days off. She said he liked to go to Vikingsholm. So I'm planning to go there and nose around a little to see if I can dig up anything that might help in my investigation. But I plan to mix business with pleasure and have a little fun while I'm there. It is my day off, after all."

He turned to Rylie with a smile. "Would you like to join me Rylie? It might be useful to have two sets of eyes checking things out. Sometimes one person sees things the other person missed."

She swallowed hard, then tried to compose herself.

"Um, sure. I'd be happy to join you, Detective. I want to do whatever I can to help find out who killed Colin. Just let me go get my purse and put Bella in my house. Unfortunately, they don't allow dogs at Vikingsholm."

"Please, call me Mark. Why don't you meet me at my SUV in a few minutes then?"

"Okay. Bye Elizabeth. I'll see you later Gillian and Liam."

Gillian smiled broadly. "Have fun!"

Rylie took Bella back to their house. "Bella, I'm going to go to Vikingsholm with Detective Felton for a while. You watch the house for me while I'm gone, okay? You're such a good girl."

She pet Bella's head and scratched around her ears. Bella wagged her tail.

She grabbed her purse and a lightweight jacket and went to join Detective Felton.

Chapter 17

Detective Felton smiled at her as she walked up to his SUV. She got up into the seat next to him and put on her seat belt.

"Have you ever gone on the tour at Vikingsholm?" he asked.

"No, I haven't. I've just walked around the grounds and up to Eagle Falls. I rented a kayak to go out to the Tea House on Fannette Island once."

"Let's do all that," Detective Felton said. "We can go on the tour and then have a picnic lunch at Eagle Falls. Then we can rent kayaks and go out to Fannette Island to see the Tea House."

"Sounds good to me."

"Great! Let's go to Safeway first to pick up some stuff for our picnic lunch. Then we'll head down to Vikingsholm."

They got sandwiches, chips, drinks, and a couple bags of ice at the grocery store. Detective Felton loaded everything into the cooler in the back of his SUV. Then they drove south on Highway 89 down the west shore of the lake toward Vikingsholm. He parked in the parking lot at the top of the mountain above Emerald Bay. He transferred their picnic lunch into a backpack, and they started walking down the steep mile-long trail to Vikingsholm.

"Oh look," he said. "There's a really nice view of Fannette Island through the trees."

"That is a nice view." Rylie smiled. "I want to get a picture."

They stopped while she took a few photos and then resumed their hike down the mountain. The trail brought them to the back wing of Vikingsholm. The wings that comprised Vikingsholm formed a square around a grassy central courtyard. They walked past the south wing with its dark wood siding and sod roof and continued past a round granite tower until they reached the front of the building that faced the lake. They turned to admire the granite-walled main wing.

"The carvings in the wood around the windows and doors are incredible," she said.

"I know. I'm interested to see what it looks like inside. Let's go find out when the next tour is and buy some tickets."

They got tickets for the next tour and sat on one of the granite benches flanking the entrance to the main wing while they waited for the tour to start. The tour guide came out the front door a few minutes later. They joined a small group of people as they shuffled into the front hallway by the living room. The tour guide stood behind the rope barrier dividing the hallway from the living room and addressed the group.

"Hello everyone," she said. "My name is Gayle Edwards. Today I want to share with you some of the special features of this beautiful property. I've been coming here since I was a little girl. My parents were good friends with the woman who built Vikingsholm."

"All the rooms in this house are furnished with Scandinavian-style furnishings," Gayle continued. "Some of the furnishings are antiques and some are reproductions like this hand-painted Bridal Table. If you look up at the ceiling, you'll see hand-carved beams with dragon heads at their ends on both sides of the living room. In ancient times, only the man of the house and his male guests were allowed in the area between the two dragon beams. The area outside the dragon beams was for women and children. In this house, the dragon beams were hung strictly as decorative pieces."

Gayle led the group to the back foyer. "This is Selma," she said. She pointed to a life-sized carved wood statue of a Scandinavian peasant girl in folk costume with a clock in place of her face.

"Selma the clock was named after Selma Lagerlöf. Selma Lagerlöf was a Swedish writer and the first woman to win the Nobel Prize in Literature in 1909." Gayle stepped back into the living room to make space for all the people in the foyer.

Rylie studied Selma the clock's folk costume with interest. The peasant girl was dressed in a white, long-sleeved blouse with a short black bodice laced up in the front with red laces. The front of her long blue skirt was covered by an apron that consisted of wide horizontal yellow, red, white, and black stripes. A small purse painted in the same colors as the apron hung from a strap on her waist.

"I wonder why they carved the peasant girl with her hand in her purse," she said. "Do you think the purse has some special significance? I wonder what Scandinavian peasant girls kept in their purses."

Gayle stepped over to join them in front of Selma the clock.

"Hi, Gayle," Detective Felton said. He extended his hand to shake hands. "I'm Detective Mark Felton. We enjoyed your presentation today. I've lived in Tahoe for a long time, but I've never been on this tour before."

Rylie smiled at Gayle. "Hi, Gayle. I'm Rylie. I grew up in the San Francisco East Bay area. I've been coming to Lake Tahoe since I was a little girl. I'm not sure why I never took this tour before, but I'm glad I finally did. It was very interesting."

"I was wondering if you've ever seen this man." Detective Felton pulled out a photo of Colin Matthews and showed it to Gayle.

Gayle smiled. "Oh, yes. That's Colin Matthews. He's been coming here for years. He comes a number of times every summer. He certainly is a charmer, that one. He usually comes alone. But several weeks ago, he brought a very beautiful woman with him. He introduced her as a friend, but it looked to me like they were more than just friends."

Detective Felton pulled out a photo of Katiana Flynn and showed it to Gayle.

"Is this the woman he brought with him?"

"Why yes, it is."

"Gayle, I'm sorry to have to tell you this but Colin Matthews has been murdered," Detective Felton said. "Colin's sister, Dee, told me that he liked to come here on his days off. We're looking for any information that might help us find Colin's murderer."

Gayle's jaw dropped. She stared at them for a long minute. "Could you please come back in about ten minutes after everyone in the tour group has left? Knock on the front door, and I'll let you in."

"Sure, no problem."

They walked outside through the grassy courtyard and under the raised gatehouse-style breezeway of the west wing. They slowly made their way back around to the main wing. When ten minutes had passed, Detective Felton knocked on the front door. Gayle quickly opened the door and ushered them inside. It was obvious that she'd been crying and was struggling to keep it together.

Gayle wrung her hands. "How did this happen? Why didn't I hear about it before now?"

"Maybe you hadn't heard about it because Vikingsholm is so isolated from the rest of the lake," Rylie said. "There was an article about Colin's death in Wednesday's Sierra Sun. And there was a memorial service for him at Granlibakken yesterday."

"I'm absolutely shocked. And horrified. How was he killed?"

Detective Felton exchanged a glance with Rylie. "We don't know all the details, Gayle. We're still waiting for the autopsy results."

Rylie noticed that Gayle looked a little pale. "Do you need to sit down, Gayle?"

Gayle looked like she was a million miles away. "What, dear?"

"Why don't we sit down somewhere for a few minutes?"

"Oh no, I'm fine. I don't have time to sit down," Gayle replied. "There will be another tour starting soon. I've got something to show you that might help you with your investigation, Detective. Colin and that woman he brought with him last time left something here."

They followed Gayle back to the foyer where Selma the clock was located.

"I know things about this place that no one else knows. There's a secret compartment in Selma's purse. I'd never told anyone about it until Colin and I were chatting sometime last summer. He seemed really interested in the history of Vikingsholm, and I ended up showing it to him. When he was here several weeks ago with that woman, he asked me if she could keep something in Selma's secret compartment for a little while. I thought it seemed like an odd request, but it seemed harmless enough, so I told him it would be fine. I let them into the house in between tours and left them alone so they could have some privacy. When I came back a little while later, they were gone."

Gayle slid her fingers along the top of Selma the clock's purse. The purse flipped open. There was a thick envelope inside that had been folded in half so it would fit in the purse.

"Do you mind if we look at what's inside the envelope, Gayle?" Detective Felton asked.

"Not at all. Please do."

He opened the envelope and removed a document written in a strange language comprised of symbols rather than letters. He peered into the envelope to make sure he'd gotten everything out and found a flash drive.

"I'll look through this stuff when we get back to Tahoe City. I may need to submit these items as evidence in Colin's murder investigation. Are you okay if I take these things, Gayle?"

"Of course. I want to do whatever I can to help."

He got a waterproof pouch from his backpack and put the document and flash drive in it. "We're planning on taking kayaks out to Fannette Island today, so I brought a waterproof pouch for our cell phones. I want to make sure this document and the flash drive don't get wet either."

"Please let me know if there's anything else I can do to help," Gayle said. "Here's my business card. I put my cell phone number on the back. I'd really appreciate it if you'd let me know when you find out who killed Colin."

Detective Felton took her business card and put it in his pocket. "Thank you, Gayle. Here's my card. If you think of anything else that you think might be helpful in my investigation, please call me right away."

They went out the back door as Gayle let in another crowd of people through the front door for her next tour.

"Want to hike partway up Eagle Falls and have our picnic there?" he asked.

"Sure."

They followed the path to Eagle Falls in companionable silence, both lost in their own thoughts. They hiked uphill along the stream as it tumbled down the mountain until they came to a small clearing. Mark unpacked a picnic blanket from his backpack and spread it out on the ground. She curled up on the blanket facing the waterfall. He sat down next to her and handed her a mineral water.

"Thanks, Mark." She took a drink and sat quietly watching the waterfall.

"I feel so bad for Gayle," she said finally. "I can't believe she hadn't heard about Colin being murdered. I don't know how well she knew Colin, but she was obviously fond of him."

"I hated having to tell Gayle about Colin's murder," Mark replied. "It was such a shock for her. I'll make sure to call her when we finally find out who killed him."

"I'm sure she'll appreciate that."

She grabbed her cell phone from her pocket.

"Mark! I have an idea!"

She spoke into her cell phone. "Ok, Google. Show me "let's go for a walk" translated into Russian."

"Ha! I was right!" She showed Mark her cell phone screen. "Don't these symbols look like the ones in the document that Colin and Katiana hid in Selma the clock's purse?"

He looked at the symbols displayed on her cell phone screen. Then he got out the document from the waterproof pouch and compared the symbols on it to what was displayed on her phone.

"They do look alike," he said. "Why would you think that the document is in Russian?"

"When I first met Katiana, I noticed she had a very distinctive accent. I thought it sounded Russian. Then I saw her the other day at Butter Lane Bakery. I invited her to join me at my table, and we talked a little. I asked her where she's from. She told me she's from Russia."

"That gives us a good starting point. I can have someone on my team try to find out for sure if the document is written in Russian. Once we know what language the document is written in, then it's just a matter of finding a translator."

"Great! I hope something in the document or the flash drive will provide some clue as to who killed Colin."

They ate their picnic lunch while enjoying the sounds of the waterfall dashing over the rocks on its way down to the lake. She watched some birds flitting around in the tree branches. The little patch of wilderness where they sat felt very calm and peaceful.

"It's beautiful here," she said. "So peaceful."

"Yes, it is. Are you ready to work off some of this lunch paddling out to the island?"

"Definitely! Let's go."

They walked to the kayak rental area and got in line to rent the brightly colored sit-on-top kayaks and some life vests. After they'd put on their life vests, they carefully got into their kayaks and started paddling toward Fannette Island.

Mark reached the rocky beach on the island first. He jumped out of his kayak and pulled it well out of the water to a flat area between some rocks. Then he waded out to where she was coasting in toward the beach and grabbed the front of her kayak to stabilize it while she got out.

"What a gentleman!" she teased. She carefully got out of her kayak.

Mark smiled and pulled her kayak up next to his.

"That was fun," she said. "I've always wanted to do more kayaking, but I've never gotten around to it. It's such a wonderful way to explore the lake. You get to see all sorts of things that you'd never see any other way."

"I like kayaking too. I'd like to kayak around Sand Harbor sometime. The water is so crystal clear and beautiful there. If you're interested, maybe we could find some time while you're here this summer to kayak around Sand Harbor together."

"That sounds great. I'd love to kayak around Sand Harbor."

They scrambled between granite boulders up the narrow path to the peak of the mountain where the ruined remains of the granite Tea House stood.

"I've never understood how ladies in the 1930s and '40s could make it to the top of this mountain dressed in long dresses and pearls to have afternoon tea in the Tea House," she said. "I think there might be a better trail with stone steps on the other side of the island, but I'm not sure."

She stepped inside the ruined shell of what had once been a place for elegantly dressed ladies to enjoy afternoon tea. Vandals had destroyed the roof and broken out all the windows and the door. She stepped over to one of the windows facing the mouth of Emerald Bay. The views were stunning.

"Maybe we should have brought some tea to enjoy while we were up here?" Mark teased. "I bet it was a really special place before it was so badly vandalized. It's such a shame that this place was not preserved in its original state. I wonder if they'll ever restore it."

After taking a bunch of photos, they picked their way back down the path between the boulders to their kayaks. The paddle back was hard work. The wind and currents were against them. It took them three times as long to paddle back as it did to paddle out to the island. She was a little tired when she finally pulled her kayak up onto the beach at the kayak rental area.

They hiked back up to the parking lot to Mark's SUV and headed back to her house. As soon as she opened the door to her house, Bella came bursting out and pranced around them excitedly. Then she sprinted into the woods to do her business. Rylie waited outside until Bella came running back.

"Good girl, Bella! You did such a good job watching the house for me while I was gone. Would you like a treat since you were such a good girl?"

Bella's tail wagged furiously. She panted happily.

Mark smiled. "I guess all dogs like treats, don't they?"

She went into the kitchen and got Bella a bacon, egg, and cheese doggie health bar. Bella gobbled it up so quickly Rylie wasn't sure if she'd even chewed it.

"Will you call me after you get the document translated and find out what's on the flash drive?"

"Sure. I'll let you know whatever I can without compromising my investigation. Can you put your cell phone number in my contacts?" He handed her his cell phone.

"Okay."

He bent down to give Bella a gentle scratch around her ears. Bella wagged her tail happily.

"I've got to get going now, Rylie. I'll talk to you soon."
He stood up and headed for the door. Bella bounced up and
down on her front legs.

"Thanks for a fun day Mark. Talk to you soon." She closed
the front door behind him and looked at Bella.

"He's a nice man, isn't he, Bella?"

Bella wagged her tail and looked expectantly at her.

"I'm going to microwave something for dinner, and then
we're going to call it a night, Bella. Come on. Let's go get
dinner."

She let Bella outside to do her business one last time before
they went to bed. Even though she was tired, she had a hard
time getting to sleep. Her thoughts churned as she thought
about the meeting with Dee Matthews, Garrison Taylor, and
Patrick O'Farrell the next morning.

Chapter 18

After breakfast the next day, she took Bella for a walk through the Butterfly Garden and then headed down to the lake. Bella had her nose to the ground sniffing everything in sight. She loved seeing Bella having so much fun.

She stared out across the lake and let her mind wander. Her body tensed in anticipation of the meeting with Dee Matthews and Patrick O'Farrell later that morning. She thought about the meeting she'd observed between Patrick and the guy in the expensive suit at Za's Lakefront Restaurant. If Expensive Suit Guy was an investor in Patrick's restaurant project, that could explain why he got so angry. An investor wouldn't be happy if Patrick wasn't able to get the permits required to renovate and expand the old Tavern Grill. From what she knew about Patrick, he seemed to have a quick temper. And if he was under pressure from an unhappy investor, who knows what he might do? She squared her shoulders and took a deep breath.

"Come on, Bella. Let's go home."

She walked back to her house with Bella trotting in front of her. As soon as they got inside, Bella made a beeline for her water bowl and had a nice long drink. Then she curled up contentedly on the living room floor.

A few minutes before 10:00, Rylie got her purse and headed outside to wait for Dee. Dee drove up a few minutes later. She hopped up into Dee's SUV.

"Morning." Dee smiled tightly at her, then turned her SUV around and drove down the long driveway toward the highway.

"Morning. It's such a nice day today. I took Bella down to the lake for a little while before you came," she replied.

"Oh, that's nice. Today's going to be a big day. Hopefully, everything will go smoothly and there won't be any problems with either Garrison or Patrick. I appreciate your offering to come with me for moral support. It helps to know I'll have someone there that's on my side."

"No problem," she replied. "Have you decided if you're going to sell Colin's half of the restaurant project yet?"

"I'm pretty sure I'm going to sell to Garrison. He's offered me what I consider to be a fair price. I'm already feeling overwhelmed with running the bakery. I don't think I can take on any more right now."

"I did some research online into the two restaurants that Garrison currently owns. Both restaurants look very nice and are quite popular. I feel confident that he'd do a good job of getting the new restaurant built and making it a success. And I think Colin would be happy to have his business partner build and manage the restaurant that he envisioned." Dee's voice cracked a little on her last sentence.

She looked over at Dee and saw the tears in her eyes. She didn't know Dee very well, but she felt sorry for her and everything she was going through.

"I think you're right, Dee. I'm sure Colin wouldn't have wanted you to get overwhelmed with trying to manage the bakery as well as supervising the building and management of the new restaurant. That would be a lot for anyone to take on. It sounds like Garrison is the perfect man for the job."

They arrived at The Grille at the Chateau in Incline Village a short time later. Dee let the hostess know they were meeting Garrison Taylor there at 11:00.

"Oh, Garrison's here already." The hostess smiled and picked up some menus. "Right this way."

She led them to a table near a wall of windows that overlooked the golf course. Rylie could see a glimpse of Lake Tahoe in the distance. A well-dressed man in a dark blue suit got up from the table to greet them.

"Hi!" His smile exuded genuine warmth. "How are you, Dee?"

He turned to Rylie and extended his hand. "I'm Garrison Taylor. Nice to meet you."

"I'm Rylie Sunderland. Nice to meet you, too."

Garrison helped both women into their chairs before returning to his seat. "Have either of you ever been here before?"

"I haven't," Rylie replied.

"I haven't either," Dee said. "But it looks really nice."

Garrison smiled. "It is nice. And the food here is very good. Nothing fancy, but well prepared."

The hostess handed them some menus, got their drink orders, and walked briskly away. Rylie and Dee opened their menus.

"The Sunset Salad with grilled salmon sounds amazing. That's what I'm going to have," Rylie said.

"I like their Beet Salad with grilled chicken," Garrison said. "But you have to like kale if you want that one."

"I'm not a big fan of kale," she replied. "I thought the Beet Salad sounded good until I saw that it was made with kale."

"I think a lot of people might feel the same way," Garrison said. "In my opinion, they should use some kind of leaf lettuce instead of kale for the Beet Salad. I think it would attract a larger audience."

She glanced at Dee, then looked at Garrison. "I know you own two restaurants, Garrison. Are you also a chef?"

"No. But I make it my business to know what people like to eat and what dishes will be popular menu choices. That's one of the reasons my restaurants are so successful."

She studied Garrison as he spoke. She decided his hair must be prematurely gray because he appeared youthful and energetic with lively hazel eyes, an easy smile, and a warm personality.

"I was looking at your two restaurants online," Dee said. "They both look very nice and seem to be popular."

"They're both doing quite well, I'm proud to say," Garrison replied. "They were both close to going under when I bought them. I renovated them, hired new chefs and staff, and was able to completely turn them around. I haven't ever built a restaurant from the ground up before, but I'm looking forward to the challenge."

"How did you meet Colin and end up getting involved in his project?" Rylie asked.

"I met Colin about a year ago. He approached me about his plan to build a restaurant on an empty lakefront lot that he'd purchased. He told me that he'd owned a business in the San Francisco Bay Area with Aidan Flynn but that it had gone under during the recession. He admitted that he'd made some bad business decisions that had contributed to the business failing."

"He told me that his partner Aidan had put up most of the money to start their business and that Aidan lost a lot of money when the business went under. He said he didn't want to have those kind of problems again, so he was looking for someone with a lot of restaurant experience to become his partner. I did some research and decided it looked like a good investment, so I agreed to put up the money for a fifty percent interest in the project."

"You weren't nervous about going into business with someone who admitted that he'd made some bad business decisions that cost his partner a lot of money?" she asked.

"Not really. My partnership agreement with Colin gives me the final say on all decisions regarding the construction of the restaurant and the operation of the business. I wouldn't have agreed to get involved with the project under any other terms."

"Do you think there's anything that I could contribute to the project?" Dee asked. "I don't know anything about running a restaurant other than what I'm learning on the fly at the bakery. And I certainly don't know anything about building one."

"I'm sure there are ways you could contribute," Garrison replied. "I think it all depends on how much you want to get involved. Right now you're learning how to run a bakery. You seem to be doing very well at it, I might add. I'm sure you could also learn about building and running a full-service restaurant if that's something you'd like to do. I'd be happy to share with you what I've learned about running a restaurant if you decide you want to get involved in the project."

"That's very nice of you, but I just don't know." Dee sighed in frustration. "Patrick O'Farrell's going to be here at noon. He really wants to buy the land that you and Colin own. He needs more land for additional parking so he can get the permits required to expand the old Tavern Grill. I was hoping talking with you first would give me some clarity on what I want to do with my share of the project before he gets here."

"I'm not going to sell my interest in the land to Patrick O'Farrell," Garrison said. "And I have the right of first refusal to purchase Colin's share. The right of first refusal is set out in the documents I gave you to show your attorney. You wouldn't be able to sell Colin's share to Patrick unless I decided not to purchase it. I've made you a fair offer to purchase Colin's share. It's up to you to decide if you want to sell Colin's share to me or remain in the project as either a silent or actively involved partner."

"I should warn you," Garrison continued, "that a lot more money will be needed to complete this project. Some of that money will come from the partners and the rest will come from loans. All of the money that Colin and I have invested so far has been from our own funds. But we'll need to obtain loans for a substantial amount of money in the near future."

"If you want to be an actively involved partner and continue to own a one-half interest in the project, you'll need to invest some cash and sign for loans as the project progresses. If you don't want to sell Colin's share, but you don't want to invest any money or sign for loans, then we could make you a silent partner. I could have my accountant estimate what percentage of the finished project Colin's investment would be worth. You'd own a small percentage of the finished project. When the restaurant starts to operate at a profit at some point in the future, you'd get a share of the profits based on your percentage of ownership."

"That's a lot to consider," Dee replied. "I need some time to think about it. I also need to consult with my attorney and my accountant before I make a final decision. But at least I know what to tell Patrick now. Since you have the right of first refusal to purchase Colin's share of the project, selling my one-half interest to him isn't even an option. And since you don't want to sell your interest in the project, it looks like he's out of luck. I'm sure he won't be happy about it."

The waitress arrived with their drinks and asked if they were ready to order.

"We have another person joining us that's supposed to arrive at noon," Garrison replied. "I think we'll wait until he gets here to order."

"No problem. I'll come back in a little while." The waitress hurried off.

Patrick showed up a few minutes later.

"Patrick, this is Garrison Taylor," Dee said. "Garrison was Colin's business partner in his restaurant project. He owns a one-half interest in the land and the project."

Patrick looked a little startled but managed to maintain his composure. Garrison stood and extended his hand to Patrick. "Nice to meet you Patrick."

Patrick shook his hand. "Nice to meet you too."

"And you already know Rylie, right?" Dee asked.

"Yes. Hi Rylie. Nice to see you again."

Patrick sat next to Garrison at the table. The waitress promptly appeared with a menu for him and got his drink order.

He set his menu on the table and looked directly at Garrison. "Let's get right to business. I recently purchased the old Tavern Grill. I plan to renovate it and expand it. But I've run into a problem. When I applied for my permits, I was told I had to have additional parking in order to expand the restaurant. There's no way I can do that with the land I currently have. My investors are not pleased. I'd like to buy the land that you and Dee own so I can use it for additional parking. I'll make it worth your while. I'm willing to pay a very fair price."

Rylie sensed an undercurrent of desperation in Patrick's voice. He looked like he might explode at any second. He was a big man, and he looked really strong. She had the feeling it would be dangerous to get on Patrick's bad side. She looked over at Dee. She could tell Dee was getting nervous too.

"I'm sorry Patrick, but I'm not interested in selling at any price," Garrison replied firmly. "And I have the right of first refusal to purchase Colin's interest. So Dee can't sell Colin's share to you unless I decide not to purchase it. I've already told Dee that I'll purchase Colin's share if she wants to sell. I'm afraid you'll have to find another way to move forward with your project."

She looked at Patrick. He looked devastated. And a little scared.

"If you want," Garrison continued, "I'll buy your property from you so you can get out from under it. I'd tear that old restaurant down and use the land for my new restaurant."

Patrick leaped out of his seat, grabbed Garrison by the lapels of his suit jacket, and pulled him out of his chair as if he were light as a feather. Both Rylie and Dee jumped out of their chairs and took a few steps back from the table.

"You can't demolish the Tavern Grill!" Patrick yelled. "It's part of Tahoe City's history! It needs to be preserved and restored!"

Garrison glared fiercely at Patrick. She was impressed that Garrison didn't seem at all shaken by Patrick's assault. Patrick appeared to be twice the size of Garrison.

"Back off Patrick," Garrison growled.

Patrick didn't budge an inch. He continued to hang onto Garrison's lapels and stare angrily at him. She hoped this wasn't going to escalate into a fistfight. There was no doubt in her mind that one punch from Patrick would be all it took to end the fight.

"I said. Back. Off."

Patrick let go of Garrison's lapels and took a step back. He continued to glare at Garrison for a long minute, then stomped angrily out of the restaurant.

She let out the breath she'd been holding and looked over at Dee. Dee looked stricken.

"Come on Dee," she said. "Let's sit down."

She guided Dee back to her chair and sat down next to her. Garrison sat back down too.

"I'm sorry about that, ladies."

"It's not your fault," she replied. "I think Patrick is in a very bad situation and he doesn't know how to get out of it. It sounds like his investors might be putting pressure on him. I don't condone his behavior just now, but I feel bad that he's in that situation."

"Desperation can make people do things they wouldn't normally do," Dee said grimly. "I hope Patrick had nothing to do with my brother's murder, but it looks like he may have had motive."

Rylie reached over and put her hand on top of Dee's. "I'm sorry things didn't go well with Patrick, Dee. I'll call Detective Felton when I get home and tell him about what happened here today. I think he needs to be kept informed of anything that might be relevant to his investigation."

"Thanks, Rylie."

They placed their orders with the waitress. Their lunches arrived shortly thereafter. Garrison kept the conversation going with some of his ideas for the new restaurant.

"No matter what I decide to do with Colin's share of the restaurant," Dee said, "I'd like to have something in the restaurant to commemorate my brother and his contribution to the project."

"I'd like that too," Garrison replied. "I think that would be very appropriate. Maybe we can install a water feature or some kind of artwork with a plaque recognizing Colin's contribution to the project."

"I'd love that," Dee said.

They finished their lunches and prepared to leave.

"I'll get back to you after I talk to my attorney and my accountant," Dee said.

"Thanks, Dee. I'll look forward to hearing from you."

Rylie and Dee got in Dee's SUV and headed back to Whitaker Cottages.

"I feel so bad for everything you're going through," she said. "You've had to take on a lot. But you seem to be doing a great job running the bakery, and I'm sure you'll make the right decision about what to do with your share of Colin's restaurant project."

Dee pulled into Whitaker Cottages parking lot and parked near Rylie's house. "Thanks, Rylie. I really appreciate your coming with me today."

"Sure. And please feel free to call me if you want to talk about anything."

She watched as Dee drove away, then forced herself to focus on the job at hand. Liam and Gillian were expecting her to take over at the cottages as soon as she got back from lunch with Dee.

Chapter 19

She went to her house to let Bella out. Bella greeted her enthusiastically, bouncing up and down on her front legs and wagging her tail so hard that her whole butt wagged back and forth.

"Hi Bella! Pretty girl! Were you a good girl while I was gone?"

Bella wagged her tail and looked at her hopefully.

"Would you like a treat for being such a good girl?"

Bella's tail wagged faster.

She got Bella a bacon, egg, and cheese doggie health bar and gave it to her. Bella crunched happily on her treat.

"We've got to go to work now, Bella. Let's go!"

Bella trotted ahead of her to the reception area. There was no one in reception, so she went in back of the reception desk and knocked on the door that led to Liam and Gillian's house.

Liam answered the door. "Hi! Come on in! How did everything go with Dee this morning?"

"Not as well as I'd hoped." She stepped inside.

Bella stopped for a pet from Liam and then went over to greet Gillian. Gillian smiled and ruffled the golden fur around Bella's neck.

"What can I get you to drink?" Liam asked.

"Some mineral water with a slice of lime would be great, if you have it."

She sat with Gillian at the long wooden table in the dining area. Liam handed her a glass of mineral water as he joined them.

Liam and Gillian looked at her expectantly. Bella moved close to her and pushed her warm muzzle into her hand. She glanced at Bella and stroked her head a few times before turning her attention to Liam and Gillian.

"Thanks for filling in for me this morning. I really appreciate it. How about if I work on Thursday until 2:00 to make up for it?"

"That would be fine," Gillian said.

"The meeting with Garrison Taylor this morning was interesting," she began. "He seems like a really nice guy."

She told them about Garrison's right of first refusal to purchase Colin's half of the restaurant project from Dee and how Patrick offered to buy both Garrison's and Dee's interests in the real estate.

"Garrison told Patrick that he wasn't interested in selling at any price. He offered to buy the old Tavern Grill so Patrick could get out from under it. He told Patrick he'd demolish it and use the land for his new restaurant. Patrick went ballistic. He pulled Garrison up out of his chair by the lapels of his suit jacket like he was light as a feather. I was really nervous that things were going to get out of hand, but he let go of Garrison after a minute or two and then stormed out of the restaurant."

"Oh my goodness! I wonder what Patrick's going to do now," Gillian said.

"I'm not sure," Rylie replied. "But Dee made a point of saying that someone who was in a desperate situation might do things that they wouldn't normally do. She said she hoped Patrick had nothing to do with Colin's murder, but that it looks like he may have had motive. I'm not sure what to think. I don't know Patrick very well, but he definitely seems to have a quick temper."

"We've known Patrick for some time," Liam said. "He does have a temper, but I can't imagine that he'd ever murder someone."

"I really hope that he didn't have anything to do with Colin's murder," Rylie replied. "But I'm going to call Detective Felton this afternoon to let him know what happened this morning with Patrick and Garrison. I think it's important to keep him informed of anything we learn that might possibly be relevant to his investigation."

"What happened when you and Detective Felton went to Vikingsholm yesterday?" Liam asked. "Did you find out anything that might help with Colin's case?"

"Yes, we did."

She told Liam and Gillian about Colin taking Katiana to Vikingsholm with him a few weeks ago and about the document and flash drive that she'd hidden in Selma the clock's secret compartment.

"That's disturbing," Liam said. "What was Colin thinking taking Katiana to Vikingsholm? Aidan may not be the most personable guy in the world, but no guy deserves to have his wife sneaking around behind his back like that."

She exchanged a glance with Gillian.

"When will we know what's in the document and flash drive that Katiana left at Vikingsholm?" Gillian asked.

"Mark has to find someone to translate the document," she replied. "He said he'd call me after he gets the document translated and finds out what's on the flash drive. He said he'd let me know whatever he could without compromising his investigation."

"Oh, that's good. Hey, would you like to join us for Wednesday's poker night dinner this week?" Gillian asked. "You can keep me company so I'm not the only female present."

"Sure. And I'd be happy to help you prepare dinner, if you want."

"Thanks. I haven't decided yet what I'm making, but I'll let you know when I do."

Liam's cell phone rang. He looked at the caller ID. "I have to take this."

He walked into the other room with his cell phone to his ear. He came back a few minutes later looking pleased.

"That was one of the contractors that Alain recommended for the cottage renovations. Tony Bartoletti. He said he can come look at the cottages on Wednesday. The other contractor that Alain recommended, Bob Sanchez, is coming tomorrow."

"Would you mind if I went with you when you walk through the cottages with the contractors?" she asked.

"Not at all."

"What about that other contractor you mentioned?" she asked. "The one that Colin rejected his bid to build his new restaurant? Are you having him out to give a bid on the renovations too?"

"I wasn't planning on it," Liam replied. "Alain said Steve Randall overpromises and underdelivers."

"I know. But I think it might be a good idea to have him out here anyway so we can get a chance to talk to him. Even though Colin turning down his bid doesn't seem like a motive for murder, there's a chance we could learn something from him that could prove useful to Detective Felton in his investigation."

"I guess it couldn't hurt to have Steve come out to bid on the renovations. I'll call him and see if I can get him to come on Thursday."

"Great!" she replied. "Has it busy with guests today?"

"No, it's been pretty slow," Gillian replied. "All our weekend guests checked out this morning. I think we only have one reservation for tonight so far."

"In that case, I'd like to spend a little time visiting with Elizabeth this afternoon if she's still here. Is she still here, or did she leave already?"

"She's still here," Gillian replied. "I think she's planning to go home early tomorrow morning."

"Oh, good. I'll take the business cell phone with me in case anyone calls or comes to reception. See you later. Come on, Bella. We're going to go visit Elizabeth. Do you want to go to Elizabeth's house?"

Bella wagged her tail in reply. Rylie headed over to the main house with Bella trotting in front of her. She knocked on the door and waited patiently for Elizabeth to answer. Just when she thought Elizabeth must not be home, she opened the door with a warm smile.

"Rylie! Bella! How nice to see you both. Do come in."

Bella looked up at Elizabeth expectantly. Elizabeth smiled down at her and pet her head. Bella wagged her tail and ambled into the house.

"Bella seems to be quite comfortable here." Elizabeth chuckled.

"I think she likes it here at the lake. She's been having a great time."

"I was just about to have a cup of tea in the library. Would you like to join me, dear?"

"Sure. That sounds great."

Elizabeth led the way to the library with its walls of built-in maple wood bookshelves set between tall windows that flooded the room with natural light. Overstuffed chairs flanked by floor lamps for reading were scattered around the room. A large, floral-patterned rug in muted creams and grays added to the room's charm.

"I'll be back in a few minutes, dear." Elizabeth headed toward the kitchen. "Make yourself comfortable. You're welcome to look through all the books. I won't be long."

Rylie was secretly delighted to have the opportunity to look around the library. She'd wanted to explore the library ever since she first saw it. She pulled out a couple of the books and looked through them briefly. She knew she could happily spend many hours in this room.

Elizabeth came back a little while later carrying a tray with tea and shortbread cookies. She set the tray down on the dark wood antique library table near the fireplace.

"The tea has to steep for a few minutes."

Elizabeth sat down in one of the overstuffed chairs near the library table. Rylie sat down in a chair near her.

"I'm so sorry that your stay here has been marred by Colin Matthews' murder," Elizabeth said. "I feel horrible for Colin as well as his friends and family. This has been a very traumatic experience for everyone involved. Your mother wanted you to come here so you could enjoy some time at the lake while you're figuring out what to do now that the veterinary hospital where you worked burned to the ground. I'm afraid it hasn't been a very good experience for you so far. I hope the sheriff's department is able to put this matter to rest quickly."

"Please don't worry about me, Elizabeth. I think coming here has been good for me in spite of everything's that's happened. I'm becoming good friends with Gillian and Liam. I've been enjoying taking walks with Bella down by the lake. We walked along the Truckee River the other day, too. That was fun. I've spent some time exploring Tahoe City. And I had a good time with Mark Felton at Vikingsholm yesterday."

Elizabeth's face relaxed. "I'm glad to hear that, dear. Now I'll have something positive to say to your mother about your stay here the next time I talk to her."

Elizabeth got up to pour their tea.

"How do you like your tea, dear?"

"I like it with milk and sugar. But I'll get it, Elizabeth. You just make your tea, and I'll make mine when you're done."

They sat back down in the overstuffed chairs with their tea and cookies.

"I love your library, Elizabeth. It's so warm and cozy. I'd love to have the opportunity to spend some time in here browsing through all the books. I'd like to curl up in one of these comfy chairs and just relax. I was wondering if you'd mind if I spent some time in here once in a while after you've gone back home?"

"You're more than welcome to spend time here any time you like, dear. In fact, let me get you a key to the house so you can let yourself in without bothering Gillian or Liam."

Elizabeth came back a few minutes later with a key in her hand. "Here you go, dear. Please make yourself at home here. You're welcome to help yourself to anything you find in the pantry or the refrigerator. You can make yourself a pot of tea or whatever you'd like."

"Thank you, Elizabeth. That's very nice of you. Do you mind if Bella comes with me when I come here?"

"Not at all, dear. Bella is welcome here any time."

They chatted amicably for a while, then she headed back to the reception area with Bella. She looked at the reservation that was scheduled to arrive that evening. The business phone hadn't rung once since she'd started working this afternoon. She felt bad that the cottage rentals had been so slow since Colin's murder.

Just before dinnertime, she checked in the couple that had reserved a cottage for the evening. Then she went back to her house with Bella. She curled up on the sofa with a mineral water. Her mind raced as she thought about everything that had occurred since she'd arrived at Whitaker Cottages. She was trying hard to make sense of it all

Was Colin's murderer one of the people that she, Liam, and Gillian had put on their list of possible suspects? Or was it someone that wasn't even on their radar?

Chapter 20

She got dressed and headed to the reception area with Bella just before 6:00 the next morning. Even though only one cottage had been rented the night before, she still had to prepare the continental breakfast that was included with all cottage reservations.

She saw Eric pull up in the Butter Lane Bakery delivery van. He walked into the reception area carrying a tray of baked goods. Bella bounced up and down on her front legs and panted happily as she tried to get his attention. Eric grinned and set his tray on a nearby table before he leaned over to ruffle Bella's fur.

Rylie smiled. "What delicious things have you got for us today, Eric?"

"Oh, here. Try one of my cinnamon rolls. I just made them this morning. They're still warm from the oven."

The aroma was irresistible. She bit into the warm cinnamon roll and rolled her eyes in delight.

"This is delicious, Eric! You really have a talent for baking. I hope you get to go to that school in Paris."

"Me, too. Have you learned anything new about Colin's murder investigation?"

"I've learned a lot since you brought Buddy over to play with Bella last week. It'll take a while to fill you in. Don't you have a bunch of deliveries to do this morning?"

"Yes, I do. Why don't I call you later this afternoon then?" He headed for the door.

"Okay. Talk to you later."

The couple that had stayed in one of the cottages the night before came into the reception area. They got coffee, juice, and cinnamon rolls and sat down at one of the tables to enjoy their breakfast.

Bella walked over to greet the couple slowly wagging her long, golden plumed tail. She delighted in the attention they lavished on her. Satisfied, she laid down in the middle of the reception area facing the door so she could keep an eye on things. Rylie smiled as she watched Bella playing the hostess. Even people who didn't have any dogs of their own seemed to warm up quickly to Bella and her charms. The couple finished their breakfast and left.

Liam opened the door behind the reception desk. "Bob Sanchez is here to look at the two cottages that need renovations. Are you still interested in joining us while we go through them?"

"Definitely. I'll lock up and take the business cell phone with me. I'll meet you by the cottages in a minute."

She followed Liam as he led the way through the cottages explaining to Bob the renovations that needed to be made. Bob took notes on his tablet as they went along.

"These are wonderful old Tahoe cottages, Liam," Bob said. "Do you mind if I see some of the cottages that you've already renovated so I can get an idea of your vision?"

"Not at all."

They walked through a couple of the renovated guest cottages scattered among the tall pines.

"I love this project, Liam," Bob said. "This is a beautiful property with so much character. I'll get back to you with a bid for renovating those two cottages sometime next week."

Bob typed a few things into his tablet and then looked back up at Liam. "I heard about Colin Matthews' murder. It's hard to believe something like that could happen around here. Has it had an effect on your business?"

Liam winced. "Yes, business has definitely dropped off since Colin's murder. Elizabeth Whitaker had a security system installed since then. But customers are still concerned for their safety. I can't say that I blame them. We're letting people cancel their reservations without charging any cancellation fees. A lot of people have cancelled."

"I'm glad Mrs. Whitaker put in a security system," Bob said. "Have there been any other problems here since the night Colin was murdered?"

"No. Not at all," Liam replied.

They walked Bob back to his SUV and said their goodbyes.

"I like Bob," she said. "He seems like a nice guy. I hope he comes in with a reasonable bid."

"I like him too. But we still have two more contractors coming out to give us bids. I want to see all three bids before we make a final decision."

She went home with Bella for lunch. She made herself a salad and had just sat down to eat when her cell phone rang. She saw Detective Felton's name on the caller ID.

"Hello?"

"Hi, Rylie. This is Mark. We got lucky with the document we found at Vikingsholm. You were right. It was in Russian. Fortunately, we had someone that was able to translate it fairly quickly. It's an inventory of all of the furniture, furnishings, and personal belongings of Katiana and her husband Aidan. The flash drive is a photo inventory of the same things."

"Why would Katiana want to hide an inventory of her personal belongings? Why wouldn't she have put it in a safe deposit box or something?"

"Good question. Listen Rylie, I've got to run. I'm in the middle of a million things. I just wanted to let you know what we learned about the document and flash drive. I know you, Liam, and Gillian are anxious for answers. Please don't worry. We're doing everything we can to get this investigation wrapped up as quickly as possible."

"Thanks, Mark."

After lunch, she took Bella with her to spend some time in the library at the main house. The house felt massive and empty compared to her comfortable little caretaker's house. She was glad she had Bella with her.

She went into the kitchen and made herself some tea. Bella stayed close as she moved around the house. She wondered why Bella seemed to be a little nervous and un-comfortable.

She browsed through the books in the library's book-shelves. She was particularly intrigued with the extremely old books that she found that had been left there by the original owner. She was amazed that books published in the 1800s were still in existence. She gingerly examined some of the antique books and selected a few to explore further.

When she had collected a stack of books to peruse, she set them on a side table next to one of the overstuffed chairs in front of the fireplace. She settled into the chair and took a sip of her tea.

Bella came over and put her head on her lap and looked up at her with large brown eyes. She bent over to press her cheek against Bella's muzzle and made kissing noises. Bella slowly wagged her tail and broke into a doggie grin, panting happily.

She started looking through one of the books she'd selected. Eric called a little while later. She filled him in on everything she'd learned since he'd been there last Thursday.

"Wow. That's a lot to take in."

"I know. This whole thing has been hard on all of us. But I'm sure it's been even harder on you since you were so close to Colin."

Eric didn't reply for a minute or two. She imagined he was trying to compose himself.

"Let's just hope they get this wrapped up soon. See you tomorrow."

"See you then."

The afternoon passed quickly as she explored the books she'd chosen. It was dinnertime before she knew it. She wanted to keep reading, but she knew she had to get dinner for Bella and herself.

"Bella!"

Bella raised her head from where she'd been peacefully sleeping in the middle of the room.

"Let's go get dinner!"

Bella jumped up eagerly. She took Bella back to their house, put kibble in her dog dish, and got her some fresh water. She decided to take some brie and crackers back to the library so she could read while she ate. After Bella had eaten her dinner, they went back to the library. She settled back into her comfortable overstuffed chair and munched on brie and crackers as she read.

When it got dark, she got up and closed the fabric window shades. It wasn't cold in the library, but she decided to light a fire in the gas fireplace just for the ambiance.

Bella let out a low growl. Rylie got up from where she was squatting in front of the fireplace. She saw the fur on the back of Bella's neck standing on end. Her heart started pounding in her chest. She looked quickly around the room to see what Bella was growling at.

Then she heard it. Faint rattling and thumping noises coming from the direction of the butler's pantry. She grabbed Bella's collar to keep her from running to the pantry.

"Shhhh, Bella. Be quiet."

She hurriedly made a whispered phone call to Liam. Liam and Gillian quickly joined her in the library. They huddled together and strained to hear what was going on.

A loud thump came from the direction of the butler's pantry. Bella started barking ferociously. She held on tightly to Bella's collar. She didn't want whoever was in the butler's pantry to hurt Bella.

Liam sprinted to the butler's pantry with Rylie, Bella, and Gillian close behind. They got there just in time to see a man in black clothing wearing a black ski mask disappear out the window. Bella broke free from her grasp and lunged toward the window but the man had already made it outside.

"Hey!" Liam yelled. He turned and raced out the front door after the intruder.

Gillian called Detective Felton on her cell phone. Rylie ran to the window. She saw Liam go running by, but she didn't see any sign of the intruder.

"Detective Felton will be right over," Gillian said.

Liam stalked back into the butler's pantry.

"I couldn't find him," he growled. "He disappeared into thin air. Did you call Detective Felton?"

"Yes," Gillian said. "He'll be here shortly."

They heard a knock on the front door. Liam went to answer it and came back to the butler's pantry with Detective Felton.

"Is everyone okay?" Detective Felton asked.

"Yes. We're fine. We're just a little shaken up," Rylie replied.

Detective Felton inspected the area around the window. "The evidence technicians will be here shortly to dust for fingerprints and look for anything that might help identify the intruder. We'll do the best we can tonight, but we'll have to come back in the morning when it's light out to get a better look. We'll put crime scene tape around the area to secure it until we can do a thorough investigation in the morning."

"It doesn't look like a forced entry," he added. "I think the window must have been left open. Before we run any fingerprints that the technicians find through the database, we'll need to find out if any of them belong to Mrs. Whitaker. I'll have her come to the sheriff's department so we can get a set of fingerprints on her."

"I'd suggest you go through every building on the property to make sure all the windows and doors are closed and locked and that the security system is on and working in each one. I'll make sure my guys drive by to check on the property more frequently starting tonight."

"Thank you, Detective. We'll do that right now," Liam said.

He walked Detective Felton out, then returned to the butler's pantry a couple minutes later.

"Why don't Gillian and I go with you to your house and check to make sure everything's secure, Rylie? Then Gillian and I will check the main house and all the cottages, and you can call it a night."

"Okay. Thanks."

They went through Rylie's house and made sure all the windows were closed and locked. She locked the door behind them and turned on the security system.

"That was scary, wasn't it, Bella?"

She put her arms around Bella's neck and hugged her. Then she went into the kitchen to make herself some chamomile and lavender tea to help herself relax.

I hope Mark and his team find something tomorrow to identify the guy that broke in tonight. What if it was the murderer coming back to the scene of the crime for some reason? A shiver ran up her spine.

Chapter 21

S he slept fitfully that night. She kept waking up and listening intently for any unusual sounds. At 3:00 a.m., she decided it wasn't worth trying to get to sleep anymore. She got out of bed and wrapped herself in a warm robe to ward off the morning chill.

"Coffee. I need coffee," she muttered. She looked over at Bella who was watching her through half-opened eyes from where she'd been sleeping on the floor by the side of her bed.

"Hi, Bella. You don't have to get up. I can't sleep, so I'm going to get up. I'm going to go make some coffee."

Bella stayed where she was while Rylie padded into the kitchen to make coffee. Her brain kept replaying the scene of running into the butler's pantry and seeing the man in dark clothes disappear out the window just as Bella lunged at him. She wondered what time Detective Felton and his team would get there to search for any evidence left behind by the intruder.

Bella ambled into the kitchen. She let Bella out to go potty while she put some kibble in her dog dish and got her some fresh water. After she'd gotten her coffee brewing, she let Bella back in. Bella went straight to her dish to get her breakfast.

"You don't care what time it is, do you Bella? You're happy to have breakfast any time."

Bella kept her muzzle in her dish as she continued to happily munch her way through her breakfast.

It was too early to go to the reception area, so she decided to search online to see if there had been any recent break-ins in the North Lake Tahoe area. She was surprised to find an article in the Sierra Sun newspaper online about a burglary that had occurred recently in nearby Homewood. She wondered whether the intruder last night might have been the same person who burglarized the house in Homewood or whether last night's break-in had something to do with Colin Matthews' murder.

Maybe the guy broke in to see if he could find the Zippo lighter that he lost on the night that Colin was killed? Her stomach knotted. She wondered if she should look into buying some pepper spray or some other kind of self-defense.

Then her thoughts turned to more practical matters. There weren't any guests in the cottages last night. That hadn't occurred on any of the other days she'd worked. She wondered if she was still supposed to make coffee and put out breakfast items in the reception area. What was she going to do with all the baked goods from Butter Lane Bakery? Should she call Dee and cancel the order for today?

She didn't want to wake up Gillian and Liam on their day off, and she didn't want to cause any problems with Dee, so she decided to let Eric deliver his baked goods on schedule and talk to Gillian and Liam later about how she should handle this type of situation in the future.

Just before 6:00 a.m., she walked with Bella over to the reception area. The sun had just come up. Lavender-edged puffy pink clouds stretched across the sky. She watched the birds flitting through the trees and hopping around on the ground looking for food. A Steller's Jay landed on the branch of a nearby tree and squawked at them as they passed.

She got everything set up for the continental breakfast as if there had been guests in the cottages. Then she locked the front door of the reception area and took the business cell phone with her so that she and Bella could take a walk through the Butterfly Garden.

She walked slowly along the dirt path that meandered through the garden admiring the profusion of flowers raising their blooms to the early morning sun. Small orange and brown butterflies flitted among the flowers. The garden felt so beautiful and peaceful. She drank in the calming scents of native flowers and herbs. Bella was delighting in running around and sniffing everything in sight. Rylie sat down on the weathered gray wooden bench for a minute. Then she decided to go get a cup of coffee to enjoy while she relaxed in the garden.

"Come on, Bella. I want to get a cup of coffee."

As she was heading back to the reception area, she saw an SUV drive up. Detective Felton got out. She met him by the front door of the reception area.

"Good morning, Mark. Thank you for coming. Would you like a cup of coffee or some orange juice? I have plenty to go around."

"Morning, Rylie. A cup of coffee sounds nice. Thank you."

She unlocked the door to the reception area and let Detective Felton in. He poured himself some coffee.

"The evidence technicians will be here any minute." He sat down at one of the tables in the reception area. "Now that it's light out, we'll be able to get a better look at the exterior of the butler's pantry window to see if we can find any evidence that last night's intruder may have left behind."

Eric walked in carrying a tray of freshly baked breads and pastries.

"Hi, Eric." Rylie smiled. "Whatever you have today smells amazing!"

"Hi, Rylie! Hi, Bella! Good morning, Detective."

Mark eyed Eric's tray of baked goods with interest. Eric set his tray down and leaned over to pet Bella. Rylie started transferring the baked goods from Eric's tray onto serving platters.

"Would you like some of these delicious pastries from the Butter Lane Bakery, Mark?" she asked. "We have plenty."

"That would be great." Detective Felton walked over to check out the assortment of baked goods that Eric had brought. He selected some pastries and then went back to his table to enjoy his breakfast.

She walked to the delivery van with Eric so she could explain why Detective Felton was there.

"You're kidding!" Eric exclaimed.

"Unfortunately, I'm not. I'm not feeling very safe here right now. I'm glad I have Bella with me. I was thinking maybe I should go buy some pepper spray or something."

"Oh Rylie, I'm so sorry. This is such a terrible situation for you to be in. I wish there was something I could do to help."

"The thing is that we don't know if the person who broke in last night was the person who killed Colin or if it was entirely unrelated. If it was the person who killed Colin, that's terrifying. But even if it was someone who had nothing to do with the murder who was just breaking in to rob the place, that's still pretty scary," she said.

"It sure is," Eric replied. "Look, I'm sorry, but I've got to get going. I have a ton of deliveries to make this morning. I'll call you later to check on you and make sure you're okay."

"Thanks, Eric."

Detective Felton emerged from the reception area as Eric's delivery van pulled away. "I'm going to check the area where the break-in occurred now. Thanks for the coffee and pastries, Rylie. I'll let you know if we find anything."

She went inside, poured herself a cup of coffee, and selected a pastry for herself. She checked the computer to see if there were any reservations for that night. She was happy to see that there was a large family group that had booked three of the cottages for several nights.

Liam popped his head into the reception area from the door to his house behind the reception desk and told her Tony Bartoletti had arrived to go through the cottages needing renovations.

"Detective Felton is here looking for evidence from last night's break-in," she replied. "I'll go tell him where I'm going to be and meet you guys over there."

"Okay. See you there."

She put Bella on a leash before she let her outside so she wouldn't run into the area where Detective Felton and the evidence technicians were searching for evidence. Then she locked the front door of the reception area and took the business cell phone with her. She found Mark with the evidence technicians outside the butler's pantry window.

"Have you found anything yet?" she asked.

"We found some tiny pieces of fabric on the windowsill. I'd assume they're from the intruder," Detective Felton replied.

"Are they black?"

"Yes."

"I saw in the Sierra Sun online that there was a burglary in Homewood recently. Do you think there's any chance that whoever broke in here last night was the same guy? Or do you think that it could have been the guy that killed Colin Matthews coming back to look for the Zippo lighter that we found in the Absinthe Room?"

"Honestly Rylie, I don't know. But once we get the DNA results back from the lab on this fabric, we can check to see if it matches any DNA they were able to get off the Zippo lighter."

"How soon will the DNA results be back from the lab for the fabric pieces you just found?"

"Probably not until at least the first week of July."

"Oh." Rylie sighed. "I'm going over to meet Liam and a contractor at the cottages that need renovations. Please let me know if you find anything else before you go."

"Will do." Detective Felton resumed his search of the windowsill.

She walked over to the cottages with Bella and joined Liam and Tony.

"Tony has some great ideas for the cottage renovations," Liam said. "And he just bought a lot of supplies at a huge discount from a supplier that was going out of business, so he can pass the savings along to us and save us some money."

"Great!" she replied.

They walked through the old cottages while Tony took notes on his tablet.

Tony looked up from his tablet. "I think I have everything I need now. I'll get you a bid next week."

"Thanks, Tony," Liam said.

Tony headed for his SUV in the parking area.

"I'm going to go see how Detective Felton and his team are doing," Liam said. "Do you want to come?"

"Definitely."

Bella walked sedately next to Rylie on her leash as they went back to the main house.

Detective Felton and the evidence technicians were just finishing up and getting ready to leave when they walked up.

"Did you find anything else?" she asked.

"No, just the pieces of fabric that I already told you about," Detective Felton replied. "I'll send those to the lab today and let you know when we hear back from them."

"Thank you, Detective Felton," Liam said.

"Yes, thank you, Mark," she said.

"No problem. Just doing my job."

Just after lunchtime, the large family group came into the reception area to check into the three cottages they'd rented. She helped them with restaurant suggestions and gave them brochures for local attractions. She was glad they were finally renting out some of the cottages. It made her feel more comfortable about being on the property knowing that there were people there besides herself, Gillian, and Liam.

Eric called to check up on her. She filled him in on what Detective Felton had found. He sounded relieved to learn that Detective Felton had found some evidence left behind by the intruder so that the intruder could hopefully be identified.

Around 4:00, she knocked on Liam and Gillian's door in back of the reception desk. Gillian opened the door with a smile. "Hi! Come on in. Thanks for coming early to help me get everything ready for Liam's poker night dinner."

"No problem, Gillian. What would you like me to do?"

"You can help me by peeling the potatoes. We're having bangers and mash with Guinness onion gravy for dinner tonight. We need to boil a huge pot of potatoes for the mashed potatoes. These guys can eat massive amounts of food."

"Sounds delicious. I've never had bangers and mash, but it sounds really good."

Rylie peeled the potatoes, cut them into small chunks, put them in a large pot with some water, and then put them on the stove to cook. She set the long wooden table in the dining area with Gillian's midnight blue stoneware. She lined bread baskets with blue and white checked tea towels and scattered stoneware butter crocks along the table.

Liam set out some Irish whiskey and a couple bottles of cabernet sauvignon. He put some chardonnay, Guinness, and hefeweizen beer in the refrigerator to chill and set out an ice bucket. Then he went out to the Card House to stock the mini fridge out there with more beer and chardonnay.

She inhaled deeply. The aroma of the food cooking in the kitchen was intoxicating. Gillian and Liam's home felt so warm and inviting.

Aidan, Patrick, and Alain arrived within a few minutes of each other. Liam let them in while Rylie and Gillian continued with dinner preparations.

Patrick joined them in the kitchen. "Wow, it smells amazing in here. Bangers and mash! I love bangers and mash."

Alain walked into the kitchen and broke out in a wide grin. "Gillian, if it tastes anything like it smells, you've created another culinary masterpiece."

Gillian blushed. "It's hard to go wrong with bangers and mash. Why don't you guys have a seat at the table? Liam will help Rylie and I set out the food."

When everyone was seated, Patrick spoke up. "I have some good news."

Everyone looked at Patrick expectantly.

"After some lengthy negotiations, I've been able to lease twenty parking spaces adjacent to the old Tavern Grill from the Lighthouse Center. So it looks like I'll finally be able to get the permits I need to move forward with my plans to renovate and expand the place. I'm thrilled, and so are my investors." Patrick smiled as he looked around at the group.

She looked around the table. Gillian, Liam, and Alain were smiling. Aidan's face was impassive.

"That's great, Patrick," Alain said. "It'll be nice to have that old restaurant up and running again."

"That's really good news, Patrick," she said. "I hope everything goes smoothly with your renovation plans. I'm looking forward to seeing your restaurant when it's done."

She was glad Patrick had found a solution to his problem of not having enough parking spaces to get the permits he needed. He seemed like a nice enough guy. Gillian and Liam seemed to like him. But she just couldn't shake the thought that Patrick might have killed Colin Matthews.

Innocent until proven guilty, she admonished herself.

Her mind wandered to thoughts about Colin's murder as the hum of conversation continued around her.

"I have an announcement to make too," Aidan said. Everyone stopped talking and looked at him.

"I think I know who killed Colin."

She choked a little. She heard gasps from the people around the table.

"I saw that lawyer, Blake Cunningham, and Colin leave the room together during Locals' Night on the night that Colin was killed. They looked like they were having a pretty heated argument about something. A while later, I saw Blake come back to the living room alone. He looked really angry. Since

Colin's body was found in the Absinthe Room, I assume that's where they went. Maybe they went there so they could talk privately."

She looked around the table at the stunned faces. Liam spoke up first. "Did you tell Detective Felton about this, Aidan?"

"No. When he questioned me after Colin's murder, I got the feeling that he considered me a suspect because of the rumors going around about my wife having an affair with Colin. I spent the whole time trying to defend myself. I didn't remember having seen Blake and Colin together until the next day. Then I was afraid that if I went to him to tell him what I saw that night, that he might think I was just trying to cast suspicion on someone else to get him off my back."

She studied Aidan as he spoke and tried to decide if she believed his story.

"How about I call Detective Felton right now and tell him we have some new information that might help him with Colin's murder investigation?" Liam asked. "I can make an appointment for you and I to go talk to him at the sheriff's department tomorrow."

"Okay. Thanks, Liam," Aidan replied.

"I'm sure Detective Felton will want to talk to Blake Cunningham after he hears what you have to say," Liam said. "Maybe this will be the lead he needs to solve the case."

"That would be great," she said. "I know we're all anxious to find out who killed Colin and have that person put behind bars as soon as possible."

The men offered to help with the dishes before they went to play poker, but Gillian brushed them off.

"Rylie and I can take care of it. You guys go enjoy your poker game."

She helped Gillian put away the food and load the dishwasher. Then she said goodnight and walked home with Bella.

She yawned as she walked into her house. She locked the door and set the alarm, then she collapsed onto the sofa.

"What a day. Huh, Bella?"

Bella came over and put her head on her lap. She gently scratched around Bella's ears.

She was looking forward to meeting the next contractor coming out to look at the cottages needing renovations tomorrow. Steve Randall. She thought it was likely that he would have gotten upset when Colin rejected his bid on the restaurant project. Was he the kind of guy that had a temper? It would be interesting to get a chance to talk to him tomorrow.

Chapter 22

S he was in a deep sleep when her cell phone alarm went off early the next morning. She woke up enough to wonder why her alarm was going off on her day off. Then she remembered she had to work until 2:00 to make up for having taken time off on Monday to go with Dee to see Garrison and Patrick. She turned off her alarm and drifted back to sleep. The second alarm woke her up again fifteen minutes later. She turned off the second alarm and headed to the kitchen to make coffee. Bella followed close behind.

She felt better after a few sips of hot coffee. She got Bella her breakfast and then went to her bedroom to get showered and dressed. A little before 6:00, she walked over to the reception area with Bella to get everything set up for the continental breakfast for the large family group staying in the cottages.

The coffee had just finished brewing when Eric arrived with two large trays of warm pastries. The large family group came into the reception area a few minutes later laughing and talking to each other.

The children in the group made a beeline for the pastries. The reception area was filled with the family's cheerful banter and talk of what they planned to do that day. They ate quickly and then headed off for their day of fun.

She smiled as she cleaned off the tables after the family left. She liked large families. They often seemed messy and loud, but they also seemed to enjoy a special closeness with each other that she hadn't had with her family when she was growing up.

After she'd restored order to the reception area, she checked the computer to see if there were any new guests scheduled to arrive that day. Only one of the other cottages had been reserved for that night.

Liam poked his head through the door in back of the reception desk. "Steve Randall just got here. Do you still want to join us when we go through the cottages that need renovations?"

"Yes, I do. Just give me a minute to lock the front door." She locked the door to the reception area, slipped the business cell phone in her pocket, and followed Liam into his house with Bella at her side.

Liam made the introductions. She started to extend her hand to shake hands with Steve, but she froze when Bella barked sharply and leapt toward Steve's outstretched hand. She quickly jerked her hand away and stared at Bella in shock.

"Bella!" she exclaimed.

Bella stood rigidly in front of Steve with the fur on her neck standing on end. She growled menacingly at him. Steve took a step back.

She exchanged a look with Liam. She could tell that Liam was thinking the same thing she was.

"It's probably not a good idea to have an aggressive dog on your property when you're renting out cottages here," Steve said witheringly. He kept an eye on Bella.

"Bella is not an aggressive dog," Rylie replied. She squared her shoulders. "She loves everybody. Except you, apparently."

"Bella is usually very sweet," Liam said. "I've never seen her be aggressive."

She gave him a grateful glance. She studied Steve Randall. He was a large man with a broad chest and very muscular arms. He carried himself with a sense of arrogance that put her off. And she knew by the way Bella was acting toward Steve that they needed to be careful around him.

"I'll go get a leash for Bella. I'll meet you guys over there."

She went back to her house to get a leash for Bella and then joined the two men in one of the dilapidated cottages.

"I take great pride in my work," Steve said. "You won't find anyone that will work harder for you than I will. I just need to take some measurements so I can put together a bid for you."

Steve reached into his left pants pocket. As he pulled a tape measure out of his pocket, a silver metal lighter fell out. She caught a quick glimpse of it before Steve scooped it off the floor and put it back in his pocket. Her body tensed. She glanced over at Liam to see if he'd seen it too. She could tell that he had.

She bent over to pet Bella for a minute to collect herself and compose her facial features. When she stood back up, she hoped her face didn't betray her emotions. She'd never been good at putting on a poker face.

Steve was busy taking measurements and jotting notes on a pad of paper. Liam pointed out various renovations that Elizabeth wanted done as they moved through the cottages. She silently followed the men with Bella close by her side.

"I think I have everything I need to put together a bid for you now," Steve said finally.

She quietly breathed a sigh of relief. They walked with Steve back to his SUV.

As soon as Steve started to drive away, she looked at Liam. "Did you see the lighter that fell out of Steve's pocket? It looked a lot like the Zippo lighter we found in the Absinthe Room."

"Yes, I did. Aidan and I have an appointment to talk to Detective Felton this afternoon. I'll tell Detective Felton about it then. I also noticed that Steve is left-handed. Did you see that? Detective Felton said that whoever lost their lighter in the Absinthe Room was probably left-handed."

"I did see that. And the way Bella was acting toward Steve, it made me wonder if he's the one who broke into the main house on Tuesday night. I've never seen Bella act like that toward anyone before."

"I was thinking the same thing. I have the feeling that Bella may have recognized Steve's scent from the other night and knew that he was someone who threatened her family," Liam said.

"There's something about Steve Randall I don't like," she said. "I think the way Bella acted around him has something to do with it. But it's more than that. Do you have any intention of actually considering his bid for renovating the cottages?"

"No, not really. I never did. The only reason I had him come out to give us a bid was to see if there was any reason to think he may have had anything to do with Colin's murder. Now I think we need to put him on our list of suspects, whether or not Detective Felton agrees with us. And he's a big guy. I think a punch in the face from him could definitely have sent Colin flying backward into the wall."

They went inside Liam and Gillian's house. Liam told Gillian about their meeting with Steve and about the lighter that fell out of his pants pocket.

"Oh no!" Gillian said. "So you think that Steve may have been the one who broke in here the other night?"

"Could be," Liam said grimly.

Rylie felt the muscles in her shoulders and back tighten. "I'm feeling very uncomfortable here right now. As soon as my shift is over at 2:00, I'm going to take Bella and drive someplace where we can go for a nice walk and get some fresh air."

"Oh Rylie, I'm so sorry you got involved in all this," Gillian said. "I know you came here hoping to relax and have some fun this summer. Everything has been so stressful since Colin was killed."

"Thanks Gillian. I just need to get out of here for a while. Let me know how your meeting with Detective Felton goes this afternoon, Liam."

She went back to her house with Bella to wait for her shift to be over. As soon as it was 2:00, she dropped off the business cell phone at the reception desk and texted Gillian to let her know she was leaving. She went back to her house to get her purse and a leash for Bella. She set the alarm and locked her front door on the way out.

"Let's get out of here Bella. Let's find somewhere we can go for a nice walk."

Bella's ears perked up when she heard the word "walk." She started bouncing up and down on her front legs in excitement. She stayed close by Rylie's side as they walked to the SUV and jumped up onto the back seat as soon as Rylie opened the door for her. Rylie drove down the long driveway toward the highway. She felt like she couldn't get away from Whitaker Cottages fast enough. She had no idea where she was going, but she needed to get away from there as quickly as possible.

She drove along the north shore of the lake through Incline Village until she spotted the trail that led down to Hidden Beach. She'd never been to Hidden Beach, but she'd read about it when she was searching the internet one night for dog-friendly beaches.

She found a parking spot by the side of the road, put a leash on Bella, and walked down to the beach. She felt herself gradually starting to relax as they walked.

The beach was beautiful. The crystal clear turquoise water of the lake sparkled as it wound between a profusion of rounded boulders scattered along the shoreline. They walked the length of the beach until Rylie found a boulder on the sand where she could sit and look out over the lake. Bella flopped down on the sand next to her panting happily. Rylie allowed the peacefulness of the scene to calm her shaky nerves.

She considered herself a very independent person. She was used to handling things on her own when she had problems because she'd never had anyone that she could always depend on to be there for her. But right now she didn't feel like she could deal with everything on her own. She needed to talk to someone. Someone she could trust.

She thought of calling her best friend Sophie, but Sophie was in St. Helena. She wouldn't be able to really understand what she was going through right now. She needed to talk to someone who lived here at the lake who was familiar with everything that had been going on since Colin's murder.

Gillian and Liam would be happy to talk to her, but she felt like she needed to talk to someone who didn't live and work at Whitaker Cottages. She considered calling her mother but decided against it. Her mother would worry about her and probably wouldn't provide her with the kind of support she needed right now.

What about Eric? He seems like he's genuinely concerned about me. But he's not the person I want to talk to right now.

She finally realized that the person she needed to talk to was Mark Felton. She pulled her cell phone out of her pocket and looked at the screen.

"Great. No cell phone service," she muttered.

She decided to see if she could find a dog-friendly restaurant with an outside patio where she could take Bella and call Mark. She started walking back toward the trail that went up to the road where she was parked. She saw a guy and girl taking turns throwing a stick in the water for their Goldendoodle.

"Your dog seems to be enjoying herself," she said.

"Yes! She loves coming here," the girl replied.

"Do you happen to know of a restaurant nearby with an outside patio where I could take my dog?"

"Oh sure," the girl replied. "Crosby's Tavern. It's in Incline Village in a little shopping center called Christmas Tree Village right on Tahoe Boulevard. They've got an outdoor patio in the back next to a little creek. It's really pretty. It'll be on your right-hand side as you're driving through town."

"Thanks!"

She drove back to Incline Village with Bella and found the shopping center where Crosby's Tavern was located. She parked her SUV and clipped a leash on Bella before she walked over to the restaurant. She asked the hostess if she could be seated on the back patio.

"Sure!" The hostess smiled down at Bella. "Dogs love our back patio. Right this way." She led the way to their back patio nestled among tall pine trees.

Rylie asked her for some lemonade for herself and a bowl of water for Bella. As soon as the hostess left, she checked her cell phone to see if she had any reception. She was relieved to see that she had four bars. She checked on Bella laying under the table panting.

"Do you want a nice drink, Bella?" Bella thumped her tail up and down on the ground a few times.

The hostess came back shortly with lemonade for Rylie and a large metal dog dish filled with water for Bella. Bella got to her feet quickly and eagerly lapped the water.

"I brought a little treat for your dog," the hostess said. She handed Rylie a dog biscuit.

"Thank you! Bella loves treats."

When Bella heard the word "treat," she looked up for a second, then resumed drinking.

"I'll give it to her after she has a chance to cool down a bit," Rylie said. "We just got back from the beach."

"Okay. Let me know if you need anything else." The hostess hurried off.

She waited until Bella was resting comfortably under the table, her thirst finally quenched. Then she called Detective Felton. He picked up on the first ring.

"Rylie! How are you? Is everything okay?"

"Mark! Hi!"

"What's going on? You sound upset."

She looked around the patio before she replied. There was a couple seated at another table, but they were far enough away that they shouldn't be able to hear her conversation as long as she kept her voice down.

"I am upset." She took a deep breath and continued. "Liam's been having contractors out to give us bids on renovating some of the old cottages on the property. Steve Randall came out to give us a bid on the renovations this morning. When we were going through one of the cottages with him, he reached into his left pants pocket to get out a tape measure. Both Liam and I saw a lighter fall out of his pocket that looked a lot like the one we found in the Absinthe Room."

"That's interesting."

"And when Bella saw Steve this morning, she started barking and growling at him. She never does that. She loves everyone. We think she may have recognized Steve as the person who broke into the main house on Tuesday night."

"Hmmm. I'd better have another chat with Steve," Mark replied.

She took a deep breath and let it out slowly. She was starting to feel calmer.

"Look, Rylie. Maybe it isn't a good idea for you to be alone in your house right now. I know you have Bella and that Liam and Gillian are close by, but I'm a little concerned about you. Those cottages are out in the middle of the woods. It wouldn't be difficult for someone to sneak onto the property at night and break into any one of those cottages in spite of the security system Mrs. Whitaker had installed."

"I know. I've been thinking about that too. I don't have any kind of weapon or self-defense training. Bella's the only thing I have for protection. Honestly, I'm pretty uncomfortable there right now. As soon as my shift was over this afternoon, I couldn't wait to get as far away from there as possible. I drove to Incline Village with Bella and took her down to Hidden Beach for a while. Right now we're outside on the patio at Crosby's Tavern. I think I'm going to try to find a hotel to stay in tonight. I should feel better by tomorrow."

"You don't have to look for a hotel. You probably won't find one this late in the day anyway. I've got a friend who lives at Fleur du Lac Estates. Gary Alexander. He's out of the country right now. I'll call him and ask if you can stay at his house for a couple nights. Fleur du Lac is a gated community with 24-hour security. You'll be safe there. I'm sure Gary won't mind. I'll call you back as soon as I talk to him."

She was amazed that she was being offered the opportunity to stay at one of the gorgeous homes in Fleur du Lac Estates. And it would be wonderful to not lie awake in bed all night listening for unusual noises.

Mark called back a little while later. "Everything's all set. Gary called the Fleur du Lac Estates management office and told them to open the gate for you when you arrive. He told them to get the house ready for your stay and to leave the front door unlocked with the key inside."

She felt the sting of hot tears in the corners of her eyes. "Thank you, Mark. I really appreciate this."

She hung up and headed back to Whitaker Cottages to pack. She stopped by Gillian and Liam's house to let them know that she was feeling shaken by the meeting with Steve Randall and that she needed to get away for a couple days. She told them about the arrangements that Detective Felton had made for her to stay at his friend's house in Fleur du Lac Estates.

"That was very nice of Detective Felton," Gillian said. "I'm glad you've got somewhere to go where you can feel safe. Please call us if you need anything."

"Thanks, Gillian. I will. I'll see you guys in a couple days."

She went to her house to pack everything she'd need for herself and Bella for a couple days. Then she loaded everything into her SUV, got Bella situated in the back seat, and headed to Fleur du Lac Estates.

Chapter 23

It was about 6:30 p.m. by the time she drove up to the gated entrance to Fleur du Lac Estates. She'd wondered what was behind those gates many times over the years. A little thrill of excitement coursed through her as she pulled up in front of the ornate black wrought iron gates. She pushed the button on the intercom and announced her arrival. The tall black gate slowly opened inward.

Mark had told her to stay straight on the road through Fleur du Lac Estates until she got nearly to the end. Gary's house was on the far side of the property. She found it easily. The oversized front door had been left unlocked for her. She walked into the foyer with Bella close by her side.

A wide hallway led to a spacious open plan living room and kitchen with a wall of large windows that showcased views of the beautifully landscaped lawn that led down to the sparkling azure blue waters of the lake. Log stumps standing on end served as end tables for the two sofas. A massive abstract painting hung on the wall over one of the sofas.

There was a bouquet of brightly colored Gerbera daisies and a bottle of sauvignon blanc chilling in a silver ice bucket on the large center island in the kitchen. She found a card next to the flowers.

"Ms. Sunderland. Welcome to Fleur du Lac Estates and the home of Mr. Gary Alexander. Mr. Alexander asked us to welcome you into his home with flowers and a nice bottle of wine. Please enjoy your stay and let us know if there is anything we can do to be of service to you. -The Management Team at Fleur du Lac Estates."

"That was nice, huh, Bella?" Bella looked up at her and slowly wagged her golden plumed tail.

She went upstairs with Bella to check out the bedrooms. She fell in love with the bedroom that had an entire wall of windows looking out over the lake.

"This is going to be our bedroom, Bella! It's so pretty!"

The room was furnished with a queen-size contemporary four-poster bed and two overstuffed chairs. She could picture herself sitting in one of the chairs reading a book while admiring the wonderful views of the lake.

The whole house felt warm and welcoming. The tension in her back and shoulders slowly dissolved as she walked through the house. She brought her suitcase, cooler, and Bella's bed and food inside and got unpacked.

"Come on, Bella! Let's go for a walk and explore this place a little before it gets dark."

She put a leash on Bella and went out the glass patio door. She was careful to lock the door behind her. The large flagstone patio had an umbrella table with chairs arranged around it and four lounge chairs nearby. There was a gas grill and outdoor kitchen on one side of the patio.

She walked with Bella across the emerald green lawn to a building on the water's edge called the Yacht House. She saw people enjoying drinks and chatting on the Yacht House deck. She looked around to see if there was a sign anywhere indicating if dogs were allowed on the deck.

"You're welcome to bring your dog on the deck," an older man sitting with his wife called out to her.

"Thanks for letting me know. I wasn't sure if dogs were allowed. I'm Rylie, and this is Bella."

She took Bella up on the deck and walked over to the couple. They gave Bella lots of pets and ear scratches. Bella happily soaked up all the attention.

"We used to have a golden retriever," the woman said. "She was the most wonderful dog we ever had. After she passed away, we never had the heart to get another dog. We still miss her."

"I totally understand," she replied. "I lost my yellow lab when she was fifteen years old. It was horrible. I grieved for her for a long time. When I was finally ready to get another dog, I got Bella. She's the best dog I've ever had. I love her to pieces."

She chatted with the older couple for a few more minutes and then excused herself to continue her exploration of the grounds. She went over to check out the boathouse and the boats in the boat slips. Then she headed back to Gary's house. She kept Bella on a long leash and settled into a lounge chair to soak up the last rays of the sun before nightfall and enjoy the spectacular views.

Her cell phone rang a few minutes later. She glanced at the caller ID. Her stomach clenched. A host of emotions swirled through her. She debated letting the call go to voice mail. Finally, she answered the call.

"Hi Dylan."

"Rylie! Hi! How are you?" Dylan's concern sounded almost sincere.

"I'm fine, Dylan. What's up? I haven't heard from you in over a year."

She noticed that she had a death grip on her cell phone. She forced herself to relax her grip.

"I heard that the veterinary hospital where you worked burned down, and I just wanted to check and make sure you're okay."

"The hospital burned down weeks ago, Dylan."

"Yeah. I'm sorry. I meant to call earlier. So are you okay, then?"

"Yes, Dylan. I'm fine."

I guess I should make an effort to be polite.

"How are you doing?" she asked.

"I'm doing great. Listen Rylie. I'm sorry about how things ended between us."

"Thanks for that, Dylan. I'm over it now. I've moved on."

"Well, anyway, I'm glad you're okay. Take care of yourself, Rylie. I've got to go. Bye."

She stared at the phone after Dylan hung up.

"Creep! He just needs to leave me alone."

Bella was looking at her with concern.

"Come here, Bella. I'm okay. You're such a good girl. You're always there for me, aren't you, Bella?"

She hugged Bella and wound her fingers through her soft fur. Hugging Bella always made her feel better. Bella slowly wagged her tail.

She got up and went to the kitchen for a glass of lemonade. Then she took her lemonade out to the patio and got comfortable in a lounge chair again. She gazed out over the lake and allowed her thoughts to drift. The churning in her stomach that she'd felt since Dylan called gradually subsided.

Her cell phone rang again. She glanced at the caller ID in annoyance until she saw it was Mark. She breathed a sigh of relief and answered the phone.

"Hi, Rylie. This is Mark. I just wanted to make sure you got to Gary's house safely and got all settled in."

"Yes, I did. Thank you. I'm sitting on the back patio with Bella right now enjoying the incredible views. Everything's been wonderful. Gary had the people at Fleur du Lac leave a bouquet of flowers and nice bottle of white wine on the center island in the kitchen for me. Please tell him thank you for me. I really appreciate him opening up his home to me."

"No problem. I'm glad you're enjoying yourself."

"Thanks, Mark. I'll talk to you later."

She hung up the phone with a smile.

"Bella, the handsome detective is looking out for us." Bella broke out in a doggie grin and panted happily.

She went inside the house to open the bottle of white wine that had been left for her. She poured herself a glass and took it outside so she could enjoy the sense of peacefulness that gazing out over the lake gave her. The sun slowly set, turning the lake shades of pink and lavender. She was glad she had somewhere safe to stay even if it was only for a couple days.

Chapter 24

S he slept soundly and woke up the next morning feeling better than she had in a long time. She rolled over in bed and gazed out the windows at the sparkling blue lake as it stretched toward the mountains in the distance.

I could get used to this.

Bella walked over and pushed her arm with her cold wet nose.

"Okay, Bella. I can take a hint."

She got up, threw on a shirt and some jeans, and padded downstairs. She put a leash on Bella and took her outside to go potty. Cool air softly brushed her face with the fresh scent of the lake. Bella spotted a squirrel and took off at a dead run. She almost did a face plant as she struggled to hold onto the leash. She ran behind Bella until Bella finally stopped when the squirrel bounded up a tree. The squirrel looked back at Bella and swished its tail quickly back and forth before dashing away. Slightly out of breath, she headed back to the house with Bella to make coffee and get breakfast for both of them.

After breakfast and a shower, she left Bella in the living room looking out the windows for squirrels and drove to

Safeway buy groceries. When she got back, Bella met her at the door wagging her tail.

"Hi, Bella. Were you a good girl for me while I was gone?"

Bella wagged her tail faster. She gave Bella a bacon, egg, and cheese doggie health bar. Bella made quick work of it. She put all the groceries away except for what she needed to make a potato salad for dinner. She made a potato salad with red potatoes, onions, green olives, and light mayo, then put it in the refrigerator to chill and allow the flavors to develop.

She was about to take Bella for a walk around the grounds when her call phone rang. Seeing that it was Mark, she answered her phone quickly.

"Good morning, Mark!"

"You sound cheerful this morning."

"I had a good night's sleep last night for the first time in weeks. I woke up feeling better than I have in a long time. It helps to know there's 24-hour security here. Thank you so much for making this happen."

"You're welcome. I'm glad you're feeling better. I thought you might like to know that I just got the DNA results back on the skin that was found under Colin Matthews' fingernails during the autopsy. Unfortunately, it wasn't a match for anyone in our database."

"That's disappointing."

"And I had Steve Randall and Blake Cunningham brought in for questioning this morning. They both admitted to getting in an argument with Colin on Locals' Night and punching him in the face. Steve followed Colin and Blake into the tunnel without them knowing about it and went in to talk to Colin after Blake left. Both Steve and Blake insisted that Colin was still standing after they punched him."

"What are the odds that two guys could get so angry with Colin? I only met him a couple times, but he seemed like such a nice guy. Do you believe them?"

"I've been in this business a long time, Rylie. I've learned to trust my gut. And my gut tells me they're both telling the truth. However, I did collect DNA samples from both of them to compare with the DNA from the skin found under Colin's fingernails. At this point we're thinking that there must have been another person in the Absinthe Room with Colin that night."

"Really? Do you have any idea who that person might be?"

"No, not yet. But I'm working on it. If you'd like, I can stop by Gary's house after work tonight and give you a few more details about the conversations I had with Steve and Blake this morning. I know how anxious you and Liam and Gillian have been since Colin was murdered right next to where you live, so I'm trying to keep you guys in the loop as much as I can without compromising my investigation."

"Thanks, Mark. That sounds great. Why don't you stay for dinner? I'm planning to have hamburgers on the grill, potato salad, and corn on the cob. Do you like hamburgers?"

"I love hamburgers. How about I see you tonight at about 6:00 then?"

"Sounds good. See you then."

She stood with her cell phone in her hand for a long minute trying to process everything that Mark had just told her. Then she put a leash on Bella and headed outside. Bella had a great time sniffing everything in sight as they walked along the lake.

When they got back to the house, Rylie stretched out on one of the lounge chairs on the patio to enjoy the views of the lake. Her cell phone rang again. She saw Gillian's name on the display and picked up the phone.

"Hi Gillian."

"Hi Rylie. How are you doing?"

"I slept really well last night. It's nice to have 24-hour security. And it's gorgeous here. Gary's house is stunning, and its got incredible views of the lake."

"I'm so glad you got the chance to spend some time there. It sounds wonderful. Detective Felton just called us with an update. He said he called you too. It's too bad that the DNA from the skin under Colin's fingernails didn't match anyone in the database. I was hoping the results from the DNA test would help him wrap this case up."

"I know. I was disappointed too. I've been wracking my brain since I spoke to him trying to figure out who else could be a suspect."

"You need to try and relax, Rylie," Gillian said. "Enjoy your stay at Fleur du Lac. Clear your head."

"I know. I'm working on it. Talk to you later."

She leaned back in the lounge chair to try to enjoy the views again, but she felt charged with nervous energy. She put Bella in the back of her SUV and drove into Tahoe City. She needed some strenuous exercise to help her decompress. She decided that a long walk on the bike path that ran along the Truckee River was in order. They walked briskly toward the River Ranch restaurant on the bike path and made it there in a little over an hour.

She found a table on the outdoor deck by the river and asked the waitress for a bowl of water for Bella and a mineral water with a slice of lime for herself.

Her phone buzzed with a text message. She saw it was from Laurent.

Hi Rylie. I need to talk to you. It's about Colin. Can we get together sometime tomorrow?

Sure. Where and when do you want to meet?

Can you meet me tomorrow at the Tahoe City marina at about 11:00? I'm going to take you on a boat ride. Lunch is on me.

Sounds good. See you then.

When they got back to Gary's house, she went upstairs to shower and change before Mark arrived. She dressed casually and went back downstairs to the kitchen. Bella heard someone knocking on the front door and ran to the door barking loudly with Rylie close behind. When Rylie opened the door, Bella started wagging her tail and pushed her nose into Mark's hand.

"Hi Bella." He leaned down to pet Bella's head.

"Hi Rylie. These are for you." He handed her a bouquet of bright yellow sunflowers mixed with tiny purple flowers that he'd been holding behind his back.

"Oh! How pretty! I love sunflowers. Thank you! Come in. Can I get you something to drink?"

She led the way to the kitchen as they spoke.

"Sure. What have you got?"

"Hefeweizen beer or sauvignon blanc. Or mineral water if you don't want alcohol."

"I'm off tonight. I'll have a beer. Beer goes great with hamburgers."

"My thoughts exactly." She grinned as she handed him a beer.

She started hunting through the cabinets for something to put her flowers in. She finally found a clear glass vase. She filled it with water and arranged her flowers in it. Then she put the vase in the middle of the center island.

"There! Now for dinner." She took the package of hamburger meat out of the refrigerator and set it out on the counter.

"Would you like me to make the hamburger patties?" Mark asked. "I'm not much of a chef, but I do know how to make a mean hamburger."

"That would be awesome," she replied.

"Do you happen to have any Worcestershire sauce? That's my secret ingredient. And garlic. You have to add plenty of garlic. Do you have any garlic powder?"

"I do have garlic powder," she replied. "Let me check to see if Gary has any Worcestershire sauce in the refrigerator."

She looked through the refrigerator for a minute or two, then turned around triumphantly. "Aha! Found some!"

She handed him the Worcestershire sauce she'd found and slid the garlic powder, salt, and pepper that she'd left on the counter over to the package of hamburger meat.

"How are you at cooking hamburgers on the grill?" she asked.

"That's my specialty."

"Alright, then. You're in charge of cooking the hamburgers on the grill. I have two kinds of cheeses to choose from so we can make cheeseburgers. I have sliced mozzarella and blue cheese crumbles. I'm having a blue cheese burger. I sprinkle the blue cheese on the burger after it comes off the grill. Then I put sautéed mushrooms and onions on top. So good! You're welcome to have blue cheese or mozzarella, whatever you want."

She watched as he shaped the hamburger into patties and arranged the patties on a plate. He took the hamburger patties out to the patio and fired up the grill. She followed him outside with a small plate of sliced mozzarella. Bella laid down close by so she could keep an eye on things. Mark sipped his beer while he waited for the grill to heat up. He looked good in casual clothes. Very handsome. He was a different person when he was relaxed and not in cop mode.

"Nice views here, huh?" he said.

"I know. I'd love to have a patio like this."

She went back inside to finish dinner prep. She left the patio door open so they could talk while he was grilling the hamburgers and she was working in the kitchen. She sliced some onions and crimini mushrooms, put them in a frying pan on the stove, and sautéed them with butter, salt, and pepper. She brought a large pot of water to a boil for the corn on the cob. She shucked the corn while she was waiting for the water to boil.

Soon the aromas of hamburgers cooking on the grill and sautéed onions and mushrooms filled the air. Bella pointed her nose in the air and sniffed appreciatively. Mark reached down and scratched around her ears. Bella looked up at him adoringly.

When everything was ready, Rylie arranged the potato salad, corn on the cob, and hamburgers on the center island buffet-style. They loaded up their plates and sat outside at the patio table. Bella positioned herself by their feet in case anything good happened to come her way.

"Yum! Your burgers are delicious, Mark. They're cooked perfectly. Nice and pink and juicy. Just the way I like them."

"Thanks. Your potato salad is amazing. I'm going back for seconds."

They chatted casually over dinner and cleaned up the kitchen together afterwards. Then they went back out to the patio and got comfortable on lounge chairs.

"I hate to spoil the mood Mark, but you said you'd tell me a little more about the conversations you had with Steve and Blake this morning," she said.

"I know," Mark replied. "Okay. So Blake told me that Colin asked to speak to him privately on Locals' Night. Colin took him to the Absinthe Room and confronted him about what Karalyn Ashford had told him about a real estate deal that Blake had handled for her. Karalyn told Colin that she lost a lot of money on the deal and she felt Blake was responsible. Blake said Colin got up in his face. He told Colin to back off, but he wouldn't. Blake said he lost it and ended up punching Colin in the face. Then he turned around and left. He said Colin was standing there looking a little dazed and rubbing his jaw when he left."

"That accounts for one of the bruises on Colin's face," she said. "I assume Blake was the right-handed person that punched Colin on the left side of his face? I know Steve Randall is left-handed. And Steve looks a lot more powerful than Blake, so I'd think a punch from Steve would leave a larger bruise."

"That's right. Steve said he saw Colin go into the tunnel with Blake on Locals' Night. He followed them at a discreet distance and hid in a room nearby while they argued. As soon as Blake left, he went in the Absinthe Room to talk to Colin."

"Steve was angry because he'd heard that Colin was telling people that the reason he'd rejected Steve's bid was because of Steve's reputation for underbidding other contractors to get jobs and then charging a lot more than his bid. Steve was afraid Colin would ruin his reputation and cost him jobs. He admitted he punched Colin in the face. But he said Colin was still standing when he walked out."

"Was it Steve who broke into the main house at Whitaker Cottages on Tuesday night?" she asked.

"Yes. He was looking for his Zippo lighter. He knew he'd lost it on Locals' Night. He was afraid that if anyone found it, that he'd be considered a suspect in Colin Matthews' murder."

"So you think both Steve and Blake are telling the truth, right? Brayden Hughes told us that he thought the punch from the left-handed person may have been what caused Colin to slam into the granite wall in the Absinthe Room and hit his head."

"We did think that initially," Mark replied. "But after I talked to Steve and Blake this morning and they both said Colin was still standing after they punched him, I went back through the crime scene sketch and autopsy results again. Then I had another talk with Brayden. Based on the location and nature of the injury to the back of Colin's head, we've decided that we don't think Steve's punch was responsible. The angle isn't right. That's why we now believe that there must have been someone else in the Absinthe Room that night."

"So where does that leave us? Back at square one? I can't hole up here forever. I was hired to help out at Whitaker Cottages this summer."

"I know, Rylie. Believe me, I'm working as hard as I can to find out who killed Colin as soon as possible. Why don't we just try to relax and enjoy the rest of the evening? I think we could both use a little down time."

"I'm sorry. You're right."

She discreetly took a deep breath and let it out slowly to calm herself. They chatted amicably as the sunset turned the lake to shades of pink and lavender that deepened into an inky purple night dotted with a million stars.

After Mark left, she laid on a lounge chair on the patio and let her mind wander as she stared up at the stars. She wondered what Laurent needed to talk to her about that involved Colin Matthews and why he couldn't have just talked to her on the phone.

Chapter 25

Early the next morning, she packed up her things and loaded Bella into her SUV to go back to Whitaker Cottages. She couldn't stop thinking about her meeting with Laurent later that morning. She was very curious to find out what he wanted to talk about that had to do with Colin Matthews.

Gillian was outside when she drove up to the cottages.

"Hi! How are you?" Gillian walked over and gave her a quick hug.

"I'm great, Gillian. Thanks for asking."

"Why don't you come over for a cup of coffee after you get unpacked?"

"Sounds good. See you soon."

She unpacked quickly and then went over to Gillian and Liam's house with Bella. She sat with Gillian and Liam at the dining table and filled them in on what she'd learned from her conversation with Detective Felton the night before.

"Well it sounds like he's making progress. At least we know a little bit more about what happened that night. Now we've just got to figure out who else might have been in that room with Colin," Gillian said.

"I know," she replied.

"So... First a day at Vikingsholm and then dinner with the handsome detective. Is there anything you want to tell us?" Gillian smiled.

"Mark offered to stop by after work to tell me more about the conversations he'd had with Steve and Blake. Since he'd be arriving at my house right around dinner-time, it seemed only polite to invite him to stay for dinner." She felt the heat rising in her cheeks.

Gillian and Liam exchanged a glance.

"So it looks like Steve and Blake are off our list of suspects," she continued. "But we're still not sure about Aidan. Or Patrick, for that matter. I told you about my friend from college, Laurent Theroux. When I was talking to him at Colin's memorial service, I asked him if there was anyone he could think of that might want to hurt Colin. He told me the only person he could possibly think of was Aidan. He confirmed that Colin was having an affair with Katiana, and he said they weren't always discreet about meeting in public."

"I just can't picture Aidan killing anyone, especially someone who was his friend," Liam said.

"What does Aidan do for a living?" she asked.

"He has an import/export business. He travels to San Francisco for business a lot. He leaves Katiana alone here when he travels. I guess that's probably not good for a marriage," Liam replied.

He stared at his hands on the dining table. Gillian reached over and put her hand over Liam's.

"That's no excuse for infidelity," Gillian said.

"I know," Rylie replied. "But I'm sure we don't know the whole story. I've heard from several people that Aidan has a bad temper. Do you know how he got that reputation?"

"I know he got in a fistfight with a guy at Pete 'n Peter's during a game of pool one night," Liam replied. "I also heard that one time he punched a guy who made a snide comment about Katiana. He can be kind of a hothead. I wouldn't want to get on his bad side."

She exchanged a glance with Gillian. "Interesting. Well, I'm going to take Bella for a walk down by the lake. Come on, Bella. Let's go for a walk! See you guys later."

Bella ran to the door wagging her tail and stood in front of the door bouncing up and down on her front legs impatiently. When Rylie opened the door, Bella bolted outside and headed for the lake.

"Hey, Bella! Wait for me!"

She called Eric on her cell phone as she walked down to the lake with Bella and brought him up to date with everything she'd learned.

"How'd you like to hang out at Pete 'n Peter's with me tonight?" she asked.

"Why do I have the feeling that you might have ulterior motives for inviting me to hang out at Pete 'n Peters with you?" Eric replied. She could hear the amusement in his voice.

"I just thought we could hang out at the bar and see if we could discreetly learn anything from the bartender or from people sitting at the bar. And if Aidan Flynn were to come in to play pool tonight, that would be a bonus. We could sit somewhere near his pool table and see if we could listen in on his conversations."

"You do know that Detective Felton is on the case, right?" Eric teased.

"Yes, I do. And he asked me to call him if I learn anything that might be helpful to him in his investigation."

"Somehow I don't think he meant for you to actively seek out information by chatting with bartenders or eavesdropping on other people's conversations."

She smiled. "No one would have any idea we were doing anything other than having a drink and talking. We'd be very discreet."

"Okay. You win. So how about I meet you there around 7:00?"

"Great! I'm meeting my friend Laurent at the Tahoe City marina at 11:00 this morning. He's taking me out for a boat ride. He told me he has something he wants to talk to me about. But I'm sure we'll be back in plenty of time. See you later."

Bella spotted some Mallard ducks out in the lake paddling past the beach and raced to the water's edge. She barked and bounced up and down excitedly. The Mallards barely acknowledged her other than to veer a little further from the shore.

Rylie took off her sandals and waded into the water a short distance. "The water here is always so cold!"

She slipped her sandals back on and headed out along the lakeshore path with Bella leading the way. She kept a close eye on the time. At about 10:00, she went back to her house to change and pack some things to take on the boat ride with Laurent.

She put on a bathing suit under her shorts and t-shirt and packed a beach bag with a change of clothes, sunscreen, a beach towel, and some bottled water. She tucked her cell phone and wallet in one of the pockets inside the beach bag. Bella was lying on the living room floor panting contentedly when she left.

Laurent was waiting for her when she got to the marina.

"Hi Rylie! Over here!" He waved and called out to her from where he stood on the dock.

"Hi Laurent. What a great day for a boat ride. I'm excited."

"I'm excited too. I haven't been out on the water in weeks," he replied.

He was standing in front of a 34-foot Formula powerboat in its slip.

"Nice boat, huh? Colin gave me a spare set of keys to both his boat and his house," Laurent said. "He said I could take the boat out whenever I wanted. But since he's not here anymore, I called Dee to ask her permission. She said it was fine."

Laurent helped her onto the boat and showed her where to stow her beach bag. Then he took her to see the lounge on the aft deck with its tables, cushioned bench seats, wet bar, and refrigerator. He showed her the two sunpads for sunbathing attached to the foredeck. She followed him downstairs to see the living room, kitchen, and bedroom.

"I brought a picnic lunch for us to have a little later," he said. "Let's get going."

He sat in the captain's seat and started the boat. She sat down next to him. Laurent expertly guided the boat out of the marina and headed down the west shore of the lake.

"The Washoe Zephyr winds kick up in the afternoon. They blow from the southwest side of the lake to the northeast at speeds of up to ten to fifteen miles an hour with gusts of over twenty miles an hour. That creates two to three-foot waves from the middle of the lake to the north and east shores. I don't want to get caught up in that. So we're going to stay on the west shore. We'll go down to Calawee Cove at D.L. Bliss State Park and drop anchor there. It should only take us about fifty minutes to get there. We can eat our picnic lunch on the boat in Calawee Cove. I've got something to show you after lunch."

She sat back to enjoy the ride. The boat picked up speed after they cleared the marina. Cool fresh air washed over her. She felt a sense of exhilaration and freedom. Every now and then, they were sprayed by a fine mist of water that came over the side of the boat.

"There's such an entirely different view of things from out here on the lake," she said. "I'm seeing hidden coves and beaches I didn't even know existed."

"I know. I love exploring the lake this way."

Laurent pointed out places he thought she'd be interested in as they continued south along the west shore of the lake. It was obvious that he was in his element. They chatted comfortably. It seemed so normal to her. They had taken up right where they left off all those years ago. They were still the best of friends. She was grateful for that. She wondered how she could have let their relationship slip away for so long and not have done anything about it.

Laurent slowed the boat on their approach to Calawee Cove. Calawee Cove looked like it was a popular place for boaters to drop anchor. The sparkling clear blue water looked inviting. She took off her t-shirt and shorts so she could sit out in her bathing suit. She rubbed sunscreen all over her pale skin. Laurent dropped anchor and then pulled off his t-shirt. He looked handsome and relaxed.

"What would you like to drink?" he asked.

"I'll have a mineral water with a slice of lime if you have it. This is so beautiful, Laurent. Thanks for taking me here. I love it."

"I'm not sure what Dee plans to do with this boat. I've thought about offering to buy it from her. But it would cost a lot of money to buy this boat and pay for slip rental fees. I don't know if I could convince Olivia to go along with taking on that kind of expense."

After their picnic lunch, Laurent took her downstairs to the living room.

"Dee told me Detective Felton and his team already searched the boat, and they didn't find anything," Laurent said. "The thing is, I know about a secret compartment where Colin stored things he didn't want anyone to know about. I doubt if Detective Felton or his team would have found it. It's very well hidden, and it's locked. Colin trusted me with the key, but I've never used it. I have no idea what's inside."

"I didn't think about the secret compartment when Detective Felton questioned me after Colin's murder," he continued. "I was so shocked to hear that Colin had been killed that I wasn't thinking clearly. I just remembered it a couple days ago. I want to check it out before I tell Detective Felton about it. I think I owe that to Colin, in case there's something in there that he wouldn't want anyone to know about."

He took a box of nitrile exam gloves out of a cabinet in back of the sofa. He handed her a pair and put on a pair himself.

"I bought these just in case there's anything in the secret compartment that might be considered evidence. I want to make sure that we don't mess anything up with our fingerprints."

He knelt at the bottom of the stairs and pulled back the carpet runner that covered the riser on the last stair to reveal a keyhole. He inserted a small key in the keyhole, opened the hinged wood tread, and looked inside. Rylie inhaled sharply. She knelt down beside Laurent and peered into the secret compartment.

A tiny brown teddy bear caught her eye. She lifted it out of the compartment and viewed it from all angles to see if there was anything unusual about it. She squeezed it to see if she could feel anything inside. It didn't appear to be anything more than a small child's toy. She exchanged a glance with Laurent.

Laurent picked up a photo from the compartment.

"Hey, I know this girl. She's Colin's ex-girlfriend, Melody Hamilton," he said.

She looked over at the photo in Laurent's hands. A pretty girl with a nice tan and dark blonde hair smiled happily at the person taking the photo. She was cradling a small infant in her arms.

"Melody had a baby?" Laurent's eyes widened.

He looked in the compartment again and pulled out an official-looking envelope. He removed a letter from the envelope and unfolded it.

They read it at the same time. It was the results of a paternity test. Colin was the father of the infant in Melody's arms.

She checked the compartment again and found what looked like a Hallmark card laying on the bottom. "For our son" was written across the front of the envelope. The envelope wasn't sealed so she pulled out the card and opened it. A bank deposit receipt fell out and fluttered to the floor.

Laurent scooped the receipt off the floor and let out a long, low whistle. "$50,000.00! Wow!"

Inside the card, Colin had written, "This is for Tyler. I want to make sure he has everything he needs. Love, Colin."

"I always thought that Melody was Colin's true love," Laurent said. "Colin told me once that he thought she was his soul mate. I was surprised when he broke things off with her. I think he got cold feet. He was afraid of committing to a relationship. He had a habit of breaking up with his girlfriends if they started to get too serious."

"I'd love to get the chance to talk to Melody," she said. "But we'll have to show all this to Detective Felton and let him talk to her first. I wonder if Dee knows about any of this. We need to call her and let her know what we found."

Laurent ran his hand around the inside the compartment to make sure they hadn't missed anything. He found a keychain tucked in a corner with one small key on it.

"Can I see that?" She took the key from Laurent and inspected it.

"This looks like the key I have to the lock for my storage unit," she said. "Is there anything else in there?"

She checked the compartment one more time. There was nothing else in it.

"Do you have any idea what this key might go to?" she asked.

"No, I don't. Colin didn't tell me anything about it, unfortunately."

She took photos of everything they'd found in the secret compartment with her cell phone before they put it all back. She wanted to be able to study everything more closely when she got home.

"I'll call Dee as soon as we get back to the marina so she can come and see all this before Detective Felton takes everything away in evidence bags," Laurent said. "After she's seen everything, I'll call Detective Felton. I'm sure he'll want to talk to Melody right away after he sees what we found. If he's able to talk to Melody this afternoon, I'll call her tonight and ask her if we can visit her tomorrow morning. I agree, I don't think we should contact her before Detective Felton has had a chance to talk to her. Are you free tomorrow morning?"

"Definitely."

They headed back to the marina. Laurent called Dee and asked her to meet them at Colin's boat. When she arrived, he led her downstairs to the living room and asked her to have a seat on the sofa. Rylie sat down next to her. Laurent had Dee put on some nitrile exam gloves, then he showed her what they'd found in the secret compartment.

Dee stared at the photo of Melody with the infant cradled in her arms. Her hands started shaking. She handed the photo back to Laurent.

"Colin has a son. How wonderful. And how horrible!" she sobbed. "He won't get to see his son grow up!"

Rylie put her arm around Dee's shoulders as she sobbed. She felt terrible for Dee, for Colin, and for his son. It was all such a tragedy. She shared a look with Laurent, then turned her attention back to Dee. Laurent pulled out his cell phone and went up on deck to call Detective Felton.

"I want to be a good auntie to Colin's son. Tyler. That's a nice name. I like it." Dee choked on her words.

Laurent came back downstairs. "I called Detective Felton. He'll be right over."

"I wonder what this means as far as Colin's will is concerned," Dee said. "Colin left everything to me, but he hadn't updated his will in a couple of years. I'm sure he would have changed his will to leave everything to his son if he hadn't been killed. I'll have to talk to my lawyer. Maybe we can set up a trust for Tyler, and I can manage Colin's assets until Tyler grows up."

They heard Detective Felton calling out to them. Laurent went up on deck and came back with Detective Felton a few minutes later. Detective Felton knelt on the floor at the foot of the stairs with Laurent to look through the contents of the secret compartment.

"My team and I searched this boat thoroughly after Colin's murder and never found this secret compartment," Detective Felton said. "It was very cleverly hidden. I'm glad you remembered it and had a key to open it."

He put everything from the secret compartment into clear plastic evidence bags.

"Have any of you spoken to Melody Hamilton about this?" Detective Felton asked.

"No, we figured you'd want to talk to her after you saw what was in the secret compartment," Laurent replied. "We didn't think we should talk to her until after you'd had a chance to talk to her first."

"I'm going to call her as soon as I get off this boat to see if I can pay her a visit this afternoon," Detective Felton replied.

"Let me see if I still have Melody's number in my cell phone contacts," Laurent said.

He scrolled through his phone until he found Melody's cell phone number and gave it to Detective Felton.

"Thanks." Detective Felton gathered up his evidence bags and left.

Dee left shortly thereafter. Rylie stayed sitting on the sofa deep in thought. Laurent came over and put his arm around her. They sat in companionable silence for a few minutes.

"I feel so awful for Dee. And for Colin and his son," she said finally. "His poor little boy will never get to know his father."

"I know. I feel the same way."

"I'd like to get a small gift for Colin's baby to take with us when we visit Melody," she said.

She searched the internet on her cell phone for baby items in Tahoe City and found a cute shop nearby in the Cobblestone Center called Ruffles & Ruffnecks. She stood up to leave. Laurent put his strong arms around her and held her close in a comforting hug. It felt good to have somebody that genuinely cared about her.

She walked over to Ruffles & Ruffnecks and browsed the displays. A soft white stuffed bunny with long floppy ears caught her eye. Perfect. She paid for the stuffed bunny and then headed home to shower and change into something appropriate for hanging out at Pete 'n Peters sports bar with Eric.

Chapter 26

She arrived home to a very excited golden retriever.

"Bella! Hi pretty girl! Were you a good girl for me while I was gone?"

Bella wagged her tail furiously. She let Bella outside so she could do her business. Bella made a beeline for the woods, then ran back with a huge golden grin on her face. She let Bella inside and went into the kitchen with Bella close behind.

"Would you like a treat for being such a good girl?"

Bella looked at her eagerly and wagged her tail. She gave Bella a bacon, egg, and cheese doggie health bar. Bella gobbled it up quickly.

She got Bella her dinner and made herself a salad. She sat at her dining table while she ate mentally sorting through the events of the day. She looked through the photos she'd taken of everything they'd found in the secret compartment on Colin's boat. She wondered if Melody might know something that could be the key to solving Colin's murder.

After she finished her dinner and put the dishes in the dishwasher, she showered and changed into an off-the-shoulder light gray top and dark grey pants. She added a vintage silver choker necklace and some dangly silver earrings to complete the look. She left Bella curled up comfortably on the living room floor and drove to Pete 'n Peters sports bar in Tahoe City. Eric was standing outside the entrance.

"Hi!" she called out.

"Hi yourself. Nice outfit."

She grinned. "Thank you. I don't get very many chances to dress up, so I thought I'd take advantage of the opportunity. Hey, I need to talk to you about something before we go inside."

She told Eric about Colin having an infant son with Melody Hamilton.

"What? How's that possible? Colin never said anything about it."

"Colin never told Laurent about it either," she replied. "I don't know why he didn't tell anyone. Maybe he just needed some time. I'm sure he would have told everyone eventually."

"Wow. I don't know what to say."

"Are you okay? Do you need some time before we go into Pete 'n Peters?"

"I'm okay," Eric replied. "It's going to take me some time to process this. But I don't need to do it right now. Let's go get something to drink."

Pete 'n Peters was busy with a noisy throng of people enjoying time with friends. They quickly headed for two open barstools they spotted at the far end of the bar near the pool tables. Tiffany-style stained glass lamps hanging over the bar area added a warm, quirky feel to the place. A few people were watching sports on flat-screen TVs mounted on the wall behind the bar. As they were getting seated, Eric managed to catch the eye of the bartender.

The bartender walked over and stood in front of them. "What can I get you?"

"Do you have any hefeweizen beer?" Rylie asked.

"Sure do," he replied.

"Great. That's what I'll have."

"Sounds good," Eric said. "I'll have the same. And do you happen to have any pretzels to go with that?"

"Coming right up."

The bartender put two bottles of beer and some glasses in front of them. He returned a few minutes later with a bowl of pretzels.

"Thanks!" Eric said.

"No problem, dude." The bartender hurried off.

"This is my treat," she said. "I'm the one who asked you to hang out with me here tonight."

"Thanks. Cheers." Eric clinked glasses with her.

She tried to be discreet as she scanned the room to see if she recognized anyone. She had a feeling that a lot of the people there were tourists rather than locals.

When the bartender came over to deliver drinks to some people sitting nearby, she asked, "So are most of the people in here tonight tourists or locals?"

"It's mostly tourists on the weekends," he replied. "But all the locals come here too." He strode to the other end of the bar where a loud group of young guys were hanging over the top of the bar trying to get his attention.

She glanced at the older guy with gray hair and a dark tan sitting next to her. He sat quietly nursing a beer while he watched the game on TV.

Eric also seemed to have become engrossed in the game on TV.

What is it with guys and sports? She could think of a million things she'd rather do than watch sports on TV.

She heard a familiar voice. Aidan Flynn and a man she didn't recognize were taking the barstools that had just been vacated on the other side of the gray-haired man sitting next to her. Aidan looked like he'd been drinking for a while.

She whispered to Eric to let him know that Aidan and a friend were sitting down at the bar nearby.

"Great," he whispered back.

She took a sip of her beer. The boisterous conversations around her mingled with the sounds of the sports on TV made it difficult for her to hear what Aidan and his friend were saying, but she managed to pick up some of their conversation.

"Yeah, I heard something about that."

"He did?"

"Well then, he kind of got what he deserved, didn't he?"

"Any guy who would mess around with another man's wife."

The older man seated next to her turned to Aidan. "What would you do if you found out that some guy was messing around with your wife, Aidan?"

Rylie stiffened. It seemed like everyone within earshot suddenly stopped what they were doing to listen. She'd been trying to keep her face angled away from Aidan so he wouldn't see her, but she had to see how he reacted to the jab.

Aidan got off his barstool and moved closer to the older man. His fists were curled tightly at his sides. His mouth was twisted in an ugly sneer. A muscle twitched in his jaw. She slid off her barstool and backed away from the two men. Everyone nearby also stepped back until there was a clear area around Aidan and the older man. The older man gazed at Aidan calmly.

He must have nerves of steel. Either that or he's had so many drinks that he's not really aware of what's happening right now.

Aidan's friend quickly stepped in between the two men. "Hey Aidan, why don't we go play some pool? You don't want to hit that old guy. He's not worth it."

A long moment passed. The entire bar was silent. Then Aidan's face cleared. His eyes slowly came into focus. He looked at his friend quietly for a minute. His fists slowly uncurled. He grabbed his drink, downed it in one gulp, slammed the empty glass down on the bar, and stalked out. His friend threw some money on the bar and quickly followed.

She let out her breath slowly.

"Let's get out of here," Eric said. "I think we've had enough for one night."

"Me too."

She put some money on the bar to pay for their drinks, and they headed outside.

"Wow, that was scary," she said.

"I think it could have gotten really ugly if Aidan's friend hadn't stepped in."

"I think you're right. Thanks for coming with me tonight, Eric."

"No problem. See you later."

Her thoughts churned on the drive back to Whitaker Cottages. She knew Aidan had a reputation for having a bad temper, but now she'd seen it for herself. More than once, come to think of it. She'd seen it when he stormed into Butter Lane Bakery to get Katiana and then again tonight. Tonight was worse. She wondered what Aidan was capable of when he got really angry.

Bella greeted her at the front door wagging her tail. She let Bella out to do her business and waited outside for her. Bella came trotting back quickly and they went inside. She got a lime-flavored mineral water from the refrigerator, took it into the living room, and curled up on the sofa. Bella stretched out on the floor by her feet.

"What a day, Bella."

She got down on the floor with Bella and stroked her soft fur. It helped to calm her frazzled nerves. Her cell phone rang. She checked the caller ID before answering and saw it was Laurent.

"Hi."

"Hi," Laurent said. "I called Detective Felton a little while ago and asked him if he'd talked to Melody yet. He said he had, so I called her. She was happy to hear from me. I made arrangements for us to meet her at her house at about 9:30 tomorrow morning. Does that work for you?"

"Perfect. I'm looking forward to meeting her."

"I also called Dee and asked her if we could go to Colin's house tomorrow morning after we meet with Melody. I have a key, but I felt like I should ask her permission. She said it would be fine. I know Detective Felton and his team searched Colin's house, but I still feel like it's possible that we might find something they missed. Are you up for that?"

"Absolutely. Why don't you pick me up here a little after 9:00 tomorrow then?"

After she hung up with Laurent, she called Eric to see if he'd like to take Buddy and Bella hiking somewhere tomorrow afternoon.

"That sounds great!" Eric said. "How about we take them on the Incline Flume Trail? It's a fairly easy hike with incredible views of the lake."

"Sounds good. I have somewhere I have to go in the morning, but I'll call you as soon as I get back."

Next she called Gillian and filled her in on everything that had happened that day.

"I was thinking it might be interesting to have a girls' night out with you, me, and Katiana," Rylie said. "I keep wondering if Katiana might know something that could help Detective Felton with his investigation. I think she'd feel more comfortable talking with us if she wasn't with Aidan. I don't want her to get the impression that we're interrogating her, so I think we should keep the conversation light at first. But after we're all enjoying our dinner and feeling relaxed, you or I might be able to discreetly bring up the subject and see where it goes. What do you think?"

"I like the idea," Gillian replied. "When were you thinking of doing this?"

"How about tomorrow night? I thought it might be fun to check out Bite American Tapas in Incline Village. Does that sound good? Could you call Katiana to invite her? She's known you for some time, so I think it would be better if you were the one to invite her."

"I've been wanting to check out that place!" Gillian said. "I'll call Katiana right now and see if she wants to join us. If she doesn't, then you and I can still go out for a girls' night out. I'm sure Liam will be fine with watching the cottages for the evening."

Gillian called back a few minutes later to let her know that Katiana had agreed to join them. They made arrangements to meet at Gillian's house at 6:30 the following evening.

Tomorrow was going to be an interesting day.

Chapter 27

Laurent knocked on her door early the next morning. She grabbed her purse and the stuffed bunny she'd gotten for Colin's baby.

"Hi!"

"Morning. Ready to go?" he asked.

"Yes."

She leaned over to pet the soft fur on Bella's head. "I love you, Bella. I have to do some stuff this morning, but this afternoon we're going to go hiking with Buddy! You remember Buddy, right?"

Bella pranced around excitedly as Rylie went out the front door. Rylie set the alarm and locked the door on her way out.

"I always feel guilty leaving Bella home alone."

"She'll be fine. And it sounds like you'll be having some fun with her this afternoon."

"I know. You're right."

They chatted comfortably on the way to Melody's house. Melody answered the door with her baby in her arms. She was tanned, blond, and fit, with a ready smile. It was easy to see how Colin would have been attracted to her.

"Melody!" Laurent leaned in to kiss Melody on both cheeks. He looked down at the baby in her arms. "What a handsome boy you have. I can't believe you had a baby with Colin, and I'm just finding out about it now."

"I can't believe you're just finding out about it now either, Laurent. It's good to see you. Come in."

"Hi, Melody. I'm Rylie. I brought a little bunny for Tyler. I hope he likes it."

"Why thank you, Rylie."

Melody showed the stuffed bunny to Tyler. Tyler waved his little hands around and made gurgling noises. Melody led the way to the kitchen, put Tyler in a padded baby bouncer with his new bunny, and sat down at the dining table. Rylie and Laurent sat across from her.

"It's really good to see you again, Melody," Laurent said. "It's been too long. How have you been?"

"As well as can be expected," Melody replied. "I've been trying to stay positive since Colin was killed. I don't want Tyler to see me sad all the time. I've got to be strong for him."

"I'm so sorry, Melody," Rylie said. "I only spoke with Colin briefly a couple times, but he seemed like a really nice guy. I can only imagine how you must feel."

Melody's eyes filled with tears. She brushed them away impatiently and sat up a little straighter.

"Did Colin ever get to meet Tyler?" Rylie asked.

"Yes. I told him I was pregnant when I was about seven months along. When I first found out I was pregnant, it was only about three weeks after he'd broken up with me. I didn't want to tell him then. I didn't want him to feel like he had to get back together with me out of some sort of sense of obligation. I struggled with whether I should even tell him at all for months. I finally decided it wasn't fair to Colin or the baby for them not to be in each other's lives."

"Colin was shocked when I told him," Melody continued. "I knew he was seeing someone else by then. I didn't want him to dump his girlfriend and get back together with me. I just wanted him to know about his son and have the opportunity to be involved in his life. He went to all my doctor's appointments with me after that. And he was with me when Tyler was born. He was a very good daddy. He came to see Tyler as often as he could." Melody choked up and went silent.

"I'm glad Colin was able to be in Tyler's life for at least a little while," Rylie said. "I think you made the right decision to tell Colin about his son."

"I do too," Laurent said. "I'm sure Tyler meant the world to Colin. And I know that you meant the world to him too, Melody. He told me once that he thought you were his soul mate. I think he just got scared when things started to get serious between the two of you, and that's why he bailed."

"You said that Detective Felton showed you everything we found in the secret compartment on Colin's boat," Laurent continued. "I was happy to see that Colin put some money aside for Tyler."

"Me too. I wonder when he was planning to tell me about it," Melody replied. "I didn't have any clue he'd done that."

"We found a little key in the bottom of the secret compartment. Do you have any idea what it might go to?" Laurent asked.

"Yes. Detective Felton showed it to me yesterday. It's a spare key to my storage unit," Melody replied.

"Did Colin keep anything in your storage unit?" Laurent asked.

"Just a box of old business papers. Detective Felton went through it all yesterday afternoon. Apparently, Colin and Aidan Flynn were partners in a restaurant supply business in the San Francisco Bay Area for about four years. Their business went under during the recession."

The baby started kicking his feet and getting fussy. Melody told them it was time for her to nurse him.

"No problem, Melody," Laurent said. They said their goodbyes and headed for Laurent's SUV.

"That was interesting," Rylie said. "Garrison Taylor told Dee and I that Colin and Aidan had been in business together in the San Francisco Bay Area, but he didn't tell us what kind of business it was. Did you know that Colin and Aidan used to have a restaurant supply business?"

"No, I didn't. Colin never talked about it. It was a while ago. I guess he didn't see any reason to bring it up. I wonder what other secrets Colin had. I thought we were close. But he never told me Melody was pregnant or that he had a son. That's a pretty big thing not to share with a close friend."

"Maybe he was still trying to process everything," she replied. "You told me he had a history of breaking up with women if they got too serious. I'm sure it was a shock for him to learn that he was going to be a father. Maybe he just needed to figure some things out before he let anyone know he had a son."

The first thing she noticed when they walked into Colin's house was the stale odor that hung in the air. She quickly went through the house opening all the blinds and windows to let in some fresh air and sunshine. Laurent wandered from room to room. She searched the house until she found Colin's study.

One entire wall of Colin's study was filled with built-in bookshelves. She put on some nitrile exam gloves that Laurent had brought before she touched anything. She pulled a few books down off the shelves and examined them. She looked at some of Colin's art pieces scattered among the books on the shelves.

She started going through Colin's desk. She ran her hand along the bottom of the center drawer to see if there might be a key taped to it. Nothing. She crawled under the desk to look around and make sure she hadn't missed anything. Laurent was standing in the doorway staring at her when she crawled back out.

"What are you doing?" he asked.

"Checking to see if there was a key taped under the drawer."

"You watch too much TV."

Rylie grinned. "Hey, it's not that crazy of an idea."

"And it's probably the first thing that Detective Felton and his team checked," Laurent replied.

She sat back down at the desk and started removing the drawers one by one. The drawer on the bottom right wouldn't come out. She felt around and found a small lever on the bottom of the drawer. When she pulled on the lever, she was able to remove the drawer from the desk. She found a narrow compartment behind a panel at the back of the drawer with a file folder inside. She took the documents out of the folder and started looking through them.

"Hey, Laurent! Come here! Look what I found!"

Laurent strode quickly into the study.

"I found a secret compartment at the back of this drawer with a file folder in it."

They looked through the documents together. There was a letter from Patrick O'Farrell's attorney to Colin's attorney offering to purchase the land that Colin owned adjacent to the old Tavern Grill. Colin's attorney had replied with a letter refusing the offer and providing evidence that the parking lot for the old Tavern Grill encroached on Colin's land by about ten feet. Colin's attorney insisted that Patrick remove the asphalt paving that crossed the property line immediately.

Patrick's attorney had written a scathing letter in reply threatening to tie Colin up in court for years over the property line dispute. Colin's attorney had sent back an equally scathing letter. The most recent letter was dated about a week and a half before Colin was killed. There was also a survey of Colin's land and a map showing the property lines.

"There must have been some hard feelings between Colin and Patrick over all this," Rylie said. "Did you find anything else when you were looking through the house?"

"No. I've searched every place I could think of where I thought he might have hidden something. We'd better call Detective Felton and show him all this."

Detective Felton showed up a little while later. "The evidence technicians are on their way. They'll be here in a few minutes."

She showed Detective Felton the papers she'd found. He quickly read through each of the documents.

"Did either of you find anything else?" he asked.

"No. That's it," Laurent replied.

"I'll just take this stuff back to the sheriff's department then," Detective Felton said. "Let me know if you find anything else."

After Detective Felton and his team left, they headed back to Whitaker Cottages. She told Laurent about her plans for the rest of the day.

"I'm glad you're going to get out and have some fun," Laurent said. "You really need to spend some time relaxing and enjoying yourself while you're here."

"I know. I plan to. I've missed you, Laurent. We need to get together again soon."

"We will. Don't worry."

He gave her a warm hug when he dropped her off at her house. She smiled as she headed inside to get ready for her hike with Eric.

Chapter 28

She called Eric as she stepped inside. "Hi, I just got home. I just need a couple minutes to get ready."

"Great. I'll be there in a few."

She changed into some hiking boots and packed a backpack with some bottled water, Bella's travel water bottle with its attached flip-open water dish, a first aid kit, and some sunscreen. Bella was sniffing everything she was doing, wagging her tail, and looking at her hopefully.

"Do you want to go on a hike with Buddy and Eric, Bella?"

Bella bounced up and down on her front legs. Her tongue lolled out the side of her mouth as she panted excitedly in anticipation of a new adventure. Eric knocked on the door a few minutes later.

Bella ran outside as soon as Rylie opened the door. Buddy looked ecstatic to see Bella. He rushed over to Bella to greet her, then turned and sprinted to Eric's SUV with Bella close behind. Rylie set the alarm, stepped outside, and locked the door.

"I think I'm as excited as Bella and Buddy are about going on this hike," she said. "I haven't done much hiking in Tahoe."

"I think you'll really like this trail," Eric replied. "Did you bring a leash for Bella? Dogs are allowed, but they have to be on a leash."

"I brought her 26-foot retractable leash. That way I can let the leash out sometimes so she can have more freedom to explore."

Eric drove east on Highway 28 toward Incline Village, then up the Mt. Rose Highway to the Incline Flume Trail trailhead. He parked in the parking lot across the street from the trail. Bella and Buddy bounced around excitedly in the back of the SUV as she and Eric struggled to put on their leashes. Once the dogs were safely leashed, they let them out of the SUV and set out along the trail. Bella and Buddy had their noses to the ground sniffing everything within reach.

"There should be a lot of wildflowers blooming this time of year," Eric said. "And there'll be some fantastic views of the lake as we get further along."

They hiked through meadows liberally sprinkled with yellow and purple wildflowers under a brilliant blue sky. She inhaled deeply of the fresh mountain air scented with wildflowers and the tall pine trees that bordered the meadows. She caught a flash of blue as a Steller's Jay flitted through some trees and squawked a rebuke at them for invading his territory.

They carefully picked their way over the trail as it narrowed and wound around the mountainside mere inches from a steep precipice. She kept Bella on a very short leash and stayed as close as possible to the huge granite boulders that clung to the side of the mountain. When the trail finally opened up onto a large meadow, they were rewarded with stunning panoramic views of Lake Tahoe. The translucent turquoise waters of Sand Harbor sparkled far below them as they stopped to savor the view.

They found a large boulder to sit on while they drank some water and munched on energy bars that Eric brought. She gave Bella and Buddy some water in Bella's water dish. The dogs took turns lapping thirstily. After Bella drank her fill, she flopped down on the grass near the boulder. Buddy laid down next to her. Both dogs panted contentedly.

"It looks like they're becoming good friends," she said.

"Yes it does. Buddy knows Bella's name now. He got really excited when I told him we were going to see Bella today."

"I think Bella knows Buddy by name too. I'm glad they're getting along so well."

She watched the happy dogs lying next to each other on the grass for a few minutes.

"Laurent and I had an interesting morning." Eric turned his attention away from the dogs and looked at her expectantly. She filled him in on what she and Laurent had learned.

Eric sat quietly staring out across the lake. "A couple days before Colin was killed, I was taking a tray of pastries out of the oven at the bakery, and I accidentally burned my hand. I dropped the tray, and all the pastries fell on the floor. Colin was standing right there and saw the whole thing. I felt really bad about ruining a whole tray of pastries. He told me not to worry about it. He put his arm around my shoulders and said, "Hey buddy, it's okay. You can't change what's already happened. Let it go. You just have to try to do better in the future. That's what I'm going to do." I thought it was a strange thing to say at the time. Now I wonder if he was thinking about Melody and his baby when he said that."

"It's possible. Or he could have been thinking about something else in his life. I guess we'll never really know," she replied.

"So who are we thinking are the main suspects at this point?" Eric asked. "Aidan Flynn? Patrick O'Farrell? They both had reasons that they may have wanted Colin out of the picture. It seems like Blake Cunningham and Steve Randall are less likely at this point."

"I think Aidan had a stronger motive than Patrick if he had reason to believe that Colin was having an affair with his wife. When that old man at Pete 'n Peters taunted Aidan about what he would do if he thought someone was messing around with his wife, Aidan looked like he wanted to kill the guy. He scares me. I hope Katiana can tell us something tonight that might help Detective Felton with his investigation. Gillian and I are going to try to discreetly see if we can learn anything from her. I'm sure Katiana will feel more comfortable talking with us when her husband isn't around."

"I saw Patrick get really angry with Colin when Colin told him he didn't want to sell his property," Eric replied. "I told you about that. And you saw Patrick go after Garrison Taylor when Garrison refused to sell Colin's property to him. So Patrick obviously has a bad temper too. Do you know if Dee and Garrison are aware of the property line dispute between Patrick and Colin that you found out about today?"

"Laurent said he was going to call Dee and tell her about it. I have no idea if Garrison knows, but I'd assume he would since he was partners with Colin."

A guy peddled by on a mountain bike. Both dogs leaped up and ran toward the bicyclist but ran out of leash before they reached the trail. Bella and Buddy strained at their leashes, wagging their tails furiously, when they spotted a family of four with two young sons coming toward them on the trail.

The older of the two boys, who looked like he might have been about ten years old, saw the happy golden retrievers and started jumping up and down.

"Mommy, look at those nice dogs! Can we go play with them?"

"You'll have to ask their owners if it's okay," the woman replied.

The little boy and his younger brother ran over to Bella and Buddy who were bouncing up and down with excitement. Bella gave the younger boy a sloppy wet doggie kiss. He wiped his shirt sleeve across his face, grinning with pleasure.

"Can we play with your dogs?" the older boy asked.

"Sure." Rylie smiled.

The little boys pet Bella and Buddy and allowed the dogs to thoroughly lick their faces and arms while they squealed with delight. She and Eric looked on with amusement. Eventually the boys' parents extricated their sons from the doggie love fest and resumed their hike. The boys' mother dug around in her backpack until she found some disposable wipes and attempted to clean the boys' faces. The face cleaning session was met with loud protests from the boys.

Rylie checked the time on her cell phone. "I think we should start heading back now. I have to shower and get ready for girls' night out with Gillian and Katiana tonight."

"Okay."

They headed back the way they'd come. Suddenly Buddy veered off the trail into the woods. He strained at the end of his leash and let out a bark. Bella followed Buddy as far as her leash would allow.

"What the?" Rylie held tightly onto Bella's leash.

She and Eric both heard it at the same time. It sounded like a goat bleating.

"Waaaaaa!"

Both dogs started barking.

"Bella, Buddy, no! No barking!" she said. "I think we should follow them to find out what's going on."

They found the source of the bleating a few minutes later. A little fawn was curled up under the branches of a fallen tree. They stopped a short distance away and kept the dogs close.

The fawn tried to get up from its hiding place. When it finally struggled to its feet, they could see that its right front leg was hanging at an awkward angle.

"Well I'm not a vet, but even I can tell its leg is broken," Eric said.

"Yeah, it's bad. We can't leave it here. It'll end up getting eaten by something. I think we should take it with us down to Incline Village. Then I can call some of the local veterinary hospitals to see where we can take it. It's going to need surgery on that leg."

"I have a cardboard box in my SUV that I can empty out to put the fawn in," Eric said. "And I have some clean towels that I use for Buddy that we can put in the bottom of the box."

"Great. I'll stay here with Bella and the fawn while you go get the box and towels. You might want to leave something by the side of the trail so you know where to turn off when you get back."

"Good idea," Eric replied. "I'll leave an energy bar wrapper on the ground by the turnoff. I just hope someone doesn't think it's trash and pick it up before I get back."

"If you can't find the wrapper when you get back, just start hollering and I'll holler back when I hear you."

She sat on a fallen tree near the fawn while she waited for Eric to get back. The fawn wobbled on three legs for a few minutes bleating pitifully, then awkwardly laid back down. Bella was very interested in the fawn. She knew Bella wouldn't hurt the fawn, but she didn't want her to scare the poor little thing, so she kept Bella close by her side.

Eric found his way back with no problem. Rylie arranged towels on the bottom of the box and then gently lifted the fawn and placed it inside.

She held onto both dogs' leashes on the way back while Eric carried the box with the fawn inside. They put seat belts on the dogs in the back seat and put the box with the fawn inside on the floor by Rylie's feet in the front.

When they got to Incline Village, Eric pulled into a shopping center so she could make some calls. She called a local veterinary hospital to see if they knew where she and Eric could take the injured fawn.

"You need to call Lake Tahoe Wildlife Care," the receptionist replied. "They're in South Lake Tahoe about forty-five minutes from here."

"Ok thanks," Rylie replied. "Do you happen to have their number?"

The receptionist gave her the number, and she called Lake Tahoe Wildlife Care. She explained to the woman that answered the phone that they'd found a fawn with a broken leg off the Incline Flume Trail.

"Can you bring it down here to our center?" the woman asked.

"Hang on just a minute," Rylie replied. She turned to Eric. "Are you okay if we take the fawn to Lake Tahoe Wildlife Care in South Lake Tahoe?"

"Sure. But what about your girls' night out tonight?"

"I don't have to be there until 6:30. I think we have time. If we're running late getting back, I'll just call Gillian to let her know She'll be fine with it."

The little fawn laid quietly in its box on the drive to Lake Tahoe Wildlife Care. Rylie hoped they had a veterinarian that was able to perform orthopedic surgery. Eric followed the directions on his GPS until the woman's voice on the GPS announced that they had arrived. Rylie looked around. Lake Tahoe Wildlife Care appeared to be in someone's home. She got out of the SUV and carefully picked up the box with the fawn inside.

"I'll stay in the car with the dogs with the windows down so they don't get too hot," Eric said.

"Okay. I don't think this will take long." She headed for the front door of the house and knocked.

An older woman answered the door. "You must be Rylie. I'm Brenda. Come on in. Let's see what you've got there."

Rylie set the box down. The woman peered inside.

"Oh yeah, that leg's broken all right. I was planning to take another animal over to our vet in a few minutes, so I'll take the fawn there at the same time."

"Does your vet do orthopedic surgery?" Rylie asked.

"Yes, he does. Don't worry. We'll do everything we can to help this little guy."

Rylie got the name and phone number of the veterinarian who worked with Lake Tahoe Wildlife Care so she could check on the fawn later.

"Thank you," she said. "It's wonderful that there's a place like this in Lake Tahoe. I'm sure you're very busy caring for all the orphaned and injured birds and animals around here."

"You have no idea," Brenda replied. "If it wasn't for all our volunteers, we'd never be able to do it."

"Could I give you a donation to help out with the fawn's care?"

"That would be wonderful if you could do that," Brenda replied. "Our vet gives us a good discount, but he doesn't work for free."

Rylie got her purse out of Eric's SUV and wrote out a check to Lake Tahoe Wildlife Care. She handed it to Brenda as she looked down at the little fawn one last time.

"Bye, little guy. I hope you do well. Bye, Brenda. Thanks for taking the fawn and making sure he gets the care he needs."

"Bye now. Thanks for bring him in."

She went back to the SUV and stepped up into her seat. "I'm so relieved we had someplace we could take that poor fawn. Brenda's going to take him to their vet in a few minutes."

"Is their vet going to be able to fix that leg?"

"I don't know. But I've got his name and number so I can call him later after he's had a chance to look at the fawn and take some x-rays."

They drove back to Whitaker Cottages. Eric dropped her and Bella off at their house. Buddy craned his head to keep looking at Bella as they drove away.

"Poor Buddy. I think he's going to miss you, Bella."

She unlocked the house, disarmed the alarm, and stepped inside.

"That was an exciting day, wasn't it, Bella?"

Bella wagged her tail slowly and headed straight for her water dish in the kitchen. After a long drink, she ambled into the living room and plopped down in the middle of the floor looking happy and content.

Rylie went into her bedroom to get ready for girls' night out with Gillian and Katiana.

Chapter 29

After a quick shower, she got dressed in dark blue pants with a white lace V-neck top and a waist-length light blue drape front suede jacket. She put some kibble in Bella's dog dish and gave her some fresh water. Then she headed over to Gillian and Liam's house.

Gillian opened the door with a broad smile. "Hi! Come on in. I'm ready to go. And Katiana should be here any minute."

She followed Gillian to the kitchen and sat at her dining table. Liam walked into the room.

"Hi Rylie," he said. "I hear you girls are going to Bite American Tapas in Incline Village."

"Yes. I'm excited."

"I've heard good things about it. You'll have to let me know what you think after you eat there."

She told Gillian and Liam what she had learned about Colin and Aidan having been business partners in a restaurant supply business and about the letters between Colin's and Patrick's attorneys about the property line dispute.

"Do you remember Colin or Aidan ever saying anything about having had a restaurant supply business together?" she asked.

"No, I don't," Liam replied. "That's news to me."

"Maybe they agreed not to talk about it. They might not have wanted anyone to know that their business went under during the recession," Rylie said.

"Could be," Liam said. "Listen, Rylie. Gillian and I were talking right before you came over. The business phone has only rung once or twice the entire weekend. We don't think there's any need for you to spend the next three days sitting around here waiting for the phone to ring. One of us will be here anyway. So why don't you take this week off and just relax and have some fun?"

"Really? Are you sure that's something you want to do? I'm happy to hang out here so you two can have some time off."

"We're positive," Liam replied. "It'll be good for you to get away from here. You can do some of the things around the lake that you planned to do when you came here this summer."

Rylie grinned. "Okay. If you're sure. I'll start thinking about what I might like to do this week. Thanks."

They heard someone knocking on the door.

"That'll be Katiana. Come on, Rylie. Let's go. See you later, Liam," Gillian said. She opened the front door.

"Hi Katiana," they said nearly in unison.

"Hi." Katiana's long, dark brown hair fell in soft curls over her hunter green off-the-shoulder sheath dress. She was the kind of woman that looked sexy without even trying. An image of Aidan's angry face flashed into Rylie's mind. Her stomach clenched. She quickly forced the image from her mind and brought her thoughts back to the present.

"Are you excited about having a girls' night out?" Rylie asked.

Katiana smiled a small smile. "Yes. I haven't done anything like this in a long time."

They got up into Gillian's SUV and headed for Incline Village. Rylie sat in the back seat so Katiana could sit in the front with Gillian. As they drove past Colin's vacant lot, Rylie noticed that work was being done on the site. About ten feet of the Tavern Grill's asphalt parking lot where it adjoined Colin's lot had been removed. Thick wooden fence posts set in concrete were spaced out along the property line where the asphalt had been cut. She also noticed stacks of lumber and some construction equipment in front of the Tavern Grill.

She decided to go to Colin's lot the next morning to see if Garrison was there and find out what was going on with Colin's restaurant project. Then she could go over to the old Tavern Grill and see if Patrick was there. She'd love to see what he was doing to renovate the place.

The hostess at the tapas restaurant seated them at a nice table in a far corner. They each looked through their menus and picked a few tapas to try. Rylie decided to try the sirloin cheeseburger slider, the lobster slider, and the shrimp and grits.

"I've never had grits," she said. "I've always been curious about them so this will give me the chance try them out."

"You're brave," Katiana said. "I'm always nervous about trying new things."

Their waitress came by to take their food and drink orders and then hurried off.

"I'm so glad you were able to come out with us tonight, Katiana," Rylie said.

"Me too," Katiana replied. "I haven't gone out much since we moved here. Aidan is gone a lot, and I don't like to go out by myself. I used to get out more when we lived in the Bay Area. I had a lot more friends there."

"When did you move to Lake Tahoe?" Rylie asked.

"About two years ago. A little while after Colin moved here," Katiana replied. "Aidan and Colin used to be business partners. Their business went under during the recession, but they stayed friends."

"So you and Aidan moved here to be close to Colin?" Rylie asked.

"No. That wasn't it. Aidan wanted to get away from the Bay Area. It was a constant reminder to him of all the money he lost when their business went under. We both love Lake Tahoe so Aidan thought it would be a good place for us to start over. It doesn't make any sense to me though since Aidan's new business is in San Francisco. He's always traveling there for business and leaving me here alone."

Rylie studied Katiana as she spoke. She was struck by the deep sense of sadness that seemed to emanate from her despite her natural beauty.

"What kinds of things do you like to do?" Rylie asked.

"I like to go for long walks around the lake. I'd like to go hiking, but I'm afraid to go by myself in case anything ever happened. I like to cook. And I like to read. I spend a lot of time reading. I'd rather read than watch TV."

"Do you like spending time in libraries?" Rylie asked.

Katiana's face lit up for the first time that evening. "Yes. I love libraries."

"Have you ever looked through the books in the library at the Whitakers' house?" Rylie asked. "They have a great collection. Some of those books are really old."

"No, I haven't," Katiana replied. "But I've seen their library when I walked past it on Locals' Night. I'd love to get the chance to look through those books."

"Elizabeth Whitaker is a friend of my mother. I've known her for a long time. She told me I can spend time in her library anytime I want while I'm here this summer. She gave me a key to her house so I could get in without having to bother Liam or Gillian. Would you like to come over sometime and look through the books in her library with me?"

Katiana smiled a genuine smile of pleasure. She suddenly looked years younger. "I would love that."

"Great! Why don't you put your cell phone number in my contacts? I'll call or text you so we can get something set up. Are you available sometime this week?"

"Sure," Katiana replied. "I don't think I have anything planned."

Rylie handed Katiana her cell phone. Katiana typed in her cell phone number and handed the phone back.

"That sounds like fun," Gillian said. "I'm sure you two will have a wonderful time browsing through the books in the Whitakers' library. How are your tapas? Everything I ordered has been delicious."

"Everything I've tried so far has been great," Rylie replied. She took a bite of her lobster slider.

"Mine have all been delicious too," Katiana replied. "I've been trying to figure out how I could make these at home."

"I think we should try some of their desserts," Rylie said. "I want to try their homemade ice cream sandwiches. I went hiking on the Incline Flume Trail today, so I burned enough calories to make up for a little dessert." She grinned at Gillian and Katiana.

Gillian and Katiana exchanged a glance.

Gillian smiled. "I'm not sure I burned enough calories today to make up for indulging in dessert, but hey, I'll walk faster around the cottages tomorrow."

"I'll go for a long walk tomorrow," Katiana said. "I want to try their key lime pie!"

After they finished their desserts, they headed back to Whitaker Cottages. Katiana looked more relaxed and happier than Rylie had ever seen her. They said their goodbyes in front of Gillian's house, then Rylie walked home.

"Hi, Bella! Were you a good girl while I was gone?"

Bella wagged her tail furiously and gave her a big golden grin. Rylie ruffled her soft fur and let her outside to go potty. After she let Bella back in, she went into her bedroom to get ready for bed. Bella curled up contentedly on her dog bed at the foot of Rylie's bed.

Rylie got into her pajamas and then propped some pillows up against the headboard of her bed. She crawled into bed, readjusted the pillows to a comfortable position behind her back, and texted Gillian.

Well, we didn't really learn much about Aidan from Katiana tonight, but at least she seemed to loosen up and relax a little.

Gillian texted back.

Yes. It was nice to see Katiana smile. I didn't have the heart to bring something up that might get her upset.

I know. I felt the same way. Maybe I'll be able to talk to her more when she comes to look through the books in the Whitakers' library with me. Anyway, we had fun and a nice meal. So it's all good.

Yes! We'll have to plan to have girls' night outs more often.

Sounds good. 'Night.

She got under the covers and laid there replaying the evening with Katiana and Gillian in her mind. They'd only scratched the surface in getting to know Katiana. Katiana had secrets. She wanted to know what they were.

Chapter 30

Rylie woke up early the next morning. She was eager to talk to Garrison Taylor and find out what was going on with Colin's property. While her coffee was brewing, she got Bella some breakfast. She took a quick shower, got dressed, and headed down to the lake with Bella. The early morning air was brisk and invigorating. She walked quickly to try to stay warm and burn off some of the nervous energy that was coursing through her body.

Hey, I don't have to work this week. This is great.

They turned onto the path that ran along the lake. Birds were flitting through the trees and bouncing around in the underbrush looking for food. The lake shimmered an iridescent pale blue as it stretched toward the mountains on the far shore. They walked for about half an hour, then headed back home.

She left Bella happily curled up on the living room floor and drove to Colin's property in Tahoe City to see if Garrison was there. She parked in the Lighthouse Center parking lot and walked over to Colin's lot. A couple of guys were building a fence on the property line using the fence posts already in place. She spotted Garrison right away.

"Hi Garrison!"

"Rylie! How nice to see you!" Garrison walked over to greet her. "What brings you here?"

"I was hoping to chat with you for a few minutes."

"Well come on over here to my office then," Garrison said. He led Rylie to the other side of the property where he had a couple of camp chairs and a small camp table set up.

"Either my project manager or I have to be here while work is being done on the property. If no one is here to oversee the workers, shortcuts are taken and mistakes are made. My project manager is busy finishing up another project for me right now, but he'll be here to take over sometime in the next couple of days."

"I noticed the fence going up when I drove by here yesterday," she said. "So are you starting work on the restaurant project now?"

"Yes. I hope to have the restaurant completed before winter. The fence will be finished today. Tomorrow I have a team coming in to start clearing out all the weeds and leveling the ground. Then I'll have a crew come in to lay the foundation."

"Did Patrick give you any trouble about removing part of his parking lot and putting up the fence?"

"He came over to talk to me a couple days ago when we started cutting the asphalt on the property line. I showed him the survey and the property map. The property line is clearly marked. It's indisputable. There's no sense arguing about it. I think he realized that once he saw the survey and property map. He said he'll be fine since he's been able to lease some parking spaces for his restaurant from the Lighthouse Center."

"Oh, that's good." Rylie smiled. "I'm going to go over to see what he's doing with the old Tavern Grill. I used to go to there a long time ago before they closed. I'm very interested to see what he's planning to do with the place."

She turned and gave Garrison a friendly wave goodbye as she walked over to Patrick's property.

The area around the old Tavern Grill was buzzing with activity. There were construction workers everywhere but no sign of Patrick O'Farrell.

"Do you know where I can find Patrick?" she called out to a guy walking by with a stack of lumber on his shoulder.

"I think he's in the back by the new addition," he replied without stopping.

She followed the man as he walked around the back of the building where a new addition was being framed in. She spotted Patrick talking with a guy in the middle of the addition.

"Hi Patrick!" She waved to get his attention.

Patrick turned to stare blankly at her with a slightly irritated look. His expression cleared when he recognized her. He said a few words to the guy he was talking to and walked over to where she was standing.

"Hi Rylie. What brings you here?"

"I saw signs of work going on here when I drove by yesterday, so I thought I'd stop in and see how your renovations are going."

"They're going well. We're hard at work, as you can see." He waved a hand in the direction of the new addition that was bustling with construction workers.

"I was wondering if you might have a couple minutes to show me around? I used to go here before it closed. I'd love to see what you've got planned."

Patrick looked over at the guys working on the addition for a minute while he seemed to consider her question. Then he looked back at her.

"Okay, sure. I can give you a quick tour. I can't be gone very long though. I have a million things going on right now that need my attention."

"Thanks, Patrick. I can see you're busy. I don't want to keep you."

He led the way inside the original building. It was dirty and rundown from years of neglect, but she could envision what it could become. The original dark wood bar just needed to be cleaned and polished. There was an exposed brick wall behind the bar with dark wood shelves for bottles of liquor. Vintage translucent milk glass chandeliers hung over the bar. On the wall opposite the bar, seating areas comprised of rectangular dark wood tables and tufted leather banquettes were separated from each other by dark wood dividers inlaid with panels of leaded glass in geometric patterns.

"This is wonderful! Even in this condition, it's beautiful Patrick. It deserves to be restored. What do you plan to do with this area?"

A broad smile lit Patrick's face. "I'm going to keep this area pretty much as it is. Just clean it up a little. I agree with you. It's beautiful. The addition that I'm having built will continue the original interior design with dark wood coffered ceilings and exposed brick accent walls. I found some old brick from a salvaged building materials supplier that's almost a perfect match for what's already here."

"That's great! I think you're doing this old building and Tahoe City a great service, Patrick. I can't wait to see it when you're done. I noticed that Garrison Taylor took out some of your parking lot and put up a fence. Is that going to cause any problems with your project?"

"No. I'll be fine since I was able to lease some parking spaces from the Lighthouse Center."

Patrick's eyes darted nervously toward where work was continuing on the new addition. "I've got to get going now, Rylie. I have a full crew out there that I need to supervise. Maybe I'll see you at Liam's poker night on Wednesday and we can talk more then."

"Sure. No problem, Patrick. I can find my way out. I'm sorry I barged in on you when you're so busy. Thanks for showing me around."

When she got back to her SUV, she texted Katiana.

Hi Katiana. This is Rylie. I was wondering if you'd like to look through the books in the Whitakers' library with me on Wednesday?

Sure. What time?

How about 10:00? You can meet me at the main house where we have Locals' Night.

Okay. Sounds good. See you then.

She pulled out of the parking lot and headed home. She needed to talk to Detective Felton. Something was bothering her about Colin's murder investigation. When she got back to her house, she got a lime-flavored mineral water from the refrigerator and sat at her dining table to call Detective Felton.

Detective Felton answered on the second ring. "Hi Rylie. How are you? Is everything okay?"

"Yes, everything's fine, thanks. I've been thinking about what you told me about how you didn't think that either the punch from Steve Randall or Blake Cunningham were the right angle to cause the head injury that killed Colin. You said you thought there must have been a third person in the Absinthe Room that night. What do you think that third person did to Colin that caused him to fall backward and hit his head on the granite wall?"

"I've spoken with Brayden Hughes at length about this. We think someone pushed Colin really hard. They must have taken him off guard and he wasn't able to keep his footing. That's the only thing that makes sense."

She sat quietly absorbing this information for a minute. Her stomach twisted as she envisioned the scene.

"I feel like we're getting close to solving this case, Rylie. Please try to relax and enjoy your time here at the lake. We're making progress. I'm not at liberty to tell you all the details, but we've got this. Stop worrying."

"That's easier said than done. Thanks, Mark."

"Bye, Rylie. Take care."

She looked over at Bella. "Want to go down to the lake, Bella? You can chase the ducks and run around while I read a book and try to relax."

Bella jumped up and ran to the door. Rylie laughed at Bella's enthusiasm. She picked out a book to read from the books she'd brought with her when she'd moved to Whitaker Cottages for the summer. She put on a bathing suit under her shorts and t-shirt and packed a beach bag with sunscreen, a beach towel, and some bottled water. She slipped her cell phone into the inside pocket of the beach bag.

"Come on, Bella! Let's go!"

Bella bolted outside as soon as she opened the front door. When they got to the beach, she settled into a lounge chair and got out her book. The book remained in her lap unopened as she gazed out across the water and allowed her mind to drift. After a while, she gave up on the book and took Bella for a walk along the lakeside path.

"I feel like I'm missing something, Bella."

Bella didn't look up. Her nose was to the ground as she continued to sniff all the intriguing smells of the forest.

"We're down to two suspects, Bella. Aidan Flynn and Patrick O'Farrell. But I can't imagine that either of them would push someone they were having an argument with. I think they'd both be more likely to punch them."

So who would push Colin? And why? Were they trying to kill him? Or was it an accident?

She wracked her brain trying to think of who might want to harm Colin. She kept coming up blank. After a while, she turned around and headed back to her house.

She made herself a salad for lunch and sat down at her dining table to eat. She decided to make an evidence board like the ones she'd seen in murder mysteries on TV to help sort out her thoughts. She wrote the names of each of the people that she, Gillian, and Liam considered suspects in Colin's murder investigation across the top of the page. Then she wrote what she knew about each of them under their names.

Blake Cunningham, Steve Randall, Patrick O'Farrell, Aidan Flynn. None of them seemed to fit with what Detective Felton had just told her. She wrote "Third Person in Absinthe Room" on the top right of the paper. Under "Third Person," she wrote:

Suspected to have pushed Colin really hard which caused him to fall backward into the granite wall in the Absinthe Room and sustain a fatal head injury.

She had a lot of questions without a lot of answers. Who else could have been with Colin in the Absinthe Room that night? How could a guy who seemed so warm and charismatic have gotten so many people angry with him?

Maybe she'd been going about this the wrong way. Maybe if she knew more about Colin she could find the answers she was looking for. She finished her lunch and then called Dee Matthews.

"Hi Dee. This is Rylie. How are you?"

"Rylie, hi! I'm hanging in there. What's up?"

"I was wondering if we could talk somewhere private this afternoon or this evening. I'll buy if you'd like to go out to dinner somewhere."

"Is this about my brother?"

"Yes. I've been struggling with trying to make sense of everything. I know Detective Felton and his team are working on it, but that doesn't stop me from thinking about it all the time. You told me you knew that Colin's lack of good judgment would end up costing him someday. I was hoping you might tell me a little bit more about that."

The long silence that followed made her wonder if Dee was going to hang up on her. She held her breath as she waited for Dee to reply.

"I'm not sure I'm ready to talk about it," Dee said finally.

"Oh. Okay. I understand."

"No, you know what? It's okay. You were there for me when I had to talk to Garrison and Patrick. I know you mean well. Let's talk. You're buying. How about dinner at Whitecaps Pizza in Kings Beach tonight?"

"That sounds great. I've never had their pizza, but I've heard it's good. Why don't I meet you there around 6:00 then?"

"Okay. See you then."

Chapter 31

Whitecaps Pizza was located in a charming white clapboard cottage with dark green trim and a matching green roof. The hostess asked if they would prefer to eat inside or outside on the patio.

"Definitely outside for me," Dee replied. "How about you, Rylie?"

"Outside for me too."

The hostess led the way to a large outdoor patio right on the beach with a gorgeous view across the lake to the hazy blue mountains in the distance. They were seated at a wooden picnic table shaded by a square white umbrella.

"Wow, this is great," Rylie said. "Right on the beach."

"I know, right?" Dee replied. "The pizza's not bad either."

A tall guy with an athletic build, sparkling blue eyes, and shoulder-length curly brown hair showed up to take their order a few minutes later. His cheeky grin gave the impression that he was used to charming the ladies.

I bet he gets good tips - at least from the women.

"Hi. My name is Mike. I'll be your server tonight. Can I get you ladies something to drink to start off?"

"Do you have any hefeweizen beer?" Rylie asked.

"If you like hefeweizen beer, I'd recommend our Morgan Territory Bees Better Have My Honey," he replied. "It's an American wheat ale with honey and tangerine in it."

"That sounds good," Rylie replied. "I'll have that."

"I'll have the Firefall Red Ale," Dee said.

"I'll get those for you ladies right away." He flashed them an impishly sexy grin and hurried off in the direction of the bar.

Rylie watched him walk away and then turned to Dee. "He's a charmer, isn't he?"

Dee grinned. "Yep. Kinda like my brother."

"I bet he gets good tips from the women."

"I'm sure he does."

They looked through their menus while they waited for their drinks.

"I think I'm going to get one of their twelve-inch pizzas," Rylie said. "They don't seem to have a personal size pizza. I'll take the leftovers home to have another night. I like having leftovers so I can just microwave something quick for dinner without having to take the time to make something and clean everything up afterwards."

Their cute waiter showed up a few minutes later and delivered their beers with a flourish and a flash of his pearly whites.

"Do you know what you want to eat yet?" he asked.

"I'm going to have the Soppressata Honey Drizzle pizza," Rylie replied. "But with no jalapenos."

"No problem." He scribbled something on his pad.

"I'll have the Arugula Bacon Peach Pizza," Dee said. "It sounds intriguing."

"Coming right up." Their waiter smiled quickly and then rushed off.

Rylie took a sip of her beer.

"Not bad," she said. "I can't believe I've never been here before."

"It's not far from where I live in Tahoe Vista, so I come here fairly often," Dee replied.

They sat quietly sipping their beers and enjoying the sunshine and the view for a few minutes. She looked around the patio to see if she recognized anyone but didn't see anyone she knew.

"Laurent and I went to see Melody Hamilton at her house yesterday," Rylie said. "We got to meet Tyler. He's adorable. You're going to love him."

"Oh? Why did you go see Melody?"

"Laurent wanted to ask her if she knew what the key went to that we found in the secret compartment on Colin's boat. She said it went to her storage unit. Colin kept some papers there about the restaurant supply business he had with Aidan."

"Ahh. Interesting," Dee said.

"Have you talked to Detective Felton since we saw him on Colin's boat on Saturday?" Rylie asked.

"No, I haven't."

"I called him this afternoon," Rylie replied. "He told me a few days ago that he thinks there was a third person in the Absinthe Room with Colin on the night he was killed. I called him this afternoon because I wanted to know what he thought that third person did that could have caused Colin to fall and hit his head. He told me that he and Brayden Hughes have discussed it and they think someone pushed Colin really hard and it took him off guard so he lost his footing. I've been racking my brain trying to come up with who could get so angry with Colin and why, but I've been coming up blank. I was hoping you might have some ideas."

"Look, Rylie. My brother did some stupid things. Mostly involving women. He was an outrageous flirt, but he also got involved in a number of relationships over the years. None of them lasted very long. He had a short fling with a married woman when he lived in the Bay Area. Fortunately, he broke it off before the woman's husband found out. At least that's what he told me. I told him he was playing with fire by getting involved with a married woman. I thought he agreed with me. When I heard the rumors that he got involved with another married woman after he moved here, I was furious."

Rylie surreptitiously looked around at the other tables to see if anyone was close enough to overhear their conversation. Everyone around them seemed to be engaged in their own conversations. She turned back to Dee.

"I'm sorry, Dee. I know about that. Laurent was good friends with Colin, and he told me that the rumors I'd heard about Colin's affair with Katiana were true. I'm not sure if Aidan believes his wife was having an affair, but I think if he did, he would definitely get very angry. But still. I just can't see him pushing someone he was really angry with, can you? I'd think he'd be more likely to punch them out."

"I don't know Aidan," Dee replied. "But I do know his reputation for having a bad temper. I kinda agree with you. But who knows what really went on in that room that night? I still think it's possible."

"Do you have any other ideas as to who might have pushed Colin? I wouldn't have thought that Colin had any enemies. He seemed so charismatic. But I guess he managed to get some people angry with him."

A short guy they hadn't seen before dropped off their pizzas and hurried off.

"Yum. I'm starved," Rylie said.

"Me too," Dee replied.

They started in on their pizzas. Rylie took a long swig of her beer.

"To answer your question, I can't think of anyone who might have wanted to hurt Colin - other than Aidan Flynn, that is," Dee replied. "From what I've heard, I think it would be dangerous to get on that guy's bad side. The thing is, though, that no one really knows what happened that night. Detective Felton is just assuming that someone pushed Colin. Maybe he's got it all wrong. I wish they'd had security cameras in there that night."

"You and me both," Rylie replied.

Chapter 32

After an early breakfast and a walk along the lake with Bella the next morning, Rylie curled up on the sofa in her living room to call her best friend Sophie. Bella laid down on the floor nearby.

"Hi Sophie! How are you? Is this a bad time? I was hoping to catch you before you left for work this morning."

"Hi Rylie. I'm great, thanks. More importantly, how are you? I have a few minutes before I have to leave for work. No problem."

She gave Sophie a condensed version of everything that had been going on. It had been a while since they'd talked and there was a lot to tell.

"Wow," Sophie said finally. "I can't believe how much has happened since the last time we talked. You need to call more often. Or I should call you more often. I've just been so slammed at work lately that by the time I get home at night, I'm totally exhausted, and I just want to have something quick to eat and go to bed."

"I get it. No worries. Besides, I feel like I'm the one who should be calling you more often. I know you have to get to work, and I don't want to keep you, but I was wondering if you'd like to come up for a visit this weekend? You could stay in my guest bedroom. We could rent some inflatable rafts and go Truckin' on the Truckee. Or whatever else you'd like to do."

"That sounds fun," Sophie replied. "I could use some down time. How about I come up after work on Friday night?"

"Perfect! I'll get the guest bedroom ready for you."

"Great! Look, I've got to run now, Rylie. I'll talk to you later."

"Talk to you later then. Bye."

She put her cell phone down and looked over at Bella.

"Bella, Sophie's going to come visit us this weekend! You remember Sophie, right?"

Bella's face broke into a wide golden grin, and she started panting excitedly. She jumped up and bounded over to where Rylie was sitting. Rylie ruffled Bella's fur and gave her a quick kiss. She decided to straighten up the house, run the vacuum, and dust since she was going to have company this weekend. She made up the bed in the guest bedroom and cleaned the bathrooms. She was finished by lunchtime. She decided to go to Tahoe House Bakery to get one of their sandwiches for lunch.

She left Bella napping on the floor in the living room and drove the short distance to Tahoe House Bakery. Colorful multi-colored flowers spilled from large, galvanized metal water troughs on either side of the entrance to the brown wood building.

She read the menu posted on the wall as she stood in line waiting to place her order. She decided on the homemade meatloaf sandwich with roasted red pepper aioli on a fresh baked super grain roll. After she paid for her sandwich and a drink, she wandered around looking for someplace to sit.

She found an empty table in one of the dining areas with an exposed brick accent wall and a massive fieldstone fireplace.

She sat down and took a bite of her sandwich. Yum, this is delicious.

She looked up as a middle-aged woman with a short bob of strawberry blonde hair walked by her table with a sandwich and a drink. Their eyes met. The woman looked vaguely familiar.

"Rylie? Aren't you Dr. Rylie Sunderland?" the woman asked.

"Yes." She struggled to place the woman.

"I'm Madison. Dr. Madison Lambert from Tahoe City Veterinary Hospital. We met at Locals' Night at Whitaker Cottages. You probably don't remember me. I'm sure you met lots of people that night."

"Oh, yes!" Rylie replied. "I remember you now. Would you like to join me? It's always more fun to have someone to talk to over lunch than to eat alone."

"Sure. Thanks."

Madison set her sandwich and drink on the table across from Rylie and sat down.

"So how are you enjoying living in Lake Tahoe?" Madison asked. "If I remember correctly, you're from the East Bay area, right?" She took a bite of her sandwich and looked at Rylie expectantly as she chewed.

"I love it here," Rylie replied. "But I haven't really gotten out to enjoy it much yet. I have a lot of things I'd like to do while I'm here this summer."

"Didn't you mention that you have a golden retriever? There are a lot of great places around here where you can take dogs hiking."

"I do have a golden retriever. Her name is Bella. As a matter of fact, one of my friends and I went hiking with our golden retrievers on the Incline Flume Trail this past Sunday. There were gorgeous views of the lake up there. We found an injured fawn in the woods near the trail. We ended up taking it to Lake Tahoe Wildlife Care in South Lake Tahoe."

"Oh my goodness. What kind of injuries did the fawn have?"

"It had a broken leg," Rylie replied. "The woman at Lake Tahoe Wildlife Care was going to take it to their veterinarian right away. I got their veterinarian's number so I can call him and see how the fawn is doing."

"I know their vet. He's good. He'll make sure the fawn gets excellent care. Did I tell you that I have a golden retriever, too?" Madison smiled and pulled out her cell phone. "I have some photos of her on my cell."

Rylie watched as Madison started scrolling through her photos. She saw what looked like photos of the Locals' Night party at Whitaker Cottages.

"Are those photos of the Locals' Night party where I met you?" she asked.

"Yes. I took a bunch of photos that night. Oh, here. Here's a photo of my golden. Her name is Rosy. She's a strawberry blonde like me."

"Oh, she's sweet," Rylie said. "Do you mind if I look through your photos of Locals' Night?"

"Not at all," Madison replied. She scrolled back to the photos of Locals' Night and handed her phone to Rylie.

Rylie looked through the photos with interest. A jolt coursed through her body when she saw a photo of Colin Matthews smiling and enjoying himself with the group of women flocking around him. Popular guy. At least with the ladies. She was about to scroll to the next photo when she noticed a lanky guy with scraggly dark brown hair and black rectangular glasses at the edge of the photo staring at Colin with a scowl on his face.

"Do you know this guy?" she asked.

"No. I don't recognize him."

"Do you mind if I text your photos of Locals' Night to myself so I can look at them more later?" Rylie asked.

"Not at all. Help yourself."

She sent all of Madison's photos from Locals' Night to her cell phone while Madison continued eating her lunch.

"So are you going back to the East Bay at the end of the summer?" Madison asked.

"That's the plan."

"What are you going to do when you get back? Do you have a job lined up?"

"No, not yet. I'm not actually sure what I'm going to do when I go back. I've worked at the same veterinary hospital since I graduated from veterinary medical school six years ago. I was totally shocked when it burned to the ground during the Lightning Complex Fire. I'm kind of at loose ends right now. I guess I'll give it some more thought a little later this summer. I have some time before I have to make a decision."

"Have you ever thought about doing locum veterinarian work?" Madison asked.

"No. Not really."

"You might want to consider it. I have a couple of friends who work as locum vets. They really like the freedom and autonomy of being in business for themselves. They work at veterinary practices that need temporary help because they lost one of their associate veterinarians or one of their vets is going on vacation or something like that. Sometimes they work at a veterinary hospital for only a day or two and sometimes they work at the same place for an extended period of time like if they're covering maternity leave. But they get to decide where and when they want to work. It's a different kind of lifestyle, but some people really love it."

"Hmmm. That's interesting."

"I actually have an ulterior motive for asking," Madison said. "I'm going to need some shifts covered on a couple different occasions this summer. Would you be interested?"

"I'm not sure. I'd need to give it some thought and maybe do a little research before I'd be able to give you an answer. And I work Monday through Wednesday at Whitaker Cottages, so the only days I'd be able to work somewhere else would be Thursdays or Fridays."

"I understand. How about I give you a quick tour of my hospital after lunch and introduce you to the doctor that's working today and some of my staff? Then you can let me know if you might be interested in doing some locum work at my hospital after you've had some time to think about it."

"Okay."

Tahoe City Veterinary Hospital was a brown wood clapboard building with a blue-green metal roof and a large diamond-shaped window above the glass entry doors. The reception area was flooded with natural light from all the windows.

Madison gave her a tour of the veterinary hospital and introduced her to everyone. Rylie agreed to consider doing some locum work to help Madison out while she was there that summer. She promised she'd get back to Madison after she'd done a little research and thought it over.

She drove back to her house and got comfortable at her dining table to look through Madison's photos of Locals'

Night again. The guy with scraggly dark brown hair scowling at Colin really bothered her. She called Gillian and asked if it would be okay if she came over for a few minutes. Gillian said she could come right over.

She showed Gillian and Liam the photo of the guy with scraggly dark brown hair. "Do you know this guy?"

"Yes, we do," Gillian replied. "He's the guy that used to do the weekend deliveries for Butter Lane Bakery before Eric. His name is Egan Hawkridge. I don't know what happened to him or why he stopped doing the weekend deliveries. Do you, Liam?"

"No, I don't," Liam replied. "One morning Eric showed up with our baked goods instead of Egan and that was that. I didn't think much of it at the time."

"Well he sure looks like he has some kind of beef with Colin in that photo," Rylie said. "I want to know why. I'm going to go show this photo to Eric and see if he knows anything about why Egan doesn't do the weekend deliveries anymore."

"Good idea," Gillian said. "Anyone who had a problem with Colin has to go on our list of suspects. And I think you should show that photo to Detective Felton, Rylie."

"Oh, don't worry. I plan to. I'll let you guys know what I find out. See you later."

As she was walking back to her house, she texted Eric.

Where are you right now? Are you still at work?

Yes. We're making pies. Cherry, apple, and blueberry. Want one? I have some that have cooled off since I took them out of the oven.

Sure. Hey can I come over to talk to you for a minute? I need to show you something.

No problem. Just tell Dee you talked to me and I said for her to come get me when you get here.

Okay. I'll be right there.

She showed Eric the photo on her phone of the guy with scraggly dark brown hair scowling at Colin.

"I have no idea who he is," Eric said.

"Gillian and Liam recognized him. They said his name is Egan Hawkridge and that he used to be the weekend delivery guy before you."

"Really? Huh. Ryan would know him, then. He's been here a lot longer than I have. I'll go ask him if it would be alright if I took you back into the kitchen so you could show him your photo and talk to him for a minute. Be right back."

Eric came back a couple minutes later. He took her back into the kitchen and made the introductions. Rylie showed Ryan the photo of Egan Hawkridge.

"Yeah, that's Egan," Ryan said. "He worked here for a little while as the weekend delivery guy. But after he started working here, we started having shortages in the cash drawer when we counted it at night. At first it was just $20.00 once in a while and Colin thought maybe someone was giving customers the wrong change or something. Then the shortages started getting larger and more frequent. Finally, Colin had security cameras installed. That's when he found out that Egan was stealing money from the cash drawer. He fired him on the spot."

"I wonder what Egan was doing at Locals' Night?" Rylie said. "Do you know if he got another job around here?"

"I heard he got a job working at Sunnyside as a bartender," Ryan replied. "It didn't last long. He got fired from there, too. I don't think he's been able to get another job around here since then. This is a small town. People talk. I didn't even know he was still in the area."

"Interesting. Thanks, Ryan. I don't want to keep you. I know you're busy. Those pies smell delicious!"

"What flavor do you want?" Eric asked.

"I'll take an apple pie if you have one ready. I'll go to Safeway later and get some vanilla ice cream to go with it. I'll warm up the pie and have it for dessert tonight. Warm apple pie with vanilla ice cream on top. Yum!"

"That sounds delicious," Eric said. "I'll have Dee box one up for you. See you later."

She brought her pie home, put it in the kitchen, and called Detective Felton. He answered on the first ring.

"Rylie! Hi! Is everything okay? What can I do for you?"

"I was wondering if I could meet you somewhere for a few minutes sometime this afternoon? I've got something to show you that could be important to Colin's case."

"Oh really? Great. I'm over at Sierra Vista Cottages right now talking to your friend Laurent. Why don't you meet me over here?"

Chapter 33

S he pulled into Sierra Vista Cottages a few minutes later. The charming building that housed the reception area as well as Laurent and Olivia's home was made of rough-hewn logs and had a wall of glass windows overlooking a deck on the second floor. Low fieldstone walls flanked the steps leading up to the dark wood front door embellished with hammered black iron nail heads and an iron ring door knocker.

She let herself into the reception area. Olivia opened the door to their private residence in back of the reception desk and welcomed her with a warm smile.

"Rylie! So nice to see you," Olivia said.

"Rylie!" Laurent emerged from their home and crossed the reception area in a few strides. He wrapped her up in a big hug.

"Hi Laurent." She smiled. "Hi Olivia."

"Come in. Come in," Olivia said.

Detective Felton was standing just in back of Olivia as she walked into their home.

"Hi, Mark. How are you?"

"I'm great, Rylie," he replied. "How are you?"

Olivia led the way to the kitchen, and they all sat down around the dining table.

"What have you got for me?" Detective Felton asked.

She showed him the photo on her phone of Egan Hawkridge at Locals' Night. "I thought you might be interested in this. See this guy on the edge of the photo? From the scowl on his face, I'd say it looks like he has some kind of problem with Colin."

"I know that guy. That's Egan Hawkridge," Laurent said. "He used to be the weekend delivery guy for Butter Lane Bakery. Then he stopped working there and got a job as a bartender at Sunnyside."

"That's what I heard," Rylie replied.

"I heard he got fired from Sunnyside for stealing money from the cash drawer," Laurent said.

"That's interesting," Rylie replied. "I was just over at Butter Lane Bakery to show Eric this photo. He didn't know Egan but he had me show their baker Ryan the photo. Ryan told me that Colin fired Egan for the same reason. They were having shortages when they counted the cash drawer at night. Colin finally put in security cameras and caught Egan in the act. He fired him on the spot."

"Where did you get these photos?" Detective Felton asked.

"From Dr. Madison Lambert. She's the owner of Tahoe City Veterinary Hospital. I met her briefly on Locals' Night. I ran into her at Tahoe House Bakery earlier today when I went there for lunch. We ended up having lunch together. She was scrolling through the photos on her phone so she could show me a photo of her golden retriever, and I noticed that she had photos of Locals' Night. So I asked her if I could look through them. When I saw this photo, I asked her if she'd mind if I texted her photos to myself so I could look at them more later."

"Did you get copies of all of the photos she had of Locals' Night?" Detective Felton asked.

"Yes."

"Can you please text them to me? Then I'm going to find Egan Hawkridge, and we're going to have a little chat."

"No problem." She started texting Detective Felton all of Madison's photos from Locals' Night.

"I need to get going," Detective Felton said. "Thanks for all your help, Laurent. You too, Rylie."

Olivia walked Detective Felton out.

"So I guess we now have another suspect in Colin's case," Laurent said.

"It looks that way. Was Mark discussing Colin's case with you?"

"Yes. He wanted to know more about Colin's relationship with Aidan Flynn. I guess Aidan was playing pool at Pete 'n Peters last night and some guy made a snide remark that set Aidan off. Aidan got up in the guy's face and shoved him really hard. The guy almost fell. Before it could go any further, another guy came up behind Aidan and pinned his arms behind his back. Someone called 911. The police came, but they didn't arrest anyone. Aidan got lucky this time. He seriously needs to get his temper under control."

"So what did Mark want to know about Colin's relationship with Aidan?" she asked.

"He wanted to know what kind of relationship they had after their restaurant supply business went under," Laurent replied. "He knew Aidan lost a lot of money in the deal and that Colin was partly to blame. He wanted to know if there was bad blood between them because of it. I told him I thought that probably had strained their relationship but that I thought that the rumors that Colin was having an affair with Aidan's wife probably put a lot more strain on it."

"Do you think Aidan might have found out that the rumors were true?"

"I sure hope not," Laurent replied. "He'd go ballistic."

Chapter 34

As she pulled into Whitaker Cottages, her cell phone pinged with a text. After she parked, she read the text. It was from Gillian.

Liam and I have decided to close the reception area tonight and go out to dinner. No one has called or come to the cottages for the last two days. If anyone calls, they can leave a message and we'll call them back later. We're going to Jake's on the Lake. Want to come?

Sure. What time should I come over?

Why don't you meet us at our house at 6:00?

Ok. See you then.

Bella greeted her exuberantly when she opened the door to her house.

"Hi Bella! Were you a good girl for me while I was gone?"

Bella wagged her tail furiously. She let Bella out to do her business. Bella made a beeline for the woods and came running back quickly with a huge golden grin on her face. She bent down to pet Bella's soft fur. Bella wiggled around in delight.

She went into her bedroom to look through her closet for something to wear when she went out to dinner with Gillian and Liam. She decided on a long-sleeved, cobalt blue peasant blouse over pale blue denim pants. She took a quick shower and got dressed. She hadn't eaten at Jake's on the Lake in years, but she'd always enjoyed going there. She remembered they featured dishes from Hawaii and southern California. She was eager to see what they had on their menu.

"Bella, I'm going to go out to dinner with Gillian and Liam tonight. You're going to stay here and watch the house for me while I'm gone, okay?"

Bella thumped her tail up and down on the floor from where she was laying down watching Rylie get dressed. Rylie walked over and stroked Bella's head.

"You're such a good girl, Bella."

She met Gillian and Liam at their house, and they all piled into Liam's SUV.

"I haven't been to Jake's on the Lake in years. I'm excited," Rylie said.

"We don't go out very often. But when we do, we like to go somewhere nice," Gillian replied.

The hostess asked them if they'd like to sit indoors, outside on the second floor deck, or on the patio.

"I think the patio sounds nice. What do you ladies think?" Liam said.

They all agreed on the patio. The hostess seated them along the railing with a wonderful view looking out over the Tahoe City Marina and across the lake to the rugged mountains in the distance. Rylie looked at the boats in the marina. She could see Colin's 34-foot powerboat in its slip not far from where they were seated. She turned her attention to her menu.

"I'm going to have the bison filet with garlic mashed potatoes and Pt. Reyes bleu cheese beurre composé," she said.

"I've never had bison before. Have you? And I have no idea what beurre composé is, but I love Pt. Reyes bleu cheese."

"I've never had bison, but I've heard it's good," Gillian replied. "It's supposed to have a more delicate flavor than beef. Let me know how you like it. I'm going to have the salmon."

When the waiter came to get their order, Rylie asked him what beurre composé was.

"It's a French dish," the waiter replied. "Basically, it's a mixture of butter and other things like herbs or shallots. Our chef mixes butter with bleu cheese. It just adds some extra flavor to the dish. It's delicious. If you like bleu cheese, you're going to love it."

"Sold," Rylie replied. "I'll have the bison with bleu cheese beurre composé."

Their drinks arrived shortly. Liam was having Irish whiskey. Rylie and Gillian were both having wine.

She could see the change in Gillian and Liam's postures as they relaxed. She took a discreet deep breath and tried to breathe out all the stress she'd been feeling.

"When I had lunch with Madison Lambert at Tahoe House today, she mentioned that she was going to be needing some help at her veterinary hospital at various times this summer," she said. "She asked me if I might be available to help her out as a locum veterinarian. I told her the only days I could possibly be available would be Thursdays or Fridays since I work at the cottages Monday through Wednesday. I told her I'd get back to her after I had some time to think about it and do some research. How would you two feel if I did some occasional locum work for her? It wouldn't affect my work at the cottages at all."

Liam and Gillian exchanged a glance.

"It would be fine with us," Liam said. "The most important thing is if you want to do it. You shouldn't feel pressured to do it if you don't want to or if you're not comfortable with it."

"I know. But I feel bad for Madison since she's going to be short-handed at various times this summer. I just wanted to make sure that neither of you had a problem with it before I start looking into it some more."

"It might be a good idea for you to do it just so you can see if you like it," Gillian said. "You're still trying to figure out what you're going to do at the end of the summer when you're done working here. Maybe you'd like working as a locum veterinarian."

"You mean as a career choice?" Rylie asked. "Rather than working as an associate veterinarian?"

Gillian shrugged. "I don't know. Maybe. Is that a thing?"

"I guess so. Madison said she has a couple of friends who work as locum veterinarians. She said they like the freedom of being in business for themselves. They can decide when and how much they want to work. They set their own fees. It does have a certain appeal."

A movement out in the marina caught her eye. She looked over at Colin's boat and saw Egan Hawkridge on it. It looked like he was holding something concealed under his t-shirt.

"Egan Hawkridge is over there on Colin's boat!" she exclaimed. "I think he stole something. He's got something under his t-shirt."

Liam turned to look in the direction she was pointing. "Hey!" he yelled. He vaulted over the railing and ran across the lawn toward the marina. Egan saw him coming and started running in the opposite direction. Liam was fast, but he wasn't closing the gap between himself and Egan. Rylie and Gillian ran after Liam.

"Thief! Stop him!" Liam yelled.

A guy who seemed oblivious to what was happening stepped onto the walkway a split second before Egan reached him. Egan crashed into the guy and they fell to the ground with Egan on top. Liam reached them a few seconds later, grabbed Egan's arms, and pinned them behind his back.

"Are you okay?" Liam asked the guy sprawled on the ground beneath Egan.

"Yeah, dude, I'm fine," the guy grunted. "Just get that guy off me."

Liam rolled Egan off the guy on the bottom. "What have you got there?" he asked. He pulled a laptop out from under Egan's t-shirt.

"Stealing laptops now, are we, Egan?" Liam asked.

Egan's face reddened. "Hey man, it's not like Colin's going to need it anymore. I can sell it. I need the money. Colin fired me, and I can't get a job now."

Liam clenched his fists. A muscle twitched in his tightly clenched jaw.

Gillian called Detective Felton. She seemed to have him on speed dial. "Detective Felton will be right over. He said he'll get some sheriff's deputies over here, too."

Liam handed the laptop to Gillian and hauled Egan to his feet. He kept Egan's arms tightly pinned behind him. The guy that Egan had body slammed got to his feet.

Detective Felton arrived a few minutes later.

"Hi Detective. Thanks for getting here so quickly," Liam said. "This is Egan Hawkridge. We just caught him stealing this laptop from Colin Matthews' boat."

A couple of sheriff's deputies rushed up. One of them put handcuffs on Egan.

"Ahh. Egan Hawkridge," Detective Felton said. "Where'd you find the laptop, Egan?"

Egan flushed. He stared down at his feet for a minute, then looked up at Detective Felton defiantly. "I found it on Colin's boat."

"Where, exactly, did you find it?" Detective Felton asked.

"I was looking through all the stuff around the steering wheel and a little door flipped open. I saw the laptop inside and figured I could sell it to get some money. I need the money, man."

The sheriff's deputies escorted Egan to their cruiser. Gillian handed the laptop to Detective Felton.

"I wonder what's on that laptop," Rylie said. "Maybe it has some information that will help with Colin's murder investigation."

"I hope so," Detective Felton replied. "I've got to go. I'm going to talk to Egan Hawkridge some more over at the station."

They watched Detective Felton as he walked away and then turned back toward the restaurant. All the people on the patio and the second floor deck were watching them. They walked through the restaurant back out onto the patio and sat down at their table. By then everyone else on the patio had gone back to their seats and resumed their conversations with each other. Their waiter showed up a few minutes later with their meals. Rylie took a bite of her bison with bleu cheese beurre composé.

"Yum. This is delicious," she said.

"Mine's wonderful too," Gillian said.

"That little son of a...." Liam growled. "I wanted to punch his lights out when he said that Colin wasn't going to be needing his laptop anymore. Like that made it okay to steal it."

"I can't wait to find out what Detective Felton learns when he talks to Egan," Rylie said. "Egan definitely seemed angry at Colin for firing him."

"He deserved to be fired for stealing money from the cash drawer," Gillian said.

"Of course he did," she replied. "But he doesn't seem to have the moral compass that you and I do."

"No, he doesn't," Liam said. "Or to have any moral compass at all."

Chapter 35

Early the next morning, she bundled up in some warm clothes and walked down to the lake with Bella just as the sun was starting to come up. She was rewarded with a stunning sunrise over the lake. The yellow glow of the rising sun edged the tops of the mountains on the far shore and turned them into dark silhouettes. Above the yellow glow, flaming pink clouds spread out over the lake. The dark blue lake shimmered in fiery pink where it reflected the clouds above. It was an intensely beautiful, almost spiritual, scene. She watched in silent awe as the colors shifted and changed with the rising sun.

Bella was busy exploring the area and sniffing everything in sight. A small forest creature that looked like a large chipmunk startled her as it ran for cover when she got too close to it with her inquisitive nose. Bella gave playful chase but gave up quickly.

After a while, she headed back home with Bella to get some coffee and breakfast. The hot coffee helped to warm her up after being outside in the chilly morning air. Bella gobbled her breakfast and then went to lay down in the living room. Rylie called Gillian on her cell.

"Good morning. Are you up?" she asked when Gillian answered the phone.

"Oh yes. We're always up early, even on our days off. Do you want to come over for a cup of coffee?"

"Definitely. I'll be right over."

Bella greeted Gillian at the door by pushing her nose into Gillian's hand.

"Hi, Bella!" Gillian giggled as she scratched Bella around her ears. "Come on in."

Rylie sat down at the dining table with Gillian. "Katiana's coming over to browse through the library at the main house with me this morning. She's going to meet me over there at 10:00."

"Oh, that's great," Gillian replied. "Maybe I'll join you a little later this morning, and we can have some tea and biscuits. I can bring over some biscuits when I come."

"Perfect. I'll tell Katiana you're going to join us."

They chatted until nearly 10:00, then Rylie went over to the main house with Bella. The house felt a little chilly, so she looked for the thermostat to turn on the heat. She wandered through the house turning on lights. Katiana showed up promptly at 10:00.

"Hi, Katiana! Come on in."

"Thanks, Rylie." Katiana gave her a small smile that didn't reach her eyes.

She wondered briefly why Katiana never seemed to really warm up to either her or Gillian. She led Katiana into the library.

Katiana clapped her hands together in delight. "This is wonderful!"

She watched in amusement as Katiana walked quickly over to some bookshelves and started scanning the titles. Katiana ran her fingers over the spines of a few of the books, then turned to Rylie with a genuinely happy smile. "I think I could easily lose myself in this room for quite a while."

She returned Katiana's smile. "I know the feeling. Please feel free to pull out any books you'd like to look at more closely. You can put them on a table near one of the chairs and sit down to read whenever you're ready. Gillian is going to come over a little later and bring some English biscuits so we can have tea and biscuits."

"Oh! That will be nice."

Rylie started scanning book titles on the bookshelves on the other side of the room from the shelves Katiana was perusing. She pulled out a few books to look at more closely.

"Oh look!" Katiana exclaimed. "A book of poetry by Alexander Pushkin! He's a famous Russian poet. We read his poems in school when I was a child. I can't believe they have an English translation of his works here."

She watched as Katiana flipped through the pages of the book. Katiana stopped flipping pages when she came to a specific poem. She started reading out loud in a soft voice filled with sadness:

I loved you; even now I must confess,
Some embers of my love their fire retain;
But do not let it cause you more distress,
I do not want to sadden you again.

Hopeless and tongue-tied, yet I loved you dearly
With pangs the jealous and the timid know;
So tenderly I love you, so sincerely,
I pray God grant another love you so.

I loved you once, nor can this heart be quiet;
For it would seem that love still lingers there;
But do not you be further troubled by it;
I would in no wise hurt you, oh, my dear.

I loved you without hope, a mute offender;
What jealous pangs, what shy despairs I knew!
A love as deep as this, as true, as tender,
God grant another may yet offer you.

Katiana's lower lip trembled. She seemed totally undone by the words of the poet.

And there it was.

An image of Katiana pushing her husband in the chest as hard as she could that day in the Butter Lane Bakery flashed through her mind.

"You killed Colin Matthews," Rylie said slowly. "But why? You loved him."

Katiana gave her a look of sheer terror that quickly changed to rage. Her beautiful face contorted into an evil mask of hate.

"I didn't mean to! It was an accident!"

Katiana grabbed a large ceramic art piece from the nearest table and raised it over her head to hurl at Rylie.

Rylie didn't have time to react before Bella lunged at Katiana and knocked her flat on her back on the floor. Bella barked ferociously inches from Katiana's face. Katiana screamed and dropped the art piece so she could shield her face with her hands. Rylie grabbed her cell phone from her pocket and speed dialed Gillian.

"Get Liam and come to the library right now!"

She grabbed the art piece and moved it out of Katiana's reach. Liam and Gillian raced in.

"She killed Colin! And she was about to hit me with that art piece!"

Liam strode over to where Katiana was pinned to the floor by Bella. Rylie grabbed Bella's collar and pulled her off Katiana. Katiana leaped to her feet with surprising speed and let out an unearthly banshee scream of rage and frustration as she started for the door.

Liam caught Katiana by the waist mid-stride. Katiana swung her arm into Liam's head with all of her strength. Liam recovered quickly, twisted both of Katiana's arms behind her back, and held her tightly.

"Call Detective Felton," he said.

Gillian called Detective Felton. Rylie looked at Katiana. She wondered who this evil creature was that bore no resemblance to the beautiful woman she'd previously appeared to be.

"It was an accident!" Katiana wailed. "I didn't mean to kill him. I loved him! I was just mad because he broke up with me. I thought he wanted to marry me. I was going to leave Aidan to be with him. Then one day he told me that Aidan was his friend, and he couldn't do this to him anymore."

"But I know he was lying to me. I followed him one day and saw him go to his ex-girlfriend Melody's house. I think he wanted to get back together with her. I think he was in love with her all along, and he was just using me. Just like all the others. It made me so mad!"

Katiana burst into tears just as Detective Felton walked in. Rylie filled Detective Felton in on everything that had occurred. He looked grim as he put handcuffs on Katiana.

"I'll need all three of you to come down to the sheriff's department later to give your statements," he said. He walked out with Katiana in tow.

Rylie felt her legs start to wobble. She quickly sat down on the nearest chair. Bella came over to her and put her head in Rylie's lap. Bella looked up at Rylie with huge brown eyes full of compassion. Rylie stroked her beautiful golden head.

"You were such a good girl, Bella. You saved me." Rylie put her face next to Bella's muzzle. Then she wrapped her arms around Bella and buried her face in Bella's soft fur. She felt hot tears sting the corners of her eyes.

"Come on, Rylie," Gillian said. She helped Rylie to her feet. "Let's go to my house for some tea."

They walked over to Gillian and Liam's house silently, each lost in their own thoughts. Gillian put a tea kettle on the stove to boil and got out some teacups.

"What a shock," Rylie said finally.

Gillian poured tea for everyone and passed around a plate of biscuits. The sweet tea and biscuits helped Rylie feel better. She could feel the color returning to her face.

"Can I give Bella a biscuit, Gillian?" she asked.

"Of course you can," Gillian replied. "Bella saved the day, didn't you, Bella?"

Rylie offered Bella a biscuit. Bella gulped it down and looked at her hopefully to see if any more biscuits might be coming her way. She gently scratched around Bella's ears.

"You did save the day, Bella," she said. "You're such a good girl."

They sat quietly for a few minutes.

"I never saw that coming," Liam said.

"I know. I didn't either," Gillian said.

"I'm in shock," Rylie said. "The woman who was having an affair with Colin ended up being the one who killed him. They say there's a fine line between love and hate."

"I'm glad this whole thing is finally over," Gillian said. "Now we can rest easy at night and not be afraid there might be a killer on the loose."

"Yes. Now everything can go back to normal," Liam said.

She wondered what "normal" would turn out to be.

Chapter 36

Sophie squealed as their bright blue inflatable raft bounced through the short stretch of rapids on the Truckee River. Rylie laughed and used her paddle to try to keep them from getting stranded on a rock that jutted out of the river in front of them. They were both totally soaked and having a blast. Then the river widened into a placid stretch and she relaxed. She leaned back against the side of the raft and tilted her face up to the sky. The sun felt like a warm caress on her face.

"This is so much fun." Sophie smiled.

"I'm glad you were able to come and spend a few days with me. I've been wanting to go river rafting ever since I came here this summer."

"I'm glad I was able to come, too," Sophie replied. "I think this is good for both of us. We've both been under so much stress lately. But I have to admit that I was a little nervous about coming to visit you when there was a potential murderer on the loose. It's a relief that she's finally behind bars."

"I know how you feel," Rylie replied. "Last night was the first time I've slept soundly since I found out that Colin was killed. It's so sad what happened to him. I wish I'd gotten the chance to get to know him. He seemed like such a nice guy.

But at least now everyone who knew and loved him will be able to start the healing process."

Their raft continued to glide peacefully down the river.

"So how do you like working as a caretaker at a B&B?" Sophie asked.

"It's okay. But it's not something I want to do long-term. I already have a career as a veterinarian. But it's been nice to get away from it all and do something totally different for a change. And since I only work three days a week, I'll have time to do some fun things this summer."

"Have you decided what you're going to do at the end of the summer?"

"Not yet," she replied. "But I've been thinking about it. I had lunch with the veterinarian who owns Tahoe City Veterinary Hospital on Tuesday. We met each other during Locals' Night at Whitaker Cottages. She asked me if I would be willing to help her out with some locum work this summer. I told her I'd have to do some research and think about it. If I did some locum work for her this summer, it would give me the chance to see if I like it. Then I could do locum work rather than getting another full-time veterinarian position. Or I could work as a locum veterinarian on a temporary basis while I'm looking for a full-time position."

"Hmmm," Sophie replied. "I can see the advantages of working as a locum vet. You'd get to set your own hours for one thing. So if you wanted to go on vacation, you could just not book any work during that time. You wouldn't have to ask anyone for time off."

"That's true. I'd be my own boss and set my own schedule."

"You'll just have to weigh all the pros and cons and decide if you want to go for it. You could always apply for associate veterinarian positions later if it doesn't work out."

"Well, I have some time before I have to make a decision about what to do at the end of the summer. But I'm warming up to the idea of doing locum work."

They pulled their raft out of the river when they got to the River Ranch Restaurant. Two guys from the raft rental company came and carried the raft over to their van.

They found a table on the River Ranch deck looking out over the river. A waitress came and took their drink orders and dropped off some menus. Rylie scanned the menu and decided on a mushroom Swiss burger with fries.

"You know me. I love a good burger." She smiled at Sophie.

"Me too," Sophie replied.

The waitress came back and took their food orders and dropped off their drinks.

"So how have things been going for you, Sophie? I feel like we haven't really talked about anything except about what's been going on here in quite a while. How's your interior design business going?"

"Busy, as usual," Sophie replied. She got out her cell phone to show Rylie photos of some of the houses she'd been working on.

"Wow, Sophie. These are amazing! I can't believe the transformation between the before and after photos."

"Thanks." Sophie smiled a small smile.

"How's Lucien? How's his restaurant doing? I'd love to make a trip up to St. Helena and have dinner at Vinterre one night."

"That would be fun," Sophie replied without meeting her gaze while she swirled her drink in her glass.

"Is something wrong, Sophie? You seem like something's bothering you."

Sophie regarded her quietly for a long minute before she spoke.

"Something is wrong, Rylie. But I don't know what it is. That's the problem. There's something going on with Lucien, but he won't talk to me about it. Maybe you could put your amateur sleuth skills to good use and help me out."

***

Rylie's adventures continue in Book 2 of the Rylie Sunderland Mysteries, Vengeance in the Vines.

If you enjoyed this book, I'd really appreciate it if you'd take a few minutes to leave a nice review on my book's page on Amazon (and on my book's page on BookBub and Goodreads, if you're on those sites). If you're pressed for time, just a couple of sentences will do. Reviews help readers decide whether to take a chance on a new author, so your review will really help me in my career as an author. Thanks so much for taking the time to do this.

My readers love my monthly newsletter, and I think you will too. Join us! The sign-up form for my newsletter is on my website (rachelebaker.com). You'll get info about my books, photos from my adventures, news for book lovers, and the opportunity to participate in fun contests and giveaways. You can unsubscribe at any time.

I love to connect with my readers online. Please follow me on Amazon, BookBub, Goodreads, Facebook, Instagram, and Twitter if you're on those sites.

About the Author

Rachele Baker lives in northern California close to Lake Tahoe and the Napa Valley wine country where the Rylie Sunderland Mysteries take place. She drew on her many years of experience as a practicing veterinarian when developing the main character for the series, Rylie Sunderland. Rachele's golden retriever, Savanna, was the inspiration for Rylie's golden retriever, Bella.

In her free time, Rachele enjoys exploring northern California wine country, Lake Tahoe, and areas along the California coast like Mendocino, Monterey, and Big Sur. Some of her favorite things include freshly brewed coffee in the morning, walks in nature, and, of course, golden retrievers.

Made in the USA
Monee, IL
15 August 2023

41045865R00176